THE DEAD DON'T LIE

A MIND GAMES NOVEL

MEGHAN O'FLYNN

THE DEAD DON'T LIE

Distributed by Pygmalion Publishing, LLC

Learn more about Meghan's novels on

https://meghanoflynn.com

For my baby brother Brian
I'm sorry Tommy and I convinced you that there was a game called "Houdini" which required that we tie you up in winter scarves and lock you in a Rubbermaid garbage can until you could escape on your own. Which was 100% impossible after we put stuff on top of said Rubbermaid garbage can.
I mean, it was a game, but not so much a game for you.
I'm really glad you survived.
I love you.

P.S. Let's see if we can convince Tommy that there's a game called "David Blaine." Revenge is a dish best served thirty years later, and all we need is a shovel and a little booze.
You bring your poker face.
I'll bring the winter scarves.

CHAPTER
ONE

GAUZY SUN SLITHERED through the early fog and cast murky shadows along either side of the path. Each pulsing thud of Lindsay's sneakers sent the brittle leaves crackling, the twigs snapping like tiny bones, the sparse grass wetting her ankles with dew. It was eerie, she decided, like walking over your own grave. But Lindsay didn't mind. The high-pitched screech of birdsong and the prickling flesh along her back only urged her to run faster over the rutted dirt.

She wiped sweat from her already dripping brow. Three weeks until school was out for good—three weeks until graduation and summer. In Fernborn, Indiana, the city to her west, and the neighboring town of Tysdale to her east, that meant state fairs and trips to the lake. Scary stories around a campfire.

And Jeff. Possibly without his shirt. But for now... she had this.

The fork in the road approached like a mirage, first shimmering lazily, then vanishing when her focus wavered. Straight ahead, dappled sunlight filtered through the canopy and cut the darkness with hazy gold. That was the way others would go—the only path, so far as most knew. But she wasn't "most." Heavy moss cloaked the entrance of the second path, the low-hanging branches so dense with wild kudzu that she could not see any glint of daylight beneath. The contrast was so stark that Lindsay hesitated, her feet still pounding the earth, her breath panting from her lips. Then she tightened her ponytail and hooked a right, ducking beneath the slippery vines and into the dark.

The path here was choked with weeds and spiky sweet gum pods—more brittle crackling, more snapping bones, the damp scent of rotting underbrush in her nose. Lindsay gritted her teeth. Unless she wanted to run back and forth over the same path, she had no choice but to take the trail that wound over the steeper hills closer to Fernborn. This last cross-country meet was supposed to be a doozy, and better runners than her had wound up puking on the curb. If she trained hard enough through these unmanned briars, the hilly—but weed-free—track of the actual race should be a cakewalk.

The fog condensed as she made her way along, the darkness more insistent. Fingers of chill crawled along Lindsay's spine like witches' nails, but she ignored the prickling and pushed on. She was not some character in a horror novel, some vulnerable girl who'd be easy pickings for a machete-wielding serial killer. She was Lindsay "Dash" Harris, soon-to-be winner of the Indiana Cross Country Meet—again—and a kickboxer on the weekends. Besides, what kind of serial killer would be roaming the woods at eight o'clock on a Tuesday morning? That was not how killers worked. A dark city alley, a van on a long, lonely road, a strange man at a college bar, the Supreme Court—those were the real threats. But out here? Not nearly enough victims passing through for anyone intent on harm. This was a place for high school students skipping first period so they didn't have to skip the movies with their boyfriends later. What was she going to use trigonometry for, anyway?

But as the trail veered left, Lindsay squinted

at the path ahead, her feet throbbing in time to her heart, her back sticky with sweat. She blinked away salt, her eyes stinging. What the heck was that?

Lindsay slowed as she finished rounding the gentle curve, then resorted to jogging in place. Not a killer, not a human at all, though that didn't make it any less intrusive—she could have kneed a strange man in the balls and been on her way. This was not so simple. A wall of greenery stood before her, the massive trunk taller than she was and barely visible through the thick foliage. Branches waved like kicking legs, each with enough leafy boughs to block the sun. From the black gouge along the trunk far down to her right, the giant oak had been struck by lightning and collapsed. *Quitter.*

Lindsay glanced back the way she'd come, debating. She could turn around and head back to the main path, then follow it around to her car. But she hadn't won a bookcase full of trophies for taking the easy way out.

Decision made, she approached the tree. She could not climb through—the branches were so thick, so haphazard and mean, that she wouldn't make it to the other side without getting wickedly gouged. To her right, the trunk reached who knew how far, the roots surely a minefield. And she was already in the upper boughs. Surely those leftward shadows led to the top of the tree, and the damaged earth where the oak had fallen carved out a passable aisle. She'd go around, pick up the path on the other side, and loop her way back to the fork when the time came; she knew where to cut through. Plus, she'd have a story to tell her coach, though she'd leave out the part about skipping school.

Her thighs burned as she jogged over the uneven ground, jumping the occasional extra-long branch and skirting dewberry and thistle. Above her, the canopy cleared, admitting the filtered dawn—the oak had taken some of the smaller saplings with it when it collapsed. The musk of mud and the wet heat of endurance filled her nose. It smelled like success.

Lindsay smiled. She ran on, and on, and on, letting her heart mellow into a steady ache, her lungs adjusting to the strain, her legs going numb. Euphoria rarely came easy, but once that runner's high kicked in, it was... well, even better than being with Jeff, and that was really saying somethi—

The earth vanished, her body hurtling through space. The ground smashed into Lindsay's shin like a freight train covered in broken glass. A loud snap echoed off the trees—another broken branch?

For a moment, she lay on the earth, panting. Stunned. She'd fallen, she knew that. Tripped. The shadow of the oak made the sweat on her face go cold, chilling her to the bone. She tried to force her hands beneath her, tried to push herself up, but she was shaking too badly. She collapsed in the mud, cheek against the ground, grit worming its way into her left nostril.

Then the pain hit.

It ripped through her consciousness, shattering her runner's high, a white-hot blast of pure agony. Lindsay shrieked, suddenly very aware of her solitude. She was miles from either town—she could scream for days without being heard. Perhaps she had been wrong about that serial killer lurking in the quiet woods. Maybe some murderer had set a trap and would come back for her at nightfall. The thought was delirious and irrational, but she clung to it with everything in her soul, letting it focus her.

The hell he'll come back to get me. I'm getting out of here!

Lindsay ground her teeth together hard enough to make her roots ache and shoved herself to seated, moaning, then tenderly shifted onto her butt. Her ankle was cocked at a weird angle, the bone not right—definitely not right. Her toes were hot, her shin a blistering fire poker that jabbed clear through her knee.

She snorted the grit from her nostril, gagged, choked back a sob, and blinked at the earth—too dark. Lindsay paused. She gaped at the blackness. The ground... wasn't there.

Tears leaked from the corners of her eyes. Was she imagining things, mad with pain? No. The earth near the tree was there, but several of the branches poked down into nothingness. A sweet gum pod, teetering on the edge, slipped away into the chasm. And fell.

And fell.

And fell.

She listened, frozen, waiting for the pod to hit the bottom...

Silence from the hole. Above, birds twittered, laughing at her. Blood pulsed frantically in her ears, dread tightening her chest. Was she sitting on top of the hole, protected only by the sparest tangle of dried vines? One wrong move, and she'd be swallowed up, hidden forever in the bowels of the earth.

Lindsay reached behind her, grabbing the

oak's branches for leverage—for safety—and yanked, her face slick with sweat and tears. She sobbed harder as she pulled herself away from the opening, easing back to stable ground. But the hole. She was still *so close* to the hole, her bad foot extending over the void as if begging some underworld creature to reach up and drag her, flailing, into the abyss. She grunted and moved again, her thigh grating against the ground—that wasn't dirt. Something hard, frigid, a little damp. Stone?

Lindsay shifted back again, catching her injured leg, crying out so loudly that the twittering birds took flight with a burst of staccato squawking. Her ankle burned. She hissed another inhale, panting with pain and exertion and terror. She'd calm down, *just calm down*, and then she'd fashion a cane. She'd limp back to her car. She would not be beaten by a friggin' hole—she would not be, literally, beaten by nothing.

With a final guttural heave, Lindsay hauled herself fully into the spiked web of branches, the ground beneath her solid. She blinked at the rocks, trying to catch her breath. The cavity in the muddy earth was guarded by a few rotten planks, their jagged splinters stabbing over the hole. The stones that bordered the opening were too uniform to be natural. Eroded, but stacked neatly at a concave angle. A... well?

The burst of focus might have been a distraction, her brain trying to ignore her misery, but Lindsay remained still, branches jabbing at the flesh of her back, staring. Though her leg was throbbing, fire shooting from toes to thigh, adrenaline pulsing in jagged bursts through her veins, she couldn't help but look.

Lindsey slowly shifted onto her good hip, tears coursing down her cheeks, and leaned over, craning her neck, clutching a branch for support. She squinted. At first, the foliage from the downed tree cast murky shadows into the hollow of the well. But as she watched, a shimmering beam of morning pierced the dim, blades of glitter cutting through the darkness at the bottom.

The images came to her in flashes, pulsing in time to the pain in her leg. The world stopped moving. And though she knew no one could hear her, Lindsay screamed again.

This time, she couldn't stop.

CHAPTER **TWO**

"Come on, Maggie. Why not?" Reid blinked, the rings around his amber irises glinting gold in the early sun. His red pocket square almost perfectly matched her red corduroys as if they'd planned it. A year ago, she hadn't imagined they'd end up here. Not because she consulted with the police department to catch serial killers, but because she and Reid hadn't started out as friends.

Maggie removed her reading glasses—dark cat-eyed frames. "Because you're a doofus, Reid, and I don't like you." Only part of that was true, but she tended to surround herself with doofuses, geeks, and spazzes on purpose. As her best friend Sammy would say, *it takes one to know one.* Even her glasses screamed "librarian with a penchant for *D&D*," which was pretty close to accurate.

Reid raised an eyebrow, the barest hint of stubble on his square jaw glittering. Light bounced around the items under the office window, too—her father's old sofa table, her brother's baseball still inside its leather glove. Aiden's photo shone beside it, his picture invisible behind the glare.

"Really?" Reid said. "And here I thought the chai might butter you up."

A birthday card might have worked better. Her business partner had a meeting with his lawyer, but Owen had still left her a cupcake and a fancy new ballpoint pen. Maggie tucked a long red curl behind her ear and glanced at the paper cup. She didn't need another celebration—she'd already had jalapeño toast and donut holes with Sammy and Alex, her nearest and dearest. They'd purchased a fountain for her backyard, too: cherubesque *Sesame Street* characters peeing into a birdbath. A real childhood ruiner, but she'd been in a battle of wits with the squirrels for months, and them drinking from a muppet toilet made her smile. It had been a good day so far. Until now.

She met Reid's gaze—so hopeful—and suppressed a sigh. "Do I look like I'd fit in at a police department gala?" Large groups of cops made her skin itch, and not because her father had taken an officer's bullet in the rib while protecting his suicidal patient. Nor was it because her mother was currently under house arrest.

Okay, maybe it was a little of those things. Maggie was the only one in the family who had yet to end up on the wrong side of the law. And Reid didn't know that she worked with an underground organization that helped domestic violence victims disappear. Not illegal, but she was riding that line pretty hard.

Reid crossed his ankle over the opposite knee. "They all want to meet the woman who's helping Ezra—the psychologist who solved several high-profile cases. I think they're hoping you'll work with others in the department."

I'd rather shove a cactus up my nose. "Serial killers are dramatic enough without having to break in a new partner."

He grinned and laid his hand over his heart. "You sweet-talker."

She rolled her eyes, then went on: "And I'm only treating Ezra as a favor to *you*. I'm certainly not seeking notoriety from the Fernborn PD." The boy was making progress; he was better at identifying emotions, better at conforming to the required behaviors at school. She'd never forget that Ezra had killed her pet tarantula, but he hadn't killed anyone else's pet; hadn't murdered any new humans either. Bully for him. And for Reid, too—Ezra's biological father was buried in the Fernborn cemetery, courtesy of a serial killer who'd enlisted Ezra's help. If only the boy hadn't taken to the task so enthusiastically.

Reid nodded to the cup on her desk—mostly cold now. "I knew that chai was good for something." Wait, what had they been talking about? Reid took a sip of his coffee, then leaned over to toss the empty cup into the can beside her desk. "Just think about it, okay? I know those things can be tedious, but I could use a friend. It might even be fun."

Right. A friend, not a date. Being coworkers made things sticky in the least fun sense of that phrase. Maggie shook her head. "Ask Tristan to go with you. He's a consultant too." A rich tech-businessman consultant who didn't need the job, but a consultant none the less.

Reid's gaze darkened. Instead of responding to the suggestion, he pressed his hands together, suit cuffs touching. Begging, complete with puppy dog eyes.

"You look like Elon Musk trying to get the

universe to *just love you a little more.*" Though Reid was cuter in his tall, broad-shouldered way. Not that things like that mattered to co-working friends.

"If the universe doesn't love him, it's certainly been kinder to him than he deserves." Reid dropped his hands to his lap. "I'm not asking for a favor without compensation. I'll give you anything you want."

Anything? *Interesting*. She laid her palms on her desk. "Fine. I'll go to this party with you, if you and Tristan have a guys' weekend together. No electronics, no work, just you and him, alone in the wilderness."

His brown eyes widened. He sat back in his chair in slow motion. "Are you serious?" He'd spent years trying to arrest his half-brother, until Maggie had helped to prove the man innocent. Tristan had been her patient at that time; it was how she and Reid had met.

"Serious as a mathematician on speed."

He opened his mouth as if to respond, then closed it again. His brow furrowed. "A... what?"

"A squirrel during nut season?"

He frowned. "When the hell is nut season?"

"As serious as you after three bran muffins, stuck in an elevator during a power outage." She slid her hands from the desktop and locked her fingers in her fiery curls, miming tear-her-hair-out frustration. "I don't care what metaphor you use. Even if you don't have brotherly barbecues, I think it's time you two buried the hatchet." *Hopefully not in one another's heads.*

"That is a sneaky shrink trick, using your company as a bargaining chip."

Maggie sat back and shrugged. It was a little sneaky, sure, but she had the best of intentions—she wasn't even benefitting in this bartering scenario. She was basically a saint. "I have to deal with you both every time I take a case, and it'll be easier if you get along." Tristan consulted as often as she did, taking the technical side while she worked the psychological.

Reid's eyes crinkled at the corners; he uncrossed his legs. He had this habit of crossing one ankle over the opposite knee if he was even a little anxious, and as a homicide detective, he was usually on edge.

"Fine," he said slowly. "You convince Tristan that we should go camping together, and I'll get the tents. But this is going to end badly." With a final sniff and a nod, Reid pushed himself to his feet. "In the meantime, I better get to work."

"Have a good one. And if you need a consult

about something besides partying, I'll be free first thing in the morning." *Because today is my birthday, and I'm taking the afternoon off.* She never took days off. Would he recognize this as a deviation in behavior?

Reid smiled and headed for the door. "Thanks, Maggie. I appreciate it."

Some detective you are. "Reid?"

He turned back.

"One tent," she said. "Make it a small one."

CHAPTER THREE

I SHOULDN'T BE HERE.

Maggie stared through the windshield at the strip mall. Two fast-food restaurants hulked out front, hiding the buildings in the back of the lot. A furniture store—closed down these days—sat to her left. Behind it was another building that appeared abandoned, and it almost was. Almost. The sign for psychic readings was always lit, a garish pink neon, but there was no palm reader, and no crystal balls waited behind the darkened glass. The flip sign on the door always read CLOSED. But a single stairway to the side of the building led to the basement, and beyond that...

She blinked.

Nothing said "happy birthday" like a few

hours in an underground sex club. It was anonymous, and everyone had to submit routine physicals complete with STD tests—safer than a one-night stand picked up in a bar. Plus, in the latter scenario, she'd have to go to a bar and talk to strangers. *Gross.*

Her fingers clenched, her knuckles white around the steering wheel. So why wasn't she getting out of the car? It was too early for others to have arrived, but she'd known what time it was before she drove down here. And she'd purposefully made plans with her friends this morning so she'd be alone tonight.

Maggie sighed. It wasn't that she didn't want to see her friends. Not even that she didn't want to celebrate. It was...

Her chest tightened. It was her second birthday without Kevin. The first had swum past in a haze of grief without her even realizing it *was* her birthday, but this one...

Yeah, this one. Thirty-seven, and she was fully aware that Kevin wasn't with her. Fully aware that no one had made her breakfast in bed or given her some silly gift—an RC car, a kite, an assortment of bouncy balls—while she was still in her pajamas. To be fair, it was hard to get over someone who drove themselves off a bridge when you turned down their marriage proposal. An accident? The police had ruled it as such. But when it was quiet, and the world was dark, Maggie wasn't sure.

She blinked at the psychic reading sign, the path that led to the stairwell. No one in this anonymous place would launch himself into a river because of her—no one here knew her well enough. And imagining Kevin's face over those of the masked men had eased the grief... for a while. When she'd closed her eyes, they even smelled like Kevin.

But it was dangerous to get attached, like choosing a pet at a chicken processing plant. And once she'd started seeking out the same man, once she'd begun putting Tristan's face over his leather mask, imagining that the man smelled like Tristan instead of Kevin...

None of that was healthy. She'd called it grieving when it was just Kevin's face, but it was obsessive to fantasize about an ex-patient like that. And she felt saner when she was away from Tristan and from this club; she should probably leave before she started to backslide.

The bobblehead on her dashboard stared at her: Beaker from *The Muppet Show*, his plastic eyes glaring—judging her. She had bobblehead

Bert in her drawer at work. Bobblehead Ernie had watched Kevin drive off that bridge, had watched him die, nodding the whole time.

Maggie loosened her fingers and wiped her sweaty palms on her pants. *What are you doing, Mags? Go home. Call Sammy.* But she didn't want to fight the tightness around her heart, the sickness in the pit of her stomach. She didn't want to eat cake and pretend that she wanted to be there and not wrapped in Kevin's arms. The dissonance was exhausting.

That's why I'm here. I don't want to pretend.

She glared through the windshield at the pink neon—PSYCHIC READINGS—the flip sign underneath it: CLOSED. Then she shifted her Sebring convertible into drive, wishing she still had her DeLorean. One day, she'd get a new one. Hopefully, the next one wouldn't also be destroyed by an arsonist serial killer. She wasn't sure what the odds of that were, but probably better than Reid understanding her next ludicrous comparison. *A squirrel during nut season? Come on.*

The restaurants at the front of the parking lot glared, angry with their bright reds and yellows, the colors carefully chosen to entice hungry customers through their doors. But the highway beyond was quiet before rush hour, a vast expanse of asphalt kissed by jaundiced sun.

Maggie pushed the pedal to the floor.

The late afternoon whizzed by on either side of the car, the speed reducing the dotted highway lines to a bright stripe, leading her home. She swerved around a truck that was probably doing ten above the posted limit, then slowed for a speed trap two miles before her exit.

She squinted at the officer, half hidden in the brush at the shoulder. *Sucker.* She took the ramp, checked her rearview once more as she rounded the curve onto the main road, and gunned it.

Her father's place was located on the outskirts of the city—the home where her mother and father had lived and loved and eventually divorced. Every day, it seemed more like she might stay there for good. Her house had burned down, and her father wasn't going to move back from the retirement village with or without her help. He hadn't *wanted* her to be a full-time caregiver—had forbidden it back when he was still lucid enough to forbid anything. But a little voice sometimes whispered that she should take a sabbatical from work; that maybe he'd remember her again, however briefly, if she was with him twenty-four seven.

Maybe they'd have a few days where he didn't mistake her for a nurse or the orderly. Maybe she'd get just *one more hour* where she could tell him about her world, and he could say he was proud of her. She could cling to that for the rest of her life.

Maggie swung the car into the driveway and parked along the left side of the pavement, near the steps. Reid had tried to get her to install floodlights and cameras, but it felt sacrilegious to change things from the way her dad had left them. Maybe she had a bit of a wild streak, fine, but more than that, if she had a camera, she was certain that Tristan would hack into it. That he'd... watch her. It might be ridiculous, her overthinking brain on high alert. But she couldn't shake the thought. He'd put a tracker on her phone once, so sneaking into a video feed wasn't completely out of the question.

Maybe you're just afraid that you'd like him watching, Maggie. Did you ever think of that?

Maggie kicked the car door open—of course she'd considered that. Her brain was basically a sponge that squished out bursts of racing thoughts. If someone made an action movie about her, it'd be called *The Ponderer*, and her superpower would be sitting quietly in a room while her brain worked up a million scenarios that would never actually come true.

She headed up the stairs, the wind at her back whispering against her pinstriped blouse, her corduroys humming with every step, a noise that snarled with the twittering of birdsong. She should have gone to the retirement village, but she couldn't bear her father forgetting her today. And her mother... what the heck was she doing? Mom had never been the nurturing sort, she'd left that to Maggie's father, but Maggie usually got a phone call on her birthday. Was a balloon emoji text too much to ask for?

Maggie shoved her key into the lock and twisted, but paused with her hand on the knob. A wicker chair and a small metal table sat on the porch, more for decoration than utility. But in the shadows of the eaves, sitting atop the wicker chair, was... something. Something that shouldn't be there.

She approached cautiously, squinting at the basket. A bouquet of wildflowers—she wasn't one for roses—a little yellow card nestled amidst the leaves. And in the center, a red velvet box tied in a purple bow. A strange choice, the colors clashing, but... She glanced down at her red cords, her pinstriped blouse. Fine, it was kinda perfect.

Maggie reached between the petals and slipped the card from the envelope first, black typewritten letters: "Happy birthday, Maggie." Nothing more. But she already knew who it was from; she'd known the moment she saw the gift lurking in the shadows.

Tristan. She didn't like that his attention made her feel both queasy and warm at the same time, but the flowers were... nice. Not nice enough to install an easily hackable doorbell cam, but nice all the same. And the box...

She loosened the purple ribbon. Her breath caught. *Whoa.* The bracelet inside glittered in the porch lights—diamonds. A *lot* of diamonds. He'd given her many gifts over the past year and a half, from armed guards at her father's retirement village, to deliveries of corned beef sandwiches, to airline tickets to New Orleans with passes to a Weird Al concert—her favorite musician. Maggie had never acknowledged the presents, had never said anything more than "Hey, you have to stop." A relationship forged when you were someone's shrink was not one you should engage in, especially if you'd ever superimposed his face over a masked submissive in a sex club.

Maggie swallowed hard. Flowers were one thing—acceptable, reasonable as a birthday gift for a coworker or your grandmother. The jewelry *felt* wrong. And sometimes, you had to go with your gut, especially when your logical brain was telling you the same thing.

Her cell buzzed. She placed the velvet box back inside the bouquet and retrieved her phone from her pocket. Text message. From... Tristan.

"HAPPY BIRTHDAY!"

How does he do that? Even without the doorbell cam, he always seemed to know where she was and what she was doing. Yeah, this suddenly felt a lot less nice and a lot more creepy. Her fingers paused over the keys. *Thank you?* Was that what she wanted to write? *Knock it off, stalker?* That was closer. She sighed. She'd wait until tomorrow, give herself time to ponder what to say, like any good overthinker should. As much as she appreciated the flowers, she couldn't accept any of it. She couldn't accept *him* as anything more than a coworker, and a nosy, intrusive coworker at that. Oh wait...

"Call Reid. He's taking you to the woods."

Nailed it. That'd give him pause after his creepy "I'm somehow watching you open my gifts" text. The response came immediately: a single question mark. But she wasn't in the mood to elaborate. He needed to learn to follow instructions... like a submissive in a sex club.

The phone buzzed again before she could slip it back into her pocket—he was calling her this time. But... no. Not Tristan. A local number that she didn't recognize. Maggie lifted the cell to her ear.

"Magma Connolly?"

Her spine tightened. *Magma*—her parents had hated her from the moment she was born; that, or her mom had wanted to toughen her up, a plan which had backfired spectacularly. "This is Maggie."

"Evening, ma'am. This is Detective Malone in Tysdale. If it isn't too much trouble, can you come down to the station?"

Malone... the name was familiar, though she couldn't place it. *Looks like my fame and fortune has exploded even without the police department gala.* She liked the way he talked, too, a genuine but careful kindness—*if it isn't too much trouble?* What was he, Canadian?

With a final glance at the bouquet, she said:

"My office hours are Monday through Friday, nine to four. You can call back then for an appointment, but I'm not sure I have room in my schedule for a case consultation." Maybe she could pawn him off on Owen. Owen hated her working with the police, and Reid already gave her more than she could handle.

Wow, that sounded dirty.

"Ma'am?" She didn't hear disappointment in his voice—just confusion. "A consultation?"

Not a consultation. Then why would detectives in Tysdale want to see her today...

The world stilled, the chirruping birds suddenly silent.

The man cleared his throat. "I'm not sure how to tell you this, and I really hate to be the bearer of bad news, but... it'd be very helpful if you could meet me at the station. We need you to identify a body."

CHAPTER **FOUR**

THE MORGUE WAS LOCATED at the hospital, attached to the main building via a long, dry hallway that smelled inexplicably of mustard. Surely better than the rotting corpse smell that might permeate the air otherwise, the reek of formaldehyde or rubbing alcohol or the smoked flesh of a house fire victim. No windows—apparently, it was always midnight in the corpse zone.

Maggie swallowed hard, breathing through her mouth. *Happy birthday to me.* Maybe the body she was there to identify would have a bow on it, stuck to its pale forehead like a thunderously terrible white elephant gift.

Detective Malone met her halfway down the

hall, his wide, flat mug drawn into a grimace that she had come to identify as "dead-kid" face. He hadn't told her who he thought the body was, not explicitly, but there were only so many people it might be. Alex didn't have other family —was her best friend dead? Sammy's wife would be here if something had happened to him. If her mother was dead, Maggie would be a likely first call, but she was under house arrest; she wouldn't be here in Tysdale. And if it was her brother after all these years...

She shook the thought aside. If they thought the body belonged to her brother, they should have called her mom first, and there were no other murmuring voices in this abandoned hallway. The woman might have forgotten her birthday, might not have made it to the morgue because of her tether, but she'd certainly have called Maggie if they'd found Aiden's body.

Malone's eyes remained friendly enough as he introduced himself. "So sorry about all this..." —*soory* and *aboot*. Definitely a Canadian, and with his flat, jowly face, his dark, wrinkly leather jacket, he resembled a Canadian pug. That was what he sounded like, too, the lifts in his shiny shoes clacking like dog nails against the linoleum.

She followed Malone through the swinging doors at the end of the hall and into another sterile pass-through. Three narrow doors on either side, all the swinging variety like the entry, just wide enough for a gurney. But the guard planted in the middle of the hall made it secure enough. Theft was clearly not the biggest concern in this section of the hospital. Obscuring evidence might be an issue, but screwing with a corpse was an admission of guilt. How often could that possibly happen?

Stop thinking, Maggie. But she didn't really want to. Inane thoughts about the mustard-scented hallway or the pug-faced detective or the screwing about of corpses kept her from considering what she was doing here: identifying a body. A dead body. Someone she knew.

Malone used two fingers to wave to the still-seated guard, a thin, wiry specimen with the face of a raccoon but deeper circles beneath his eyes. The man waved them past with barely a glance. They knew each other—of course they did. Tysdale was a small town, smaller than Fernborn, and even Fernborn wasn't thrumming with night lights and party people... though they might have fewer Canadians.

Malone pushed into the room at the end of

the hall. He turned sideways to let her pass, keeping his foot on the jamb.

But as she stepped nearer the threshold, Maggie's shoes went heavy, rooted to the floor like she'd stepped in a puddle of nearly set super-glue, her eyes locked on the open door—on the leaden space beyond. What waited there in the dimness of that room? Should she have asked to see the detective's credentials? Asked who they thought the corpse was, so she didn't get blindsided?

Maggie inhaled—nothing. No rotting flesh smell, no antiseptic or formaldehyde. Just the metal. And the mustard.

Malone was still watching her, waiting, his heel against the corner of the door.

Maggie swallowed hard and forced herself forward, past Malone. *Ah*—he was the one who reeked of mustard seed. The door hissed closed behind them.

Cold inside the little room, and smaller than she'd imagined. A counter ran the length of the back wall—clean now, scratched and dented, but without a single scalpel. Two people stood in front of the counter, but Maggie couldn't seem to look at them. Her eyes were locked on the silver table in the center of the room, the top covered with a thin skin of blanket. The bulges beneath the blue sheet were far too small.

Her stomach clenched. This was the body? Or was it only part of a body? A leg, maybe, or just a torso. Or maybe it was someone she knew intimately—could you identify a body from only a penis? In her experience, most were unremarkable.

"This is my partner," Malone said. "And Doctor Fran Getty."

Maggie dragged her eyes from the table to rest on those standing behind it. But the moment she registered the other faces in the room, she froze. The hairs along her spine bristled.

Maggie had never met Detective Malone, nor did she know the medical examiner. But she recognized the other man: Detective Nick Birman. Her father's age, with wrinkles that ran like tributaries through his high forehead. He had the same squinty gray eyes she remembered, the high ball cheeks, an oversized mouth—clownish, if you added a little lipstick—and plaid flannel made him look more maple-syrup Canadian than Malone. The bushy gray-streaked beard was new, presumably to hide the enormous dent in his chin. She and Sammy had spent significant time pondering how much that cleft looked like a butt.

"Are you okay, Doctor Connolly?" Malone asked from behind her.

She nodded. But she wasn't. Her chest was a twisted nest of thorny heat, her back rigid as if she had a steel rod implanted in her spine. Birman—it had to be that dingus. Which meant the body was...

The woman in the corner stepped forward, tight ribbons of black curls piled atop her head, heavy lips drawn with concern. The doctor lifted the top hem of the sheet, then pulled it slowly to rest at the base of the stainless steel table.

The bones hadn't been cleaned, not yet, the ends still bearing grainy bits of dirt and sand. Yellowed bone streaked by black, the kind of good, wormy dirt you needed to grow tomatoes. The killer had buried him deep.

Maggie's guts hardened into a knotted ball of fire. Murdered. Had to be, right?

She stepped closer, two hollow footsteps that bounced against every metallic surface in turn, a ricocheting patter she felt in the roots of her teeth.

They'd removed the clothing, if any had existed. No remnants of hair remained. So small—all of him so small.

She did not raise her eyes from the table as she asked: "Why isn't my mother here?"

"We called her a few times," Birman said. "Unfortunately, we haven't been able to locate her."

That... wasn't possible. The woman had a tether. Then again, she had been joking about absconding to the Maldives since they put her under house arrest, and that would explain the lack of balloon emojis.

But Maggie frowned, her gaze still on Birman's. Something wasn't right. She watched, studying his clownish face for twitches in the tiny muscles around the eyes—still. But his nostrils flared. A sheen of sweat glistened at his temples. Huh. He was... *lying* about contacting her mom. He wanted her here alone.

Maggie sensed the rise of heat in her chest, but she could barely feel it over the squeezing tightness around her heart.

Aiden. My brother is dead.

She swallowed hard and forced out, "Where'd they find him?" Him. Was this really a him anymore? A body. Just bones. A life reduced to a pile of calcium and mulch.

"An old well," Malone said. "Deep in the woods, smack-dab between Fernborn and Tysdale." Miles from either town. Miles from help. There were smaller sections of trees that wove themselves between the middle school and the residential streets, and she suddenly wished that he had been found there, in the woods nearer to civilization—a place less *lonely*. But the isolation was, presumably, the killer's goal.

"Who?" Her voice cracked, and she cleared her throat to cover it, then glanced over her shoulder to look at Malone.

Malone raised an eyebrow. "Sorry?" *Soory*. Birman was still glaring at her from across the stainless table. She could feel his gaze like needles on her skin.

"Who found him?" she tried again.

"Ah." Malone sniffed. "Local girl. She tripped, busted herself up pretty good, but she managed to make her way back out. Five miles on a shattered ankle." Damn if he didn't look impressed.

"I'll buy her a fruit basket or something," she muttered, turning back to the table. *I have a diamond bracelet she might like.* But her words, even the thoughts in her own brain felt as if they were coming from someone else. Her gaze dropped to the body. To the skull, the front part of the mouth where three teeth were lighter than the others. After the injury, her mother had held him in her lap on the way to the hospital, singing in her too-bright off-key way.

"Did he have any distinguishing marks?" Malone asked as if reading her mind. "We're reasonably certain because of the clothing found with him, items he was last seen wearing, but if he had broken bones, injuries that might be—"

"He knocked them out," she said. "Slipped on a puddle in the kitchen and hit his mouth on the counter."

The other three followed her gaze to the skull. To Aiden's spacer, cemented to his other—real—teeth.

"So, you believe this to be your brother?" Malone said, stepping toward the table into Maggie's peripheral.

Maggie nodded. She didn't just believe this was Aiden—she was positive. All the times she'd hoped they'd find him, dead or alive, just so she'd know for sure... she regretted that now. Sometimes it was better not to know. Sometimes it was better to believe the worst hadn't happened—that if he was really gone, it was fast and painless. That he hadn't seen it coming.

Maggie didn't want to imagine him dying

slowly—suffering. But though her insides were shaking, though bile was burning her throat, though her heart was popping like firecrackers in her chest, she couldn't stop herself from asking: "Do they know what happened? How he—"

She looked up in time to see Birman squint his beady eyes at her. "We'll be going over everything with a fine-toothed comb in the coming days." That was a good thing, but his timbre was all wrong, laced with threat. "But preliminarily..." He turned to Dr. Getty.

Dr. Getty nodded, her eyes on the bones. She gestured with thin fingers—piano player's fingers. "From a distinctive puncture in the jacket and a similar tear in the shirt beneath, I believe he was stabbed in the chest. In all likelihood, such an injury would have pierced his heart. It would have been fast."

Stabbed. In the heart. But though the doctor clearly hoped it had been quick, she didn't *know*. Maggie closed her eyes, and in the darkness behind her lids, she could see her brother, tears on his cheeks, his lips trickling a steady stream of red—slowly bleeding out. She could hear him, too, screaming for her from the bottom of that lonely well. Because she was supposed to have been there, she should have been with him, she was supposed to walk him home—

Her eyes snapped open. She didn't want to know about his last minutes on this earth. Absolutely not.

"We might not have all the information yet," Birman said, "but it's clear that he was murdered. I'm sure you already knew that."

Dr. Getty frowned. Malone blinked.

An interrogation—of course. After all, that was why he wanted her here alone; why he lied about not being able to find her mother.

Maggie's fists balled at her sides. *Don't hit him, Maggie. Don't do it.* She was not generally quick to anger, but Birman had been there when Aiden vanished, he'd made it a hundred times worse, and now he wanted to screw with her head while she identified Aiden's bones. *What an asshole.*

"You were pretty beat up that day," Birman said. "If I remember correctly."

Oh, he definitely remembered correctly. And he didn't know the half of it. The scar on the back of her head pulsed, once, twice—a deep, warm ache. She could feel the blood on her hands, too. But that blood wasn't hers.

"I was a dork, detective." *Was—past tense?* "I

got beat up all the time." Not really true, especially after her and Sammy had become friends, but that wasn't why she'd been injured the day her brother died.

The scar pulsed again, sharp and angry, and this time she hissed a breath through clenched teeth. She should call Sammy. No, Alex. Her face burned. Her mother was probably eating dinner, blissfully unaware of her son's dirty bones, busy forgetting all about birthdays and daughters, except step-daughters, whom her mother had said were "a few bricks short of a wall."

I wish I could call Kevin.

She blinked at the detective, but Birman was carefully avoiding her gaze, frowning at the body. Was there a sign of a struggle on those bones? "Why'd you ask about getting beat up? Do you think he got into a fight with his killer?"

"You fed us that line the first time," Birman said. *I'd love to feed you a knuckle sandwich.* "We looked at every punk in that school—every bully."

Doctor Getty's nostrils flared, her lips tight. She was used to dealing with bodies, but clearly less so detectives harassing the families of murder victims. "It wasn't a line," Maggie snapped. "I answered your questions."

"Either way, it's a little early to make definitive statements about what happened here." Birman's clown lips peeled back, almost a snarl, and her shoulders went rigid. "You need to level with me. I know you're hiding something."

Maggie balked, but before she could retort, Birman went on: "Where is your mother?"

"At home—she has to be at home. And if you think my mom did something wrong because she didn't answer your call, you're a terrible detective. Maybe she just thinks you're a jerk."

Malone snorted, and she turned his way, but he wasn't watching her. His gaze was locked on Birman, eyes hot with accusation, more agitated than she'd seen any Canadian. It seemed he didn't like his partner's antics any more than she did.

Birman cleared his throat. "Miss Connolly? We really need to know where your mother is. If there's nothing to hide, she wouldn't be avoiding us."

That wasn't necessarily true. "You don't know anything about my mother." But her mother was under house arrest. If she wasn't home, if she *really* wasn't home...

"Miss Connolly," Birman repeated.

"*Doctor* Connolly." The voice did not belong

to her, nor did it belong to the detectives. She turned.

The door swished open, surely a less dramatic entrance than he'd intended. Reid stalked in, his face pink with irritation, staring daggers at Detective Birman.

CHAPTER **FIVE**

"I'm sorry it took me so long to get there," Reid said. The tips of his fingers left divots in the side of the paper coffee cup. That had to hurt—her chai was hot enough to burn her palm.

The coffeehouse had been their meeting place before anyone had said the word *partner*, before anyone had imagined that they might work together regularly. Even she hadn't seen it as a long-term thing. Then again, she'd never expected to identify her brother's remains on her birthday. Life was full of surprises.

"I didn't expect you to show up at all," she said. "How did you even know about the...?" *The body.* It still didn't feel right to say it aloud, like she was reducing everything her brother was to a single, literally dirty word. In her mind's eye, she saw dark striations of filth clinging to what was left of him.

"Clark called me," he said, settling his cup beside hers.

"Oh." She frowned. Detective Clark Lavigne was a detective here in Fernborn, so he knew that Maggie consulted with the department, that she and Reid worked together. But why was he in Tysdale? Had they temporarily joined forces because a body in those woods might have been a resident of either town? "Well, it meant a lot that you were there. And just in time to save me from that clown of a detective."

Reid palpated the side of his coffee cup as if trying to undo the damage he'd inflicted. He failed. "What was he on about, anyway?"

"Just typical clown stuff," she muttered, dropping her eyes to the table.

"Unicycles?"

"You're thinking of bears." A tiny drop of condensation glistened on the wood near her pinky. She smeared it into a comma with her fingernail, then sighed out: "He said that he couldn't find my mom. To tell her about Aiden."

"Did you call her?"

The comma stretched into an exclamation

point. Maggie nodded at her fingers, then raised her head. "Yeah—twice on the way here. No answer. But she's under house arrest. Whether she picked up the phone or not, they can see where she is. She didn't take the tether off, or they'd know that too. And she's already violated once; if she goes outside the boundary of that tether again, she goes back to jail." Would she do that? Not on Maggie's birthday, right? Then again, you'd think the seventeen hours of labor would at least mean a balloon emoji. *Why am I so obsessed with balloon emojis?*

"For now, let's keep my Incredible Vanishing Mother between us," she said. "Birman was lying about her, about contacting her—I could tell by his face. But I don't know why yet, and if she's home, I don't want to send up any red flags." *And if she's not, I don't want to be the reason she gets locked up—not today.* Maybe tomorrow, though.

Reid tugged at the neck of his button-down; he'd already tossed his jacket over the back of the chair. "My lips are sealed. Like a squirrel during nut season."

"You don't know crap about squirrels, Reid."

He lifted his coffee and took a tentative sip that felt less like drinking and more like stalling.

"Yeah, I'm no zoologist. But I do know that what I heard at the morgue wasn't about your mom."

Yeah… that. The scar—the bite—on the back of her head spasmed sharply, as if the missing flap of skin had returned to attack. Exhaustion tugged at her limbs, begging her to go home. But she had to tell him—had to tell *someone* what really happened that day so they could tease apart the timeline. The only other person who'd ever known was Kevin. When they were teenagers, she'd been too afraid to tell anyone, and later, she'd worried about Kevin's sobriety too much to risk discussing it. The days it popped into his head on its own, how he'd left her in that building to be attacked, how they'd left that boy bleeding on the floor afterward… those were hard days for him. Hard weeks. Months.

Maggie's eyes grazed the front counter where a pair of twenty-somethings were ordering enough cookies to feed an army. "Birman was accusing me of homicide, the same way you did the day we met." She watched the pair take their snacks and vanish into the night, then turned her face toward Reid.

His lips had tightened—guilt? "I didn't accuse you of murder. I accused *Tristan* of murder and accused you of knowing about it."

She raised the chai to her lips and cut her eyes away, examining the third chair, the concave shadows on the wood, anything but Reid's face. It wasn't the sorrow that was so acutely etched into the folds around Reid's eyes, but the understanding that radiated off him like a cloud of perfume. If she allowed herself to breathe it in, she might not be able to breathe at all, and she did not have time to succumb to sorrow. Because now that Aiden was dead, now that she knew for sure...

Now she had to catch a killer. She'd been a frightened child back when he'd vanished, but she was no longer afraid of the consequences of her actions. And as long as Nick Birman saw her as a suspect, he wasn't focused on finding the person who'd actually killed her brother.

"You had a reason to suspect me, Reid. He does too." She kept her eyes on the chair, but she heard him straighten; saw his fingertips edge onto the table in her peripheral vision. She could almost imagine Aiden sitting in that empty chair, watching, laughing, shoveling cookies into his maw. Her lungs ached.

"What possible reason would Birman have to suspect—"

"The day my brother disappeared, I was attacked. My ex, Kevin... we were screwing around at this abandoned building. It had been vacant for years, but it was set to be demolished the next day, so we were breaking windows, smashing stuff. Pretty typical, I guess."

He inhaled sharply—*what kind of delinquent sees that as typical?* But she'd always had a bit of a wild streak. So had Kevin. *God, I miss him. And Aiden.*

Her throat tightened, itchy and hot, but she forced out: "Kevin left for a few minutes, and this... guy came in. At least three years older than I was, maybe sixteen? Only a year or so older than Kevin." She could suddenly smell the dust, kicked up from the building's floor in the struggle, see the slanted light from the grimy windows superimposed over the wooden curves of the chair. "He threw me onto the floor, his knee in my back. I elbowed him. He... bit the back of my head."

Her scar brightened with heat, a searing bolt of lightening. And though she knew it wasn't real, she felt the heat of her own blood running over the back of her neck.

Reid shifted again, probably crossing his ankle over his knee, but then she felt his fingers on hers. Warm. Maybe from the coffee. Maybe not.

"There was glass on the floor from one of the interior windows. One shard was bigger than the others, and it was just... glittering like a beacon, you know?"

Reid said nothing; he squeezed her hand the way Kevin had when he dragged her out of that building.

"I managed to kick myself onto my side. The glass went right through his cheek—opened up the whole side of his face below his cheekbone. Kevin came back and found me on the ground, bleeding, and the guy face down in the corner."

Reid pulled his hand back and leaned toward her, his elbows on the table. "Maggie—"

"I had blood on my shirt"—*just let me get it out, Reid!*—"and the wound on my head..." She swallowed hard. "It wasn't visible beneath my hair, but my clothes were gross. We had to go over to the school gym to clean up. When I got home, I snuck in and took a shower. Made sure I was presentable, so no one would know what had happened—what I'd done to that guy. I didn't even think about Aiden until a few hours later when my dad started knocking on the door, asking me where my brother was."

Reid waited a beat, perhaps expecting to be interrupted again. When she remained silent, he said, "So, Birman saw your injuries and thought you had something to do with your brother vanishing? I would have assumed that someone attacked you both, not that you were guilty of harming Aiden."

That... was a great point. Why hadn't she considered it? Probably because she felt so guilty about not walking Aiden home. Birman's accusations, while unfounded, had felt like just desserts.

She sighed and finally looked into Reid's face. His eyes were glittering with sympathy and sadness, but not pity. "You'd have to ask him, I guess," she said. "Especially since there were witnesses who cleared me. A teacher saw us heading into the high school locker room right around the time Aiden was leaving the middle school."

"Ah." He nodded, barely discernible. "That means... you thought your attacker had an alibi for the time Aiden vanished, too. That even if he left the building right after you did, he was injured and would have needed to tend his wounds instead of kidnapping a child. Which is another reason you didn't say anything."

She cleared her throat; her windpipe felt too small. "I thought it might pull focus from my missing brother. But it wasn't just that. I panicked for days that the guy would... I don't know. Tell the police I stabbed him? And Kevin was pretty distraught about it, too, begged me not to say anything. He thought we'd get into trouble, and his dad was a lot meaner than mine." She shrugged. "But once I knew Aiden was missing, it seemed inconsequential. The best-case scenario was that I'd be in trouble for vandalizing the building and stabbing a dude in the head, Kevin's dad would beat him for breaking windows, the guy would be in trouble for biting me, Aiden would still be gone, and my mom... I mean, she had always been a little off, but after Aiden, she kinda lost it. Pulled away from me, from my dad. We've only recently begun getting closer again, but that was before she violated her tether."

Maggie put her palm on the table and wiped away the condensation, then grabbed her cup. No longer hot; were her fingers numb? "Anyway, Birman started giving me shit, and I stopped talking altogether. I'm sure that looked suspicious." And as the months passed, there was less reason to talk about it—why implicate herself in a crime no one was investigating? They'd torn the building down the next day as planned, as if to erase the events from Fernborn's history. "If I'd thought for even a minute that this was connected, that my admission would help catch Aiden's kidnapper"—*killer*—"I would have told them."

"Didn't you think it was weird that someone attacked both you and your brother on the same day?"

She sipped the chai—watery. Cold. "Not really. I thought it was a terrible coincidence. Why would some random kid attack me and then kill my brother?"

"Without knowing who he was, that's hard to say."

Fair enough. "I'm no help there. I'd never seen him before. He didn't go to my school, and even if he wore a disguise, Kevin would have recognized a kid with a knife wound to the face at Fernborn High."

"A... disguise?" He raised an eyebrow.

"Like a fake mustache or something."

Reid blinked. *What did I say?* Finally, he shook his head. "I'll get Tristan poking around the hospital archives, looking for that injury." He leaned back, rocking the chair on two legs. "Do you remember what he looked like? Any distinguishing characteristics?"

"Yeah, he had half a face."

One corner of Reid's mouth turned up, but it didn't reach his eyes. *Too soon?*

She squinted, trying to remember, but witness accounts degraded after a few days, if they were ever right to begin with. Plus, he'd been sixteen at most; whatever she remembered would have changed drastically in the past twenty-four years.

"He had bright green eyes—that's really all I know for sure. I don't want to be responsible for sending Malone on a wild goose chase." Why not Birman? *Because I have a weird feeling about that guy—my gut is telling me that he's all kinds of wrong.*

Reid's voice brought her back. "Or maybe you don't want Malone looking for this guy because you still don't think it's possible for your attacker to have taken Aiden."

She shook her head. "Aiden wouldn't have walked past the building to get home—the middle school and the woods are on the opposite side of town. There's no reason they would have crossed paths, even if that green-eyed devil left right after me. And I can't imagine he'd have been physically capable of carrying Aiden five miles through the woods after being injured." Her hands felt hot—

sticky—the broken glass biting into the meat of her palm. She glanced down, but saw only the waxed paper coffee cup, her fingertips pale against the side.

"Eventually, we'll have to tell Birman, but let me do a little digging," Reid said. "Any other shady characters around? Could Aiden's murder be related to your father's work? Or to your mother?"

She snorted and jerked the cup to the table hard enough to send drops of tea exploding through the hole in the lid. Maggie winced and rubbed at the stains on her blouse, then gave up and crossed her arms. "They pulled my father's caseload apart. Or rather, he did, back when they were trying to find Aiden." That was one reason he and her mother had divorced. He'd spent all his time locked in his office, poring over case files, looking for clues to her brother's disappearance. Her mother had just wanted them to forget.

"I had to ask," Reid said. "About your parents. Especially with their criminal histories. Your dad working with convicts, and your mom..."

And her mother, being a convict herself. Her mother, who had originally been arrested for providing illegal weapons to abuse victims, who'd violated her tether and spontaneously vanished just in time to avoid identifying her son's remains. Where the hell was she? She had to be at home—Birman would have thrown "we have an arrest warrant out" in Maggie's face otherwise, just to put her off her game during his stupid morgue interrogation. House arrest was a last-chance scenario, one last shot for her mother to, as she said, watch Maggie get married and have kids. Maggie believed she was more likely to fall madly in love with that clown Birman... or Bozo. Maybe *IT*. At least Pennywise had a bad-boy past, which seemed to be her thing.

Reid was still watching her. "I know you had to ask," she said. "I asked myself that too. But no, I don't think Aiden's murder is connected to my parents' work." Maggie glanced once more at the extra seat. Not even a hint of the ghost she'd imagined earlier, as if Aiden had already erased himself from the blackboard of her memory. Her chest tightened.

She pushed herself to her feet fast enough that she almost toppled her chair. It clattered back onto four legs as she said: "I should try to get some sleep."

"Can I drive you home?" Reid's voice rang hollow—far away. She suddenly felt profoundly alone. Like Aiden must have.

"No. I'm fine to drive."

"I can follow you," he said, grabbing his suit jacket. "You have to be hungry; it's nearly seven. I'll call the babysitter and—"

"Don't bother."

Reid frowned, his eyes tight. "Maggie, you shouldn't be alone right now."

She shook her head, but he was right—she shouldn't. Which is why she had no intention of staying that way.

It would be cruel to let her mother find out about Aiden the same way she had.

CHAPTER
SIX

MAGGIE TOOK the long way to her mother's, traversing the snarl of fading rush-hour on the highway, then the heavy traffic along the strip where the shopping mall was located. Even the tiniest of towns had a strip mall and a few pockets of entertainment. In Fernborn, it was family-owned restaurants. Bowling. Ax throwing.

Smashing windows in vacant buildings. Stabbing people in the face. Burying children in the woods.

She tightened her fingers on the wheel until her knuckles went white and her palms burned and the thoughts subsided. The middle school passed on her left, a long single story of gray bricks and maroon trim. She'd met Sammy in elementary, so she could not credit Fernborn Middle with her most significant childhood friendship, but she had met Alex there, in the bathroom. Alex had been cleaning the wound on her chest after a radical mastectomy—an extremely early cancer diagnosis that had led to the loss of her breast. A one in a million chance, maybe one in two million. She'd never actually looked it up, but she did know it was rare, like losing a brother. Focusing on the other's pain had helped them both.

Maggie hooked a right and made her way toward the bleeding horizon. The floodlights beneath the high school's billboard made the grass glitter like diamonds in an unwanted bracelet, the sign screaming: CONGRATULATIONS SENIORS! Maggie's back tensed as she approached. More gray brick, more maroon doors and trim. She could practically see herself making her way down the sidewalk, limping, bleeding, Kevin putting pressure against the back of her head, acting like he was innocently hugging her whenever anyone glanced their way. The gym had smelled of old socks, the locker room of yeast and sweat. But there had been clean towels there. And Kevin's spare jacket, which had more effectively covered the evidence—the blood. It had been enough to get her home without arousing suspicion. And while she was busy sneaking through town, while she was busy hiding her wounds, her brother was...

Aiden's bones blinked in her mind's eye, dull like the bricks, covered in soil and bugs down at the bottom of that lonely well. The high school faded in her rearview. Maggie forced her fingers to relax and turned left at the next light.

The site where the vacant building once sat was within walking distance of the high school, but it felt exceptionally close while driving. The expanse of green space rolled from the gloom, barbecue grills glinting amidst the picnic tables, the setting sun multiplying the metal rungs of ladders and monkey bars, elongating their black shadows until the swing sets looked like prison cells. She and Kevin used to come here at night, Maggie pumping her legs on the swings while silvery threads of moonlight gently erased the unspoken horrors of that building, replacing the dust, the blood with the smell of Kevin's skin, the feeling of his hand on her low back, the taste of his watermelon bubble gum. She'd loved him since that day. She loved him still.

I should have said yes.

Maggie braked at the curb hard enough to lock her seatbelt. The city council had preserved the old building's foundation and repurposed it for a single-story indoor gathering area. Basic, like the school, just bricks, a bunch of long wooden tables, and a shingled roof, but they'd trussed up the front walk with perennials and flowering bushes.

Why are you here, Maggie? Old time's sake?

No. She needed to think. She needed the reverent silence that she had not gotten in the morgue.

Maggie climbed from the car and approached, the wind rustling the brush, wafting sickly sweet lilac air toward the end of the walkway. She stared down the flowering tunnel until the bushes and the swings faded in her peripheral. Soon all she could see were the six stories of murky brown bricks, brown trim, half the windows busted out, the others glinting dully beneath a coat of yellow grime.

The back of her head throbbed. It was not the sharp pang of a fresh wound, but the heavy ache unique to dead teeth and remembrance. The police department had lobbied hard to tear that building down because they'd known the lot was dangerous. For her, demolition had come a single day too late.

She stood on the sidewalk, watching the

building fade from brown to black as twilight eased into night. And as the uplights came on around the foundation, as the moon finally pulled her head from beneath the cover of gauzy clouds, Maggie felt the sharp pressure of his knee against her spine, the muggy heat of his breath on her neck. The salty musk of his sweat stung her nose. She could taste the dirt off the floor, gritty, dry, feel the jagged glass against her palm. If she hadn't caught her shirt between the glass and her flesh, she'd have torn her hand open, too.

Her chest constricted, the air thin—too thin. But the tightness in her lungs wasn't about the teenager who'd come after her in that building. Who had killed her brother?

She knew the statistics. In cases where the child was over five, the perpetrator was almost always someone outside the family. Children were usually murdered within seventy-two hours after an abduction. In most cases, they were killed less than two hundred feet from the dump-site, generally within a two-mile radius. But she did not want to consider the most common motivation: sexual assault.

Maggie stared, feeling teeth in her scalp, smelling that boy's rank body odor. *Who did this to you, Aiden? Who did this to me?* Not the same someone, almost certainly not, but she trusted Reid's judgement. And he seemed to think the attacks were too coincidental.

Was it possible that Reid was right? That the guy who attacked her had somehow run into her brother, and... what? Killed him in a fit of rage? Most child abductions were opportunistic; that would fit the profile. She'd thought him badly wounded, enough to incapacitate him—she could see the glass protruding from his cheek in her mind's eye, the sharp end piercing into his tongue. Was she misremembering? Had he been less injured than she thought?

Maggie inhaled deeply, focused on the saccharine flowers, trying to settle her racing heart. She sneezed. Birman wasn't going to let her anywhere near Aiden's case, but she could put a profile in writing. The suspect was likely a white male, an opportunistic killer, unknown to the victim. And he had to be strong to carry the body that far through the woods. The paths were much too narrow, too overgrown for a four-wheeler. Someone smaller in stature would have buried him close by instead of risking discovery by dragging the body through the trees—that could take a full day, and every minute made arrest more likely. Plus, they'd have seen evidence of dragging on the bones, right? So, a younger male, twenties or thirties, with good stamina. And to know about the well, the killer had to be intimately connected to the area; even Maggie herself hadn't known it existed.

Her rib cage tightened. The killer was one of them—someone from Fernborn. Or Tysdale.

The building suddenly felt too close, the shadows too dark. The air was sickly sweet, cloying and putrid in her throat. She eased back from the flowery walk, one step, then another, and—

Her arms windmilled, flailing, but she managed to catch herself as she stumbled into the street. She cringed, waiting to get hit by oncoming traffic. The road remained quiet. Deserted. Lonely. She righted herself, then turned on her heel and hustled to her Sebring.

Smooth, Maggie. Real smooth.

Maggie slammed the door and leaned her head back against the seat, her heart pounding in her temples. Something was wrong, and it wasn't this place. Had Birman tried to find her mom—really tried? She'd felt the lie in her guts, and even Malone had looked pissed when Birman said they couldn't locate her.

Heck, maybe the killer *was* Birman. What

killer wouldn't insert themselves into their own case if it meant they controlled the narrative? And psychopaths loved to join the police force, the military, the clergy—anywhere they could enjoy unchecked power.

Maggie... Birman? Really? He looked like a clown, but that didn't make him a monster, no matter what clown-phobic Sammy thought. She tugged her cell from her pocket and tapped on her mother's number.

The phone rang. And rang. And rang. Maggie sat straighter when the cell clicked, but it was only a robotic voice: "You've reached the voice mailbox for—"

Maggie hung up and blinked at the surrounding landscape. Long shadows crouched beneath the monkey bars. Lilacs swayed, languishing in the night air. *Where are you, Mom?*

But maybe it didn't matter. Maybe it had always been inevitable that her mother would run off to the Maldives and forget her too. She'd spent years telling Maggie to forget Aiden. Haranguing her about going to his gravesite, telling her to move on with her life. Reminding her that though they didn't know what had happened to him—not for sure—he was gone.

Forever.

No. Maggie couldn't handle her mother vanishing too. Not on her birthday. Not on the day she identified her brother's bones.

She shoved the keys into the ignition and sped off into the night.

CHAPTER SEVEN

The gloom outside the car provided no reprieve from the drama in her skull. Every time she blinked, she saw Aiden's bones on that table, Nick Birman standing over them, glowering, a man who was such an asshole that he'd grown a butt on his chin.

Maggie sighed and took the highway exit hard, the cacophony of her own squealing tires and the plinking of gravel against the car's undercarriage echoing in her ears. Her eyes burned. She'd tried her mother three more times—nothing. Each unanswered call made her chest constrict as if she were wrapped in rubber bands. It was probably the result of staring at those bones and obsessing over past traumas, pondering

Aiden's murder, but Maggie could not shake the thought that something terrible had happened. She just wanted her mother to answer. Hell, she was so frustrated right now, that maybe she wouldn't even tell her about Aiden—maybe she'd hang up once she verified that Mom wasn't a pile of bones, too. That'd teach her... until tomorrow when Maggie would have to call back and tell her Aiden was dead so they could plan the funeral.

Maggie parked across the street from her mother's driveway, though she didn't need to—no cars blocked her path. The ranch glowed with lamplight, a basketball hoop swinging lazily on the front of the garage, a pair of wicker chairs on the front porch. The chairs were new since last she'd been here. Maggie used to have breakfast with her mother a few times a month, but Maggie hadn't been by since she violated her tether to go to dinner. They had been *this close* to Mom being able to visit her office or meet her at a coffeeshop or actually be *involved in her life*, and her mother hadn't been able to stop herself from breaking the law.

Maggie glanced at her phone, hit the button to call the landline, and listened to it ring. Nothing shifted inside the house—no shadows moved to answer the call. The machine picked up: Jerry's voice.

Maggie punched the *End* button. Where was she? Maybe at dinner with a friend—eating more Thai food, the *very important* thing that had led her to meander past the boundaries of her original tether. Mom had always been a bit of a free spirit, an unapologetic rule-breaker, and she'd never seemed quite content in her new life. She hadn't been content since Aiden died.

She kicked the car door open and marched across the quiet street, the oils on the asphalt glittering with artful iridescence beneath the streetlamp. She rapped her knuckles against the wooden door so hard that her hand ached. The birds cawed; the night exhaled its sultry breath against her neck. But no one answered her knock.

Her stomach sank. Mom was gone. Yes, in theory, she might be unconscious, maybe injured, maybe even sleeping, but Maggie felt the emptiness of the house in her blood, the silence louder than the birds. If authorities caught Mom outside the house, they'd send her back to jail just in time for the funeral, the responsibility of which was now squarely on Maggie's shoulders. *Neat-o.* It was even possible that her mother had already been arrested.

She pulled out her phone, frowned at it, then scrolled to her mother's contact numbers. Again. But she couldn't bring herself to punch the call button—couldn't risk that hollow ringing, not one more time. She hit the number below it instead.

"Hello?"

The low, nasally voice answered immediately, and Maggie startled and almost dropped the phone. "Hey, Jerry, is my mom around? I tried her cell"—*about a hundred times*—"but I can't seem to get ahold of her. She must have shut it off."

"Yeah, she does that," her mother's husband said with a sigh. "I'm sure she's at home. It's not like she can run off. I mean, she did once, tried some aluminum foil trick with that tether, but... she won't risk it again."

You're obviously wrong there, Jer. She leaned her head against the doorframe—a few inches of wood, not nearly enough to contain her mother. Perhaps jail would prove more effective. But...

She would know if Mom had been arrested. Reid would have heard, or Sammy—he worked with the district attorney's office. The last time, Sammy had Maggie on the phone before they loaded her mother into the squad car.

Maggie righted herself and dropped her gaze,

the glint of light from the front windows tinging against the doorbell, the knob, the lock. The air thinned.

"Did you try the landline?" Jerry went on. "I'm in Maryland with the kids, visiting my sister."

"Oh." She had to force the word out. The breeze had taken on a faint metallic odor; she could taste iron on her tongue. Maggie bent toward the doorknob, squinting, and traced the metal with her fingertips. The perimeter of the lock was run through with jagged gouges, scratched deep into the brass plating. "When was the last time you talked to her?" she croaked. How long had he been in Maryland? How long had her mother been gone?

A pause. "We spoke last night to discuss..." The silence stretched.

"Jerry?"

"I might as well tell you—you'll find out eventually." He sighed. "I've filed for divorce. She's taken up with another man."

She dropped her hand. *Another man?* "Who?"

"I don't know, but I'm sure you can figure it out if you go by there. The doorbell cam has been on the fritz since I left, and I doubt that's a coincidence."

Ah. He thinks her mother tampered with it to hide the identity of her lover. Maggie raised her eyes to the doorbell, but the camera was not... visible. A tiny square of black tape covered the lens, so small she wouldn't have noticed if Jerry hadn't mentioned it. He was right: that wasn't an accident. But had her mother done it? The affair wasn't a secret; they were already getting divorced. And her mom wouldn't screw with her door locks.

Maggie's mouth was dry, her throat tight, but she managed: "Have you had any break-ins around the neighborhood lately?"

A pause. "Break-ins? Why would you—"

"Oh, you know, just something I heard on the news." *And I'm standing outside your house, where the door has clearly been tampered with.* One thing she was sure of: Jerry didn't know anything. If her mother had been planning to leave, she wouldn't have told him ahead of time, and if someone had busted in and taken her...

Get him off the phone, Mags, go find your mom. She swallowed hard. "Uh, thanks, I guess. Have a good night!" Much too cheery. *You had to make it weird. Remember that time you asked him how it was hanging and accidentally looked at a stain on his pants, but he probably thought you were looking at his crotch?*

She hit the button to end the call and shoved the cell into her pocket. The doorknob was cold in her hand.

Maggie wasn't entirely sure what she thought might happen, but she gasped when the knob turned in her palm. A crack appeared. No, this was not right, not usual. Her mother used to be a high-powered attorney, her father a renowned psychologist—they both saw people at their worst. A lock was not a magic force field, but... it helped.

She pushed her way inside, stepping carefully over the flowered doormat and a pair of pink tennis shoes. "Mom?"

Nothing. The foyer lights glared at her, accusing her of trespassing.

I'm not trespassing. I'm just... visiting. Unannounced.

Her shadow crept through the spacious living room, slinking down the white walls. The brilliantly green breakfast nook made Maggie feel she was drowning in a sea of Astroturf, but nothing was amiss—no upturned chairs or overturned furniture, no opened drawers or scattered papers. The velvet couch, garishly teal, was tacky, but that was usual—not suspicious. The rugs were bright and geometric, but unstained by blood or other mystery fluids.

Mystery fluids? Ew.

She made her way through the kitchen; no glasses in the sink. The trash was empty. Someone had cleaned up. A forest green hallway connected the bedrooms to the kitchen, the walls adorned with pictures of Mom and Jerry and his two girls. None of Maggie and her brother. None of her dad.

She strode past the girls' rooms, one on either side of the hall. Her mother and Jerry shared the room at the end, though Mom had recently told her that he'd been sleeping on the couch more often than not.

The door to the master was already open, but walking into her mother's bedroom felt a little skeevy—a little too private. The bed was neatly made, the blue duvet tight around the mattress, the green pillows fluffed. The end tables and the dressers were neater than Maggie's own, the drawers shut. Everything closed up tight. Everything except... the closet. Slightly ajar.

Maybe the intruder is hiding there.

Right. After all the ringing and the knocking, no self-respecting criminal would stay a sitting duck in this house. It'd be more likely to find a bear on a unicycle.

"Hey, dummy!" she called, just in case. No reply from the closet. Not a sound from the room, the house, nothing from outside. She didn't feel eyes on her back. If someone had been here, they were gone now.

Maggie squared her shoulders, stalked around the bed before she could change her mind, and toed the bifold doors. As expected, no intruder waited inside. No bears either. Saddest of all, no unicycles. Just a long rod full of clothes, bisected dead center by a narrow row of floor-to-ceiling cubbies stacked with folded jeans and sweaters.

She stood on her tiptoes, pawing through the items on the shelf above the clothing rod. Her mother's suitcase was still here—no cruise to a non-extradition locale like the Maldives, not tonight, unless her things were stashed at her new boyfriend's place.

Is that what you think happened, Maggie? That your mother ran off with her lover after breaking into her own house? She had mentioned the Maldives more than once, but with that broken lock, a few off-hand remarks weren't setting Maggie's mind at ease.

Maggie lowered her arms slowly, the air too thin, her head fuzzy. Dizzy. She grabbed the door for support, inhaling deeply until the haze cleared, staring straight ahead. Probably a good thing, or she might have missed the object the way she'd almost missed the tape on the doorbell camera.

A tiny *Star Wars* figurine sat on the middle shelf. One of Aiden's toys—she'd recognize it anywhere. But she hadn't seen it since he vanished.

Maggie wheezed, her guts twisting. Her mother had always been one to let go and move on—she'd constantly pushed Maggie to leave Aiden behind. And on the off-chance that this item held some special meaning for her mother, she wouldn't keep it in the open where her "dumb as socks" step-daughters might come upon it and break it.

Maggie reached out and moved the toy to the shelf below, trying to ignore the way it clattered against the wood—the way her hand was shaking.

The sweaters left no breathing room in the cubby, wool and cotton taking up every inch. She grabbed at them, tore them from the shelf, her heart in her throat, not feeling the least bit sorry about trashing the place. Especially once she saw what was behind them.

Maggie wasn't immediately sure what it was, just that it was tiny, glinting dully in the dim lamplight. She snaked her arm into the cubby, wincing, prepared for the steel teeth of a booby trap to clamp down around her flesh. Instead, her fingers closed on the item: cold, metal, heavy. It felt heavier still when she pulled it into the light.

Her mother's jade ring—her favorite piece of jewelry. No way she'd leave it behind without a good reason; she wore that thing in the shower, for god's sake. No finger in it, ransom-warning style, but the scrap of paper rolled inside like a tiny napkin in a holder was more confusing. There were only so many ways to interpret a severed finger. Well, maybe more if you knew sign language.

Maggie used her nails to tease the note from its metal holder and unrolled it. One line graced the sheet, definitely her mother's handwriting:

"He's coming for you. I'm sorry."

What the hell? *It's code, Maggie. In case someone else found it instead of you.* She blinked at the scrap for a single heartbeat, then at the cubby. In the far back was a tiny blinking light. The tether. Armed, still tracking, but clearly tampered with since it seemed to believe her mother's ankle was still inside it—it still thought her mother was here.

Nope, forget this tomfoolery; I'm done. Speculating might make her puke. She yanked out her phone, fumbled it against her thigh, and finally managed to dial.

Reid answered on the first ring, as Jerry had. "Hey, Maggie, are you home yet—"

"She's gone, Reid. My mom's gone. The house was unlocked, the doorbell cam covered, her ankle monitor is here, and her husband said she's taken up with some other guy. 'Taken up with,' those exact words, like he's some nineteen-forties mobster and—"

"Whoa." A single huffed syllable, gruff and confused.

"There's more. There was a note." *Slow down, Maggie, you sound like a crazy person.*

"A note?" More confused.

"In the closet." She read the words aloud, the paper rattling with the tremor in her hand. "It's for me; it has to be." No one else would understand the significance of the toy she used to mark the cubby. "But I have no idea who she might be referring to—who might be coming. I think I'd notice if someone was after me." Was that really true? Stalkers were sneaky by default. Like politicians.

The silence stretched. "I'm coming over there."

"Don't bother. I'm leaving." She eyed the ring. Was it the last thing her mother would ever give her? Her guts twisted, sharp. Prickly. The walls were edging nearer—closing in.

"Maggie—"

"I just want to go home."

"Okay." Another pause, this one so long, she thought he'd hung up until he said: "So, what would your mother be sorry about?"

She wasn't sure if he was trying to calm her down or trying to solve the mystery, but it loosened the thorny vines choking her intestines. "For running away?" Did that make sense? She hadn't fully registered her conclusion before now, but the abandoned tether meant Mom *had* run away, right? Hopped a plane bound for the Maldives. The timing was unfortunate with Aiden's body, but Jerry *was* conveniently out of town. Yet... that lock. *That stupid lock.*

"Running off doesn't explain the warning," Reid said, his voice coming to her as if underwater. "It sounds like she's the reason this mysterious *he* is on your case."

But there was a scenario that explained both. What if her mother believed someone was after her, decided to abscond for safety's sake—she'd likely been planning to leave anyway—and left the note for Maggie as a warning? And for this threat to be coming for Maggie, too, it was a foe they had in common. Their only current commonality was that they were part of a network that helped to ferret abuse victims out of town—helped them vanish when their lives were in danger. An abusive partner of someone they'd helped? If he thought he'd find information on his victim's whereabouts, that was a good reason to break in here.

"Her marriage is over; her son is gone," Maggie said slowly. "She has nothing left to keep her here." *Except her daughter.* Maggie frowned at the ring, so lonely without its note. Without her mother's finger.

He inhaled and blew out a breath—a loud hiss. "She's under house arrest, so I can send out some flatfoots. But if she did leave of her own accord, and they find her..."

Go to jail, go directly to jail, do not pass go.

"I'd rather err on the side of her safety," Reid went on.

"If she was kidnapped, she wouldn't have had time to leave me a note. She wouldn't have removed the tether and set everything up in the closet." And Jerry had spoken to her the night before. Last night, she was fine.

"But she obviously thinks that danger exists —for her, and now for you. Do you think... she knew someone would be coming after her and left before they got there?"

Damn him and his mind-reading ways. But she didn't want to tell Reid about their abuse victim vanishing service. In that context, it was not a shock that her mother had managed to disappear, but the more people who knew, the more risk there was for the women they were trying to protect. If her mother had left of her own free will, and it appeared she had, then Mom was safe. But was Maggie?

When Maggie remained quiet, Reid sighed. "I'll see if I can find this other man, the one Jerry was talking about. I'll even call my favorite camping buddy, get him on the technology—trace her last twenty-four hours. Can you shoot me Jerry's number? He might be angry about the infidelity, but he'll—"

"Relish the chance to drag this cheating punk's name through the mud."

"Right."

She nodded, realized she was nodding at a phone, then cleared her throat. "I'll send you the contact." The ring was heavy in her palm. The closet smelled of sage. It smelled like her mom.

"Maggie?"

"Yeah?"

"Go home. I'll get on this, I'll get Tristan on it, but you just identified your brother's body. You need to eat, to sleep. I'll send a patrol now. And if you need me, I can be there in twenty minutes. Do you want me to come?"

"No. Thanks, but no. Just please call if you find something—anything at all, even the barest whiff of a clue."

"Even the shadow of a clue. I promise."

"Thanks, Reid. You're a good friend."

Another pause. She didn't realize he'd hung up until the phone blinked off. Or maybe she'd hung up. It was hard to say.

Maggie carefully rolled the note and slipped it back inside the ring. She set it on the shelf and made quick work of refolding the sweaters, placing them back in the cubby, her eyes gritty, her chest on fire. Reid would call with new information, but she didn't want to be the sidekick—a lame Scrappy-Doo to his Scooby.

She opened drawers, ran her hand beneath the mattress, searched inside each of her mother's shoes. Maggie repeated the search in the bathroom, the kitchen, the living area, the garage, but there was no hint as to where she might have gone, or who this boyfriend was. Perhaps she should have expected that; her mother was not stupid. Mom hadn't even written Maggie a clear message, just a cryptic line of text for her daughter to decipher. Like Maggie didn't have enough to do. On her *birthday*.

When everything was exactly as it had been when she'd arrived, Maggie retraced her steps back to the front door. She paused with her hand on the knob. Maggie left the door unlocked, too, exactly how it had been when she'd arrived.

Her pocket buzzed as she escaped onto the porch—*Mom?*—but it was not her mother calling, not Reid either. Sammy. She raised her thumb above the button to answer, but froze. Electricity prickled along her spine.

Maggie lowered the cell and scanned the surrounding landscape, straining her eyes as she peered into the trees, then the pockets of inky black behind the neighbor's garage. The driveway oils were still shimmering. Somewhere up the road, a dog howled, one long, keening wail of yearning. The shadows in the bushes were alive with hidden things—dangerous things. Threats. But she could not see any figures lurking nearby. The amorphous shapes were surely just the rustling leaves made more vital, more secretive, by the encroaching night.

She slid the phone back into her corduroys. She'd call Sammy soon—she'd intended to call him first thing tomorrow morning, after she told her parents about Aiden. But her father's dementia was going to make that tricky, and she'd done her best to tell Mom. Besides, her mother had accepted Aiden's death long ago. Confirmation would likely prompt a nonchalant shrug, leaving Maggie even more alone than she already felt.

Or maybe she's already dead, Maggie. Maybe you and your brother were the targets back then, and the killer came back to finish the rest of the family off.

Her flesh was shivering, but not with cold. She hustled back to the car feeling eyes on her back. Whoever had hurt Aiden wouldn't have a reason to hurt her mother. They had no reason to come after her either, especially not so many years later. It didn't make logical sense.

But that didn't stop the hairs along her spine from prickling. Because though she understood that she was overreacting to the shadows, that her nervous system was an electrified bundle of overwrought emotion, she was also well-aware that imagining her mother alive was a valid way of coping.

It would not be the first time she'd tried to convince herself that the worst was impossible.

It would not be the first time that she was horrifically wrong.

CHAPTER EIGHT

THE LONELINESS of the road offered an uneasy equilibrium—the desolate night outside matched her insides. Clearly an overdramatic thought. She had the best friends in the world, a business partner who'd do anything for her, and Reid, who had offered to be with her tonight even if he had forgotten her birthday. But after staring down at her baby brother's bones, after finding her mother's abandoned ring stuffed with that cryptic warning, everything felt heavier. Darker.

Perhaps she should go to Sammy's house. But though his family was as close to her as her own blood, she could not bring herself to make the turn when it came up. Alex's exit went by, too, Maggie's jaw so tight she could hear her molars grinding together. The resistance to seeking them out was a needling sensation deep in her guts, at odds with the thoughts in her head. Her closest friends would want to know about Aiden. They'd feel this as deeply as she did. And... *oh*. That's why she was putting it off. *I'm giving them more time.*

Maggie straightened, her hands fisted around the steering wheel. She didn't want Sammy, a man who had been her surrogate brother for more than thirty years, to worry about her mother when there was nothing he could do. If Mom had run away, she was gone until she wanted to be found. While Maggie would try to figure out who this elusive "he who will be coming for you" was, she might soon be at an impasse if it was a domestic abuser. By design, she did not know most of those her mother had helped to vanish. And neither would Sammy.

No, telling Sammy wouldn't help. She also wanted him to have one more night where he didn't know Aiden had been murdered. Alex had never met Aiden, but she'd be sad for Maggie all the same. It was a small mercy to give them a few more hours—one extra night of good sleep before she ruined their week with all this loss.

She'd tell them in the morning, after she told her dad.

But as she pulled into her father's driveway—was it hers now?—her headlights glinted off the metal bumpers of two other cars already parked in the drive. A Jeep and a Volkswagen Bug. The tightness in her belly melted into a pool of not-quite-calm... something relief adjacent.

Sammy climbed out as she slid her Sebring into park, half off the drive so as not to block their vehicles. He looked extra tall from his angle, his bald head shining in the moonlight. Alex barreled from her Bug as Maggie made her way around the Sebring's hood. With blonde hair and slender bones and oversized dangly earrings, Alex was a sparkly little pixie—they all assumed that the treatments for an early cancer diagnosis had stunted her growth. But she more than made up for her short stature with the overzealous way she threw her body around.

"Birthday surprise party!" Alex said, rushing at Maggie like a defensive lineman. Her sweater was wrapped around her waist, making her thin arms feel even more spindly.

Maggie staggered back at the impact, but returned Alex's hug, and the moment she was in her friend's arms, the heat in her chest wrapped around her lungs and bled upward into her cheeks. Her eyes stung. "How did you..." Her voice cracked. Because they were not here for her birthday, not after their breakfast celebration. They would not be here now unless they knew about Aiden.

Alex released her, and the night air hit Maggie like a wave of cold water. But it did not have time to cool the sweat against her flesh before Sammy had her in his arms. "I talked to Reid," he said into her hair.

Wait, what? Reid had called Sam? She frowned through her tears, her face planted against Sammy's broad chest. That felt presumptuous—overbearing. "What exactly did he say?"

"Actually, I did most of the talking. Imani heard about Aiden from the Tysdale DA, but she didn't have all the details." *Ah.* Sammy and his wife both worked with the district attorney's office; they were well-acquainted with the attorneys in neighboring towns and with the detectives in Fernborn. It's not like Reid had hacked into her phone to get Sammy's number—that, she'd expect from Tristan.

"As for Reid, he didn't know much more since he's not the lead on that case." Sammy's words rumbled against her cheek. "But he casually mentioned that you were on your way home. I think he wanted me to make sure you ate. Though that might be difficult after... what you saw today."

What I saw... yeah. That. "It was awful. Aiden... he was just bones on a table."

"Shit, really?" he said. "Not even his clothes, like a hoodie to preserve his... modesty?"

Aiden hated hoodies. Anything with cords around the throat had made him feel like he was being strangled. "Crazy, right?" Maggie sniffed. Her cheeks were slippery with tears. "I'm screwing up your shirt, Sammy."

"Just don't get snot on me, weirdo."

She snorted in jest. Sammy groaned—"Eww, gross, Mags!"—and took a step back to stand beside Alex, who was fussing with her hair, wrapping it into a ponytail. He grimaced, brushing at his T-shirt—at the damp spots, which were probably not snot. "Imani wanted to be here, but the kids have to be up early for school. She'll stop over tomorrow, if you're up to it. We called you earlier, but I guess you were busy with... everything."

Maggie nodded. "Maybe we can do lunch." Imani would provide some much-needed level-headed conversation between telling her father that his son was dead, making funeral arrangements, and god knew what else she had to do since she had no family to lean on because...

"My mom's gone."

Sammy's eyebrows hit his hairline. "Did she finally hop a one-way flight to the islands?" Sammy knew her mother as well as Maggie herself, and right-off, he'd assumed that she left of her own free will—that she had planned this.

Alex released her ponytail, her blue eyes wide, and lowered her hip against the hood of Maggie's car. Her hands... was Alex shaking? Yeah, this nonsense was bad for everyone.

"All I know is that she slipped out of her tether and vanished. But there was a note in her closet, like this weird cryptic warning, and she left Aiden's toy and her favorite ring, and the lock on the door was busted..." Had she told Reid that part? About the door? She had, right?

He blinked; he looked as confused as Reid had sounded. Alex just stared. She really needed to get better at relaying information. "A note?" Sammy prompted.

Right. "It said someone was coming for me, and that she was sorry, but she neglected to specify about what. Reid's sending a patrol over, in case. Did he tell you that?" Actually... they should go inside. Why were they standing in the driveway?

Sammy's brow furrowed. "He forgot to mention that part."

Maggie hit the button to lock her car, but she couldn't seem to move, her brain filled with things that needed to be said, all her energy rerouted from her legs to her head. "The detectives in Tysdale have been looking for her"—if Birman was telling the truth—"so she'll be outed soon if they don't already know she's gone."

"Does she know about Aiden?" Sammy asked. When Maggie shrugged, he went on, "If so, Birman's always been on your case. She might have figured he'd be on you like weed on Afroman when he realized she was gone. Birman will surely, and I quote, 'come for you' now, interrogate you about Aiden *and* about your mother, and he'll feel justified doing it." He shook his head. "I can't imagine that she'd leave you in a risky situation, especially after Aiden. There's no way in hell I'd leave my kids alone if I thought they might be in danger. If she meant someone besides Birman was after you, she'd have given you a name, right?"

"And you just said the police were looking for her," Alex cut in. "Maybe they went by, messed with the door. Was there evidence that she was like... kidnapped?"

Was there? Maggie frowned. "No. Just the door. And that note."

Sammy leveled his gaze at her, his eyes tight—worried, but not overly so. "If someone busted in the door and took her, she wouldn't have had time to leave that note for you." Maggie had thought the same. Her shoulders relaxed as Sam went on, "She probably set it up, kept it cryptic on purpose so she could claim kidnapping if she got caught on her way out of town."

Maggie blinked. The breeze sighed at her back. From the increasingly desperate way Mom had been talking since her last arrest, the hints about running, his assessment rang true. It was a smart move, even if it was cruel to do to a daughter.

"I'm sure we'll get postcards from Thailand or..." He squinted. "Where was it that she was always talking about?"

"The Maldives." Her voice sounded weak. Tired. There was relief at not having to shoulder this alone—at having others who believed her mom was still okay. Of course, she'd need to be on high alert until she knew for sure who her mother meant—until she identified this mysterious "he." But there would be a patrol along momentarily, and tonight, with Sammy and Alex at her side, she was safe. No one was coming after her with them here.

I should tell them about that day in the building, finally get it all out in the open. Kevin wouldn't mind her spilling the secret now—not like he could relapse over it. But... maybe tomorrow. Or after the funeral.

Sammy stepped to her side again, wrapped an arm around her shoulders, and squeezed. "Maggie, are you okay?"

"I..." She shook her head. "I can't stop thinking. I need to... stop for a few minutes."

Alex pushed herself off the car's hood. "Yeah, we know. That's why I brought tacos. You can settle that giant brain of yours with cold Mexican and room-temperature ice cream." Alex grinned and turned toward her Bug, her loose tank top fluttering, revealing the tattoo on the left side of her upper back. A free-form heart, artistically lopsided in multicolored swirls; she'd had it since high school. Heart tattoos were a little "sailor," but to each her own.

Alex ducked inside her passenger door and returned with a pair of large paper bags—one with the Mexican takeout logo, one standard-issue grocery. "Let's go. I'm starving, and this melted ice cream isn't going to slurp itself."

The porch steps felt steeper than they had earlier—a few hours ago, she hadn't been carrying this dead-brother-missing-mom weight. Inside, Maggie hit the lights and turned to re-lock the door behind them as her mother had trained her to do. *I can't believe she did this. How dare she do this to me, and on the day I had to identify Aiden's bones.*

"Who sent the flowers?" Alex called from the kitchen. She settled the bags on one side of the countertop, opposite Maggie's birthday gifts.

Maggie opened her mouth to respond, but Alex was already squinting at the card. "A secret admirer? It's Reid isn't it?"

"No. They're not from Reid."

"That guy is into you, Mags." Alex tossed the card onto the counter, then reached into the first paper bag. "I don't care what you say, you need to jump on that train and ride it hard." She turned to slide the ice cream into the freezer, flitting around faster than usual. Pressured. Trying to force Maggie to think about something else—anything else. Maggie loved her more for it.

"Trains are for old white men in western movies," Sammy said.

"And vampires who need a quick lift through the Transylvanian countryside." Maggie shook her head, then met Alex's eyes as her friend returned to the counter.

"So, what *did* Reid get you?" Alex asked.

"Nothing. Because Reid doesn't know it's my birthday."

"Damn," Sammy and Alex said at the same time. "And here, I was just starting to forgive him for being a dick the night your house burned down."

Maggie raised an eyebrow, and Sammy shrugged. "I'm just sayin'... he's leveled up his worry game enough that I don't think he'll screw you over."

"Unless she asks him *really* nicely," Alex said over her shoulder, heading for the living room with a stack of take-out containers.

Maggie pulled extra napkins from the cabinet —they never had enough napkins. "To be fair, the night of the fire, there *was* a dead body in the garage." Macabre, but the banter was soothing the pain in her head, the pressure in her chest.

"Like you'd leave your victims in your own house," Sammy scoffed, grabbing cups. "You're smart enough to burn a body at the neighbor's place."

Maggie rolled her eyes. "The neighbor's? Ridiculous. I'd throw my victims down a well." *Too soon?* Yes, obviously too soon.

"I hear a well can buy you twenty-four years before discovery," Sammy said. "A ravine might get you forty. But a chasm that deep might suck you in, too."

"Your mama said the same thing last night."

He grinned.

"Are you morbid bastards coming to eat, or what?" Alex called from the living room couch. "You're worse than Kelsey."

"Who the hell is Kelsey?" Sammy asked as they sank onto the sofa beside Alex. But Maggie knew. She'd helped Alex pick out a new dress for their first date.

"We've only been out twice." Alex shrugged. "He's cute. Funny, like you crazy punks. Not much to tell yet—we barely kissed. But if he lasts another week, I'll invite him out with us so you guys can scare him off properly."

Sammy frowned. "What if I'd rather scare him off before date three? What's this boy's number?"

Alex rolled her eyes and gestured to the television screen. "You down for *Gremlins*? Maybe *Ghostbusters*?"

"*Spaceballs*," Sammy said.

"*Spaceballs*," Alex and Maggie agreed.

They watched. When the food was finished, they piled pillows on the pull-out couch, Sam lying across their feet as he had when they were children—as he had after Aiden went missing. Showing that he was there, showing her that she still had a brother. When her eyes began leaking, she let them. Sammy handed her napkins without a word, Alex laced her fingers through Maggie's own, but they could do nothing for the achy pulse in her head, the scar beneath her hair throbbing, throbbing, throbbing. And that was okay. It felt like the end of an era—like the past trying to say goodbye.

But in the early morning hours, the scent of spice wafted over her from the crack in the living room window, a whisper on the breeze that should not exist.

Kevin was dead.

But she smelled him all the same.

CHAPTER NINE

Maggie woke with a cricked neck and an uneasy emptiness in her guts. Sammy made eggs with onions and jalapeños; Alex had brought PopTarts. Maggie brewed the coffee extra strong. When life was punching you in the face, food and drink all tended to taste a little dull, but there was no denying the bitterness of espresso, the pure-sugar appeal of processed pastry or the burning spice of peppers.

When her friends had left, she typed out her thoughts on Aiden's killer; a more rudimentary profile than she'd prefer, but they were still waiting on evidence—evidence she might never be privy to. Maggie emailed the pages to Reid anyway, with an addendum that she'd amend it once she gained access to the forensics, and called her mom a few more times before leaving the house. Nothing.

She hadn't expected an answer. Her mother had probably left of her own accord, which meant answering the phone might reveal her whereabouts to Maggie and, more critically, the police. But the note was eating at her. Was Mom really worried about Birman asking a few extra questions, harassing Maggie, as Sammy suspected? Or was she concerned about a domestic abuser? Maggie had poked around on the abusers she knew by name, but the list they had in common was short; few of those Maggie worked with had contact with her mother. Of those, most were locked up—no longer threats. And why not come after Maggie the moment they realized her mom was gone? Sammy's assessment was making more and more sense.

Maggie sighed and shoved her feet into her flats. No matter who this notorious "he" was that was coming for her, her mother couldn't come home without getting arrested. Whether a threat existed or not, whether she sent the occasional postcard, by any practical definition, Maggie was motherless. Should she grieve her mom along with Aiden? Perhaps that was why the droning ringtone made the peppers and eggs and PopTart frosting churn in Maggie's belly like a washing machine full of oily cottage cheese.

The highway felt dystopian before eight, like the other cars had been sucked into a black hole. The patrol behind her was unmarked, but he had a flasher inside the windshield—Reid's guy? She jammed the pedal to the floor, but he didn't pull her over, just hustled to keep up even when she hit fifteen over the speed limit. Definitely Reid's guy. She eased off the gas, unwilling to test fate and the officer's patience.

Maggie made it the rest of the way to the retirement village on autopilot and parked in the front of the lot. She'd called last night to alert them to Aiden's death, in case the detectives came by. She hadn't wanted any surprises, not for Dad and not for the staff. Her father was already walking a fine line staying here without full-time nursing care. Soon, he'd be in the adjoining nursing home.

Bright inside, brighter than the early sun. Maggie nodded to the nurse behind the circular counter in the lobby—Candace was her name. She nodded back to Maggie, but her eyes were sad. *Poor you*, they said.

Maggie decided she did not like Candace as

much as she'd imagined just moments ago. Empathy was one thing, sympathy another, but pity implied a no-way-out kind of sadness—helplessness. That was enough to make her spine bristle. Just a sympathetic nervous system reaction, a defensive maneuver to feel a little less out of control, but Maggie disliked the sensation all the same.

Her father's room was down the hall on the right; she could hear the television from outside the door. Probably awake. Good. Or bad, depending on whether she felt like making an old man cry. Who was she kidding? He wouldn't react to her as if she were family. He'd probably feel more about the sickly plant on his piano than he would about the name "Aiden."

She shoved the thought aside, then the door. The giant leaves on the wallpaper greeted her with their extravagance, but the rest of the room was typical, even boring—a mahogany bistro table with three chairs that Sammy had helped her pick out, an upright piano topped with a pot of spiky Mother-in-law's Tongue. A picture of her and Aiden as children sat beside the pot, the wooden frame adorned with carved leaves that matched the walls. Her father did not look up as she entered, his stark white curls run through with a rusty hue that matched Maggie's own hair —his bushy beard was rustier still. His eyes were the same amber shade as hers, too. But he wouldn't notice.

Maggie made her way to the piano to retrieve the framed picture, then slipped into the second La-Z-Boy, the photo of her and Aiden in her lap. Her father's chair was already in a semi-reclined position, the remote on the arm, his index finger poised over the volume button.

"Hey there." She had to raise her voice to be heard above the television. It made her throat sting. "Do you mind if I watch with you?"

Her father glanced over, one fiery eyebrow raised. "Do you like *World's Most Baffling*?"

She smiled. "Who doesn't?" The show had been a favorite of theirs over the past ten years. An *Unsolved Mysteries* knock-off that didn't quite pass muster, it was enjoyable enough to watch over and over. She'd heard a new season was in the works—exciting stuff. It killed the suspense when you knew who all the bad guys were.

Dad narrowed his eyes at her, but nodded. "You've got that right. I heard they were thinking about replacing Harris Overstreet, but they came to their senses, thank god."

She already knew that; she was the one

who'd told him that fun fact. Maggie cocked her head, but his eyes remained the same. Friendly, but without the glint of affection that recognition would have elicited.

"Have you seen my mom lately?" Maggie asked. It was highly unlikely that her mother would have come here—she hadn't come to see her father since they'd divorced, so far as Maggie knew. But her mother had never run away before either.

"Who's your mom?"

"Older woman. Sometimes wears a giant green ring." *Unless she leaves it wrapped around a cryptic note.*

He snorted. "Nah. But it sounds gaudy, like she's got something to prove."

He wasn't wrong. And it was answer enough. The photo in her hand felt heavy. Hot, too, warmed with her body heat. "Do you mind if we turn the television down a little? I want to show you something."

He sniffed, frowned, and finally did as she asked, tapping the buttons extra hard as if to express his annoyance by way of aggressive volume control.

Now or never. Oh, who was she kidding? No matter what happened, she'd have to tell him again before the funeral. In case he wanted to... go. Would he? If he did, would he remember why he was there once they arrived?

Shit, I have to plan a funeral.

Maggie turned the photo to him, her hand trembling. He glanced over, frowned, then turned back to the television.

"I remember when he went missing," she said slowly—testing. "I remember feeling like there was something I should have done differently. That if I'd been with him... he'd still be okay."

Her father grunted. She waited for some other response, but her dad's eyes were locked on the screen.

"Do you remember how bad I felt after he vanished? I cried for weeks."

"Have you seen this episode?"

She swallowed hard. *He doesn't remember, Maggie. Doesn't know his son vanished, won't remember the child even if you tell him that Aiden is dead.* But her mouth was already moving, talking whether the logical side of her brain thought it was stupid, irrelevant, maybe even cruel. "No, I haven't seen it." *For the thirty-fourth time.* "And I'm excited to watch it with you. But first..." She leaned closer. "I have to tell you something." She was not one to push him to remember—she never even called him "Dad" if she could help it. But this... She had to say it. She had to at least say it aloud, even if he had no idea what it meant. She could not deprive him of a piece of information so crucial. "Aiden's dead."

He tapped the remote; the volume increased two clicks. He blinked at the TV screen.

"Did you hear me?" She had to make sure he'd heard. Then, for his sake as well as her own, she'd never say it again. She'd let him forget as her mother had insisted they do since the day Aiden vanished.

Anger burbled in her guts, so hot and sudden and unexpected that it stole her breath. Her mom—she'd run off and left all this on Maggie's head. Even as a child, she'd left Maggie alone with her pain, insisting that Maggie forget every time she tried to bring up her brother. And it was common psychologist knowledge that telling someone not to think about a white polar bear immediately makes them think about white polar bears. Tell an already anxious teen not to think about their dead brother, and you had a perfect recipe for obsession.

Her father blinked at the screen again as Harris Overstreet strode down a long, wooded road, the trees at his back making his words all the more sinister. She pulled the photo back and settled it into her lap. *I tried.* She wasn't here to torture him, so she might as well make the best of what was left of her visit—

"I never thought it was you, you know."

She blinked. "Me?" Did he know who she was? Did he know what they were talking about? It was hard to say—it was always hard to say. "Thought *what* was me, D—?" *Dad.* She covered the slip with a cough.

He glanced over at her. "I'm trying to watch this show."

Of course you are. Maggie's head spun; her stomach churned. "Never thought what was me?" she tried again.

"Quiet, would you?"

Her jaw tightened. Maggie repressed a sigh. Any glimmer of remembrance was gone. But she could imagine what he meant. Nick Birman had talked to all of them, had interrogated Maggie herself, asked her parents questions for hours. He'd surely insinuated that Maggie'd had something to do with Aiden's disappearance, brought up whatever minor injuries he'd seen as evidence that she'd struggled with her brother. He hadn't known about the more significant injuries—no one had ever looked under her hair.

Maggie leaned back in the recliner, set Aiden's photo on the arm of the chair, and pulled out her phone. Harris Overstreet was droning on about the suspect—a baker in this episode—but all she could see was Birman's twitchy clownish face, his lying eyes. His butt-chin.

She tapped the cell's screen. Maggie rarely used social media, but she was curious about Birman and his partner—what type of man would spend his days with a jerk like Birman? Malone couldn't possibly be as nice as he seemed. Online, the Canadian had a wide, friendly smile, no hint of the grim pug face she'd seen at the morgue. His nose looked less smashed when he was at a wine tasting. There were pictures of him with three different women over the course of the last year, photos of his food, vacations in... Montreal and Italy. The fact that he had a public profile seemed to hint that he didn't have many secrets. Unless that was a ruse.

But Birman... nothing. She tried other social media sites with the same results—no Nick Birman, at least not the right Nick Birman. It was possible that he had a private profile based on his position as a homicide detective; Reid didn't have public social media pages either. She googled Birman instead, but outside of a few brief mentions in local newspapers, the man was a ghost. Low profile, sure, but the lack of accolades made her think that maybe he sucked at his job. Not the man she wanted working her brother's case.

Maggie frowned. She hated to ask Tristan for information on the detective—hated to ask him for anything, just one of many complications of working together. If she knew anyone else who could do it, she'd ask them instead, but as it stood... Tristan was it. She didn't want to tell Reid she was investigating cops. He might be fine with it, but if he wasn't—

"I'm hungry," her father said suddenly, and Maggie jumped, startled. "Can you run down and get us some popcorn? Extra butter." He nodded, just once. Resolute.

She blinked at her phone, then at her father. He never asked for popcorn—it hurt his teeth, and he had a partial denture that didn't take well to kernels. But popcorn had been their thing when she was small. Back when Aiden was still alive, they'd sprawl out on the couch, often with Sammy, and watch the original *Unsolved Mysteries*. Harris Overstreet couldn't hold a candle to Robert Stack.

He was still watching her—waiting for an answer. She pushed herself to standing and headed for the piano to replace the picture. "I'll see what I can do." The vending machine in the cafeteria might have some.

He grinned—long in the tooth, the enamel yellowed, but his smile was genuine. "Good girl."

She paused halfway to the door, her heart twisting. *Good girl.* That was an old family phrase, too, though it was most often said in jest. Even if he didn't fully, consciously, understand what Aiden's death meant, there was a part of him that was trying to hold on to his son. To hold on to her.

Her eyes burned. Pain in her chest, her ribs aching to split wide—a dam breaking. Yeah, she'd find popcorn, real popcorn, even if she had to run to the store. Fake butter, but her father wouldn't notice. They'd sit here and watch *World's Most* and share snacks, and she'd try to remember, just for a few hours, what it was to have a brother, a father.

What it was to have a family.

CHAPTER
TEN

When the struggle didn't belong to you, emotional challenges had the ability to force concentration and distract you from your own nonsense. Such was the life of a psychologist the day after her brother's body was found.

Janice smiled, but only the left side of her lips responded. The shiny burn on the right side puckered, crinkling her skin from chin to cheek.

Mom had referred Janice to Maggie initially—one of the few cases they'd worked together. But Janice had wanted a day to think about leaving, and a day was a day too long. Sixteen hours after Maggie had met her, the day after Janice had refused the offer to abscond, her husband had attacked her in the restaurant they'd owned. Now, he was in jail, and Janice owned the restaurant, though she hadn't come out unscathed. She'd also lost mobility in three of her fingers when he'd shoved her into the deep fryer.

"I've been working with the support group you recommended," Janice said. "Lots of other moms, which is both terrible and refreshing in terms of camaraderie."

Maggie nodded, but the word "mom" made her chest ache. She had so much to grieve, and no time to do it. "I'm glad it's working out for you. I'm sure you're helping more people than you know."

"Might as well use this gorgeous mug for something, right?" Janice smiled again, but Maggie could see the tightness at the corners of her eyes. The burn treatment and subsequent skin grafts were painful. And she wasn't even close to finished with them, which meant the anxiety still, necessarily, existed.

The session with Janice bled into one with a veteran suffering from PTSD, then a lovely woman with agoraphobia who had only recently transitioned from online sessions into the office space. By the time lunch rolled around, Maggie's ribs had loosened just enough to allow her to breathe normally, even when her mother's phone went to voicemail. Again. Why was she still trying?

Tap-tap-tap!

Maggie looked up in time to see Owen step into her office carrying a brown take-out bag with plastic handles—broad shoulders beneath his professor-tweed blazer, platinum blond hair, bright blue eyes, very surfer meets librarian. "Got us Reubens," Owen said. "Since I kinda missed your birthday." He winced—an apology.

Maggie waved him in, but the heavy reek of corned beef reminded her of Janice's burned face. Had the restaurant smelled of frying meat in the aftermath? Had the customers sniffed with watering mouths, wondering what that delectable scent was?

Stop thinking about it, Maggie. But she might as well tell herself not to think about a white polar bear.

Maggie swallowed against the bile in the back of her throat and forced a smile. "You did plenty for my birthday, dude. But have a seat." *I have to tell you about my dead brother anyway, and my missing mother, and the note that implies I'm in danger. Also, you might see some patrol cars in the lot. I'd rather you be sitting.*

She could have called him last night, but Owen was her college friend, her business partner, and he was straight-laced—traditional. He wasn't into adult slumber parties. The rest of them leaned into togetherness to ease heavy burdens; when Imani lost her grandfather, when Sammy's dad died, when Alex got fired. When Sammy's babies had colic, Alex and Maggie had stayed over with Imani, taking turns rocking and patting and singing while Sam was on a business trip.

It wasn't the same with Owen. He thought slumber parties were bizarre, and he hated her working with the police, hated her working with the prison, hated any whiff of danger. Aiden's murder would disturb him in more than an "I'm so sorry" way. To his credit, he'd told her about that sex club—he'd heard about it from his ex-wife and been scandalized. If he found out that she'd actually gone, he'd have a stroke. Sammy would make fun of her if he knew... but he'd accept it. Alex would probably ask for the address.

"How was the cupcake?" Owen said now. He settled the bag on the corner of her desk and removed the Styrofoam containers—one for her, one for him.

"It was delicious. And I love my new pen. Thank you."

He smiled, but it only made the bags under his eyes puff up—pronounced today. Dark purple bruises.

"Owen... are you okay?"

He slumped into the chair across from her and popped the top on his sandwich container, but made no move to eat. Owen shook his head. "I'm not great. Katie filed for full custody of the girls. Can you believe that? Everything I've done for her, for my daughters, and she just..." He sighed, his bloodshot eyes tight. "I guess that's what happens when you have a fancy new lawyer boyfriend who wants you to move to California with him. If she wins this, she can take my kids wherever she wants. I'll only get to see them a few times a year."

Maggie's jaw dropped. "That's insane! Your children adore you; she can't just take them away." His children were his life. She'd only met Katie twice, both at holiday gatherings—Katie never wanted to hang out with Owen's friends, had always seemed jealous of Maggie herself. She didn't want her kids to hang out with Owen's friends either. Hell, maybe Katie had always been the problem, and once the divorce was final, he'd join their crisis slumber parties.

Owen's lips were pressed tight together, a single bloodless line. Staring at his sandwich. He'd still made no move to pick it up.

She reached for hers as if to lead by example, the Styrofoam warm and oily. "I'm so sorry, Owen. But she won't win this; we won't let her. We'll talk to Sam, okay? I'm sure he knows some awesome divorce attorneys." She was surprised Owen hadn't asked Sammy or Imani already, but he was the optimistic sort—he'd thought they'd be able to handle things with a mediator. But once Katie started dating some big-shot lawyer... well.

Maggie opened the top on her sandwich box, and the salty air rose like a fog of grease into her nose. Her belly rolled. She sat back in the chair and let her eyes graze the desk, then the far wall where Aiden's baseball glove sat, the photo of her and her brother. Her dead brother.

Owen was still staring at his sandwich.

Yeah, she'd save Aiden for another time. Instead, they spent the next twenty minutes discussing Owen's options, processing his feelings in true shrink style, and then they both abandoned their mostly uneaten lunches for their clients.

Unlike her morning, the afternoon crawled by. But working helped keep her mind off the fact that someone had murdered her brother and tossed him down a well... mostly. Took her mind off of her missing mother... mostly. Made her forget that she could still smell Kevin in her sinuses even over the corned beef. And Bert the bobblehead watched it all, nodding, nodding, nodding.

By the time her last patient left, Maggie's bones were heavy with exhaustion. She had missed two text messages from Alex, one a joke about a donkey, the second three words: "Love ya, dork." Maggie smiled, texted back a horse emoji and a peach, then scrolled her missed calls. Scam likely, and... scam likely. Neat. The final call was from Reid.

She punched the button to call the last number back.

"I found out why Birman was questioning you so hard," Reid said before she could say hello.

She rested her elbows on the desk and leaned over them, the phone caught against her palm. "I already told you why. I was all beat up—"

"No, you didn't. I mean, you thought you did,

but..." In the background, a car horn honked, one high, sharp bleat. "I'm almost to your office, unless you'd rather meet at the coffeehouse. Or we can get dinner."

She glanced at the still-full sandwich container. "I have to work late tonight, and I'm not hungry. Just spit it out."

He paused. Then: "You thought Birman was suspicious because of your injuries—he didn't even mention them to me. According to Birman, they thought Aiden had been kidnapped because *your mother* told them that someone had been watching him."

What? She straightened, suddenly more awake, like a sleeping frat boy who'd just taken a flyswatter to the face. "You're wrong. You have to be—"

"I saw the original report myself. I even talked to the officer who filed it. Birman isn't making this up."

Maggie stared at the desk, stunned. "That doesn't make sense. If someone was watching Aiden, why wouldn't she be more careful, pick him up from school, watch him more closely? Even if she thought she was being paranoid, once he vanished, why not watch out for *me*?" Just because she liked him better? If Aiden's very normal name was any indication, Mom had preferred him from birth. *Magma? Who does that?*

"That's the same question Malone and Birman are asking themselves. Why, if she thought Aiden was being watched, she didn't adjust her level of protectiveness, either before or after he was taken. But with that note... maybe she's trying to watch out for you now."

"Shitty job she's doing. She couldn't guarantee that I'd find the note at all. And if that note is related to Aiden, it implies that *his killer* is after me. Why would she protect them by not giving me a name? Why not call the police?" It was one thing to write in code, but that note didn't come close to identifying the culprit. If Maggie knew who'd killed her child, she'd out them before they could hurt anyone else. Hell, she'd out them for the sake of justice—even revenge.

"I have no idea what your mother's thinking. I wish I did."

Maggie blinked; at some point, she'd begun stroking Bert's head. The toy jiggled, but Maggie couldn't tell if the nod was accusatory or supportive.

The silence stretched—uneasy quiet. She dropped her hand to the desktop.

"Reid, what aren't you telling me?" What didn't he *want* to tell her?

He sighed. "Birman wasn't especially forthcoming, but it seems that someone called in a tip about Aiden from Yarrow soon after the all-points bulletin went out."

Yarrow? "That's three hours away."

"Three and a half. The woman described what Aiden was wearing to a T, his backpack, everything. And for him to be in Yarrow when that call came in, the killer left Fernborn soon after you arrived home."

Her head was spinning. "But... why? I mean, what if it was just the killer trying to throw the cops off?"

"It's possible. Birman said it was an old payphone—bad connection, and the money ran out before they got a name, which is inherently suspicious. But the following morning, the Yarrow PD found Aiden's notebook out behind the gas station where the caller reported seeing him. It's possible that someone dropped it after they buried the body, but Birman wholeheartedly believes that your brother was in Yarrow with his kidnapper. With his killer."

Maggie stared until Bert's bobbling head went still. How had she not known? But maybe it was better not to know. If Aiden was alive three and a half hours later, the killer had dragged it out. Her lungs spasmed then released. "If Birman thinks that the killer took Aiden out of town, then why is he still being such a jerk to me?" It sounded like she was with Birman himself when the call came in.

"Well, there's another issue with the... body. Especially if the killer traveled with him." He paused. "There were no defensive wounds on the bones. I'm still verifying the information, have requests in with the phone company, but the witness in Yarrow said he was just standing by the gas pumps."

Maggie frowned. "Whether the call was real or not, no defensive wounds means that Aiden died fast, right? Too quick to suffer?" But the rest of it. Aiden standing, free. And how could that possibly make her a suspect?

"Yeah, it happened fast—a single knife wound from a Bowie-style blade. Aiden didn't have time to fight. But..." A sharp inhale. In the background, tires shrieked. "If the call was legit, Aiden didn't try to run when he had the chance. Birman believes that Aiden didn't fight the kidnapper because he didn't know he should."

She leaned back against the seat in slow motion. "What are you saying, Reid?" But she knew, didn't she?

A hollow clunk, his car door opening, then a slam that echoed in the evening outside the building. "It seems that your brother went with the kidnapper willingly. Which is why Birman and Malone both think that Aiden knew the person who killed him." He paused. "And so do I."

CHAPTER **ELEVEN**

Reid hadn't brought coffee this time, no chai either. She was glad for it. The lingering scent of her uneaten corned beef was making her stomach slither around. She sipped from the glass bottle on her desk—a gift from Alex—but the sparest trickle of water made her insides clench.

Reid's hair stuck up along the left side, the result of running his fingers over his head as he did when he was properly stressed—when he was trying to figure something out. He crossed his ankle over the opposite knee. Maggie followed suit, mirroring his movements as if by doing so she could get into his brain. She felt strange, like an imposter, like a bear on a tricycle.

She uncrossed her legs and leaned over the desktop instead.

Aiden went with the kidnapper willingly.

Aiden knew the person who killed him.

"Birman knows that I can verify the Yarrow call, and I will, so lying about it would be stupid at best. For now, let's hash it out as if your brother was in Yarrow; get everything out on the table. I know it sounds unlikely, but—"

"If he went with the kidnapper... I don't know who could have taken him," she said. "I didn't have friends with a car at thirteen; Aiden certainly didn't at eleven. Kevin was the closest I had to a driving friend, but he was only fifteen—no car. That leaves an adult, and..." She shook her head. "A teacher, maybe? He wouldn't have gone off with a stranger."

Reid sniffed, shook his head. "They investigated the hell out of the school, the teachers, anyone Aiden had regular contact with for the reasons you just mentioned. Then there was the stalking your mother reported. Whether or not the detectives shared this with your family, Birman definitely believed, even then, that the person who took Aiden was someone known to him."

Maggie dragged her hands from the desktop.

They left foggy palm prints on the wood. She watched the humidity evaporate, then said: "It doesn't make sense."

"A stranger would have had to drug him; he would not have been standing at that gas station if—"

"No, not that part." She glanced down at her fingers, hot and sticky in her lap. "Why would the killer bring him all the way back to Fernborn to" —she swallowed hard, trying to force the word— "dispose of him? I mean, if they got him out of town, well away from those who were searching... why come back to kill him in the woods?"

"He might have been dead before they got back to Fernborn. Maybe the suspect figured it was a good dumpsite since the officers had already cleared out of the forest. But you're right— it's a risk. And a strange one to take." He uncrossed his legs, recrossed them on the other side. "And on top of some splinters and tree sap, expected trace from the woods, there were remnants of chemicals on his body, indicative of a specific kind of insulation. You wouldn't have it in your house, and I checked with the school personally. They never used that kind of insulation. It's older."

Older, like... *the kind you'd expect in an about-to-be-demolished office building?* She met his eyes, pools of amber, liquid in the gilded lamplight. "If the killer laid Aiden in the office and moved his body to the well later, it would explain why they didn't find him when they scoured the woods."

"Exactly." Reid nodded.

She let her gaze drift to the table beneath the window, to her brother's baseball glove. Whether the killer brought him to Yarrow or not, it would have been easy enough to sneak him into that dark building. Aiden was...

Small. She saw the bones in her mind's eye. The tiny pile on that stainless table.

Reid was watching her, waiting for her to respond; she could feel his gaze boring into her flesh. She blinked once more at the glove, then the photo of her and her brother, their frozen smiles, and turned back. "It was smart to dump him in a place the police were no longer looking, but this feels more like remorse—wanting Aiden to be near his family, even in death. I don't know why they'd take that risk otherwise. And all of this shows more planning than I'd expect in an opportunistic abduction." But if someone had been watching Aiden, as her mother said, it wasn't exactly opportunistic, was it? And back then, her mother wasn't helping domestic violence victims escape, which tossed that theory out the window. Plus, those who hurt children usually killed them in the first few hours. Even making it to Yarrow alive would be an anomaly, and... Maggie frowned. "It sounds more like panic, doesn't it? Running off like that, moving the body around."

"So, not a seasoned killer."

"No. I'd say on the younger side—maybe even an older teenager." *Like the guy who attacked me.* Her throat constricted. Had she been wrong all this time? Had that jerk left the office immediately after her, come across Aiden by some freak accident, and murdered him? "Was the insulation transferred from the person who killed Aiden? Or was it from the building itself?"

Reid shrugged one thick shoulder. "It was just trace, so it could theoretically be either." His voice was tight, his jaw tense. He coughed, then went on: "You've said that Aiden wouldn't have gone near some weirdo with a giant shard of glass in his face. But what if he thought the guy needed help?"

"I can't see Aiden getting into a car with him, but at eleven..." Kids could be dumb. She'd certainly been stupid at thirteen. Yes, it was *nearly* impossible for her attacker to have driven to the other side of town in time to meet Aiden in the woods, but was it really more likely that someone else had taken him? Maybe their family had been targeted, maybe not, but one vicious suspect was an easier explanation than multiple, unconnected attacks. She'd never believed that before, but maybe she just didn't want to be the one who'd left a killer free to murder her brother.

He wanted to kill me. I fought back, and he had to find another way to slake that bloodlust. And instead of wrestling or biting, he'd stabbed Aiden straight in the heart. Driving out of town didn't make sense, the remorse seemed unlikely, but...

It should have been me.

"If the man who attacked you was as injured as you say, there would have been blood on Aiden, on his clothes. But DNA degrades out in the elements—that won't help us much. So, let's look at it from another angle." He met her gaze. "This man you stabbed... are you sure he got out of the building? Tristan is poking around the hospitals, but so far, nothing. And the injury you described would have looked like foul play. The hospital should have called it in."

That was an abrupt change of subject. The

Bert bobblehead on her desk stared. "You're asking... if I killed him?" Then who the hell did he think went after Aiden?

"I'm asking if you saw, for certain, that you didn't." The temperature in the room had increased; sweat prickled on the back of her neck. "When you saw him last, where was he?"

"Laying in the corner."

"Kevin didn't ask who he was, check if he was breathing?"

She blinked. "No."

"That seems weird, doesn't it?"

At the time, it hadn't seemed strange—they'd both been so panicked it had felt right for Kevin to help her up, to run off with her, to patch her wounds. He'd been protecting her. But after the fact... yeah, they'd both questioned their decisions. Kevin had always felt guilty.

"Did *you* go to him?" Reid asked when she didn't respond. "Check to see if he was alive?"

"I didn't kill him, I just *cut his face*." Her back was so stiff that she could barely breathe. She had no idea what had happened to that boy, but he had surely been gone by the time the building was demolished the following day. Someone would have noticed a dead kid in the rubble;

would have seen carrion birds in the days following.

"How long did it take you and Kevin to get you back home?"

"I… I'm not sure. I just know it was getting dark." She felt like Reid was asking questions in circles.

"Did Kevin drive you?"

The Bert bobblehead nodded—her leg was vibrating against the desk. "Kevin was barely fifteen. He didn't have a license, let alone a car. I told you that."

"I can't recall… did you pass the building again after you cleaned your head? Did you cut through the woods?"

Her muscles were screaming, the tendons in her arms tight as piano wires. "Should I get a lawyer, Reid?"

One corner of his lip turned up. "Just humor me, okay? I don't suspect you, but this… helps me think. Interrogating a suspect and talking to you about a case are my go-to tactics."

Her spine loosened. She was projecting—she felt guilty and was assuming he believed her guilty, right? But when her back was once more pressed against the chair, her arms crossed of their own accord. "No, we did not pass the building again. We went to the high school to get his coat from his gym locker and cleaned my head. We wanted to make sure I was... presentable before we started toward home."

"And you took the long way? The woods would have been faster, right?"

"My... knee hurt after the attack. My back, too. And the sun was setting by then. The woods are treacherous after dark."

"So, this guy attacked you while your brother was at band practice. And while you were walking to the high school to get cleaned up, your brother was just leaving the middle school a few blocks away and on his way home—he was seen heading into the woods. Tell me again why your attacker couldn't have left that building and met your brother in the forest?"

"I thought it was unlikely because the building wasn't near the woods. My attacker would have had to drive to the other side of town, park, then race through the trees to find my brother. All while bleeding profusely."

"If someone was watching Aiden, maybe they were watching you both—knew where you two would be and set out with an agenda." When she balked, he went on, "Alternatively, what if the guy who attacked you went into the woods to collect himself? He'd at least have needed to stop the bleeding. Maybe he got in his car the moment you left, drove to the first isolated spot he could find, and Aiden came across him there."

"So, in those scenarios, I didn't kill him, right?" *Didn't kill the guy in the building? Or your brother?* She went on, "Him walking away seems more likely than him dying in the office. The carrion birds around the rubble would have been a dead giveaway." Get it? *Dead* giveaway?

"So, you *have* considered that he might be dead." Welp, that pun had fallen on deaf ears. But it felt nice to hash it out. It felt nice to be *involved* in the case—in finding the man who'd killed her brother.

Reid planted his feet on the floor and his elbows against his knees. "Maybe we should poke around."

She frowned. "Under the... park?"

"You're probably right about him walking out. If he died there, there should have been scavengers to alert the workers. But..." He sighed. "A few cadaver dogs can't hurt. I'll call over to Tysdale for their hounds—Fernborn has never had any. And I want to be sure."

"To be sure I didn't kill a man."

"To be sure the man who attacked you didn't get what he deserved."

She raised an eyebrow. It almost sounded as though, if someone hurt her, Reid would kill them himself. No wonder he'd sent a car to watch her. No wonder Sammy approved.

"Would Kevin have gone back to the building after he walked you home?"

She shook her head, suddenly exhausted. "Why would he have gone back there?"

"To make sure the guy was okay. But, again, we haven't found any reports of someone with that injury in a neighboring town. And he'd surely have needed medical attention." He sat back in the chair, his face grim. "What if Kevin went there to check on him, found him dead, and decided to hide the body because he didn't want to be an accessory to murder? Or maybe they got into it, and Kevin finished him off by mistake."

What? "Then who killed my brother?"

Reid shrugged. "What would Kevin have done if your brother walked into that building looking for you?"

The air thinned; her heart lodged itself in her throat. "You think... *Kevin* went back to the building, finished off the guy who attacked me, and my brother happened by in time to see it? And then what? Kevin killed him too? Are you insane?" Kevin had always felt guilty about not checking on the guy; he'd have killed himself if he'd murdered Aiden.

Who says he didn't kill himself?

Maggie squared her shoulders. *The medical examiner. That's who. The police said he got drunk and drove off a bridge.* But had she ever fully believed it?

"I'm just asking questions," Reid said, shaking his head. "The timeline is a little... mushy. And if your brother stopped to buy candy after band practice or even walked around the block looking for you, it might fit. I think that's where Birman is going with this—where he will go, once he finds out about your attack. He'll assume it's all connected, and maybe he should."

Her face was on fire. "Kevin wasn't a psychopath."

"I didn't say he was. We don't know how it all went down. But Kevin fits the profile. *Your* profile. He was a young male, an older teenager, white, someone known to the victim—someone Aiden would have gotten in a car with. Someone who might have had something to hide. Driving to Yarrow in a panic would fit, and he'd feel guilty in the aftermath. Kevin is exactly the kind of person you'd expect to bring Aiden back and bury him near his family. He probably at least had a learner's permit, could have borrowed his mom's car. Or taken the keys from your attacker."

Her insides were trembling with a rage so caustic that she could barely catch her breath. "Kevin didn't kill my brother," she insisted, more quietly this time. "If he'd dragged Aiden through the woods, you'd see injuries on the bones. Kevin wasn't a big guy at fifteen; he wasn't strong enough to carry him for miles. And I was his" —*girlfriend*—"friend at the time. Everything he did that day was to protect me."

"You're too close to be impartial. Maybe he wheeled Aiden out there on the back of a bicycle." Her jaw dropped, but he raised a hand before she could protest again. "I'm just trying to get all the pieces to fit."

"But this *doesn't* fit. Kevin obviously wasn't stalking Aiden in the weeks before he was taken. And my mom isn't worried about Kevin being after me now." *Because he's dead.*

"Your mom had no evidence to back up the stalking claims. She had vague feelings of being watched, said she saw a dark truck one time, a green sedan another time. But from her behaviors, she obviously didn't think anything about it until after he was gone, and she barely considered it then except to tell the police. She didn't even take extra precautions with you. I'm more inclined to believe she was mistaken—that whatever she saw wasn't connected to Aiden's death, and that the note, her current disappearance, isn't connected to this killer. If you take your mother's statements out of the equation, everything else fits."

Did it? Maybe. Especially if Sammy was right about that note—if her mother was trying to set herself up in case she got caught running away. *Dammit, Mom, couldn't you have,* just this once, *been straight with me? I don't need this shit right now. I have to bury my brother.*

Her insides trembled, her blood sizzling. Reid leaned forward, his elbows on his knees once more, his gaze boring into hers. "Kevin might well have grown into the good person that you fell in love with, but kids make stupid, sometimes horrific, mistakes."

So do mothers. But this wasn't about kids, wasn't about her mom, wasn't just about that day. It felt like he was tearing her whole life apart, her memories, her history, reducing the man she'd loved to an evil caricature—a villain.

Every word he spoke seemed to make her more responsible for her brother's death.

Tears burned behind her eyelids. She inhaled deeply, trying to force them down. No, a childhood mistake did not make one unredeemable.

But was she?

CHAPTER TWELVE

He squinted through the night at Maggie's Sebring, the dull blush of her rear lights fading as she swerved into the left lane and gunned it up the highway past two trucks and a little Honda with a scuffed rear panel. No brakes for his girl—she was asserting her position. Taking control.

Watching her was rarely a surprise these days, but it was always fun.

She slowed abruptly behind a Mack truck with a yellow sun logo, the brake lights twin blasts of red beneath the bright yellow circle—bloody water at sunset.

The Sebring jerked back into the right lane, mere feet in front of a blue pickup, which leaned hard on its brakes and its horn. But she was already gunning it again, out of his line of sight, skirting that beast of a semi. He leaned on his brakes, too, like the truck, following the yellow sun. No way he could squeeze around the way she had.

He liked that about her, this tendency to push boundaries, to forge her own path. Was she listening to Weird Al, blaring "White and Nerdy" as she roared down the highway? Was she twisting her curls around her knuckles? It was not a habit that he'd seen in real life, but he often imagined her doing it, her hair like flames between her fingers as if she had tamed fire.

He had no doubt that she was capable. She was capable of anything. Though it was hard to imagine looking at her—her geeky reading glasses, her polka dots and pinstripes and corduroys—she was a *bad* girl, all right. He knew that better than anyone.

He checked his rearview. A line of cars stared back, headlights bobbing. It was possible that the detective's patrol was still back there, somewhere, but it was more likely that they were changing guard—that the next one would meet her at home. Either way, he had no mind to draw attention to himself.

Careful. He hit his turn signal, heart rate increasing, his tongue dry. The chase always made him hard, but the thrill had recently become more intense—too intense, crossing the line into oppressive. Some nights, he could hardly breathe.

Lately, she was less a rabbit—a known entity, tangible prey—and more of a gnat, flitting through the air around his head. Things had changed. He had never liked the unknown, but he'd always been able to orchestrate the playing field, bending it, twisting it to his will. And now...

He frowned at the truck. The garish sun stared back, striations of orange and yellow reaching for him as if asking what he was waiting for. Was he merely addicted to the chase the way the grass was addicted to the sun? Of course not.

But he was missing something.

Why haven't you come back to the club, Maggie? She had no idea that when she put on that mask, when she took his hand and led him away from the throng, that she was embracing his soul as much as his body. It had taken him longer than expected to get Maggie to choose him, and once she had, she'd been as enamored as he. But now...

But now, indeed. It had been months since he'd stood in the back of the club, waiting for her to appear in those tall leather boots. Waiting for her to choose him once again. Yesterday, he'd thought she had returned, and he'd watched, his heart throbbing in his head, in his groin, but... no. She'd been in the lot, then she was gone before he could taste her—the worst kind of tease. He'd driven home, aching with what might have been, hot with need and frustration in equal measure.

But no matter. They had all the time in the world. Didn't they?

A break in the line of cars. He edged into the right lane, escaping the judgmental sun. Where was she? He squinted. Ah, there, four cars ahead in front of a green Scion. He smiled. She drove fast, dangerously, but Maggie wasn't hard to track. She did that on purpose: made herself available to him.

Though she'd never admit it, she thought about him as often as he considered her. She might be imagining him at that club, putting his face over those masks he always wore, but she'd never called out his name, so he had no way to verify. Probably though. Who wouldn't be thinking of him?

Are you thinking of me right now, Maggie?

He hit the gas. Perhaps her thoughts were elsewhere this evening, understandable under such profoundly distressing circumstances. He'd forgive her that. They'd just found her brother's bones, after all.

Took them long enough.

Did she find it strange that Nicholas Birman, the detective she despised, had switched precincts soon after Aiden's disappearance, but had still caught the case at his new locale? Did she wonder what strings he'd pulled to make it happen? Hopefully not. He didn't need her mind on detectives and procedure. She'd get antsy, go into crime-fighting mode, and forget all about affection—connection. And that was where he would shine if he got the chance.

He frowned. Should he tell her where to find her mother? Perhaps that would help her to see him as a confidant, a person worthy of more than the occasional stint in a sex club. But no, not once she realized how he knew. And especially not once she realized the where.

Definitely not then.

He blinked, refocusing on the highway as Maggie swerved into the left lane once more, hit the gas, and vanished up the road. This time, he let her go. He knew where she lived.

Yes, they had time. Plenty of time. They had a past, and now, they'd have a future.

Once this was all over and her brother was

buried, their lives could finally begin. It took a long time to heal from the things she'd been through, and this would take longer than most. But he'd wait for her at that club every night if he had to. He'd take that pain away.

Though she was always the one with the red bracelet, she belonged to him.

She just didn't know it yet.

CHAPTER THIRTEEN

WAS SOMEONE FOLLOWING HER? Maggie frowned at the rearview mirror, the little hairs between her shoulders vibrating. The blue-white brights of a little sports car glared from the crest of the hill along with giant floods from a pickup, yellowed headlamps bobbing through the night from sedans and SUVs. Nothing suspicious. No one driving erratically, no one except her. But the tension along her spine refused to relent.

She'd swapped lanes, bobbed and weaved through traffic, pulled off the highway to get a drive-through smoothie, but in the dark it was near impossible to tell if the headlights at her back were the same cars or different ones—if any of them were bobbing and weaving along behind her. And even if they weren't, there were still a million and one things that needed her attention —a million different traumas, a million different threats, and she had no idea which were coming for her now.

Maggie's brain felt like a mushy mess of information and thoughts that didn't want to congeal into anything resembling facts. Her mother had seen someone watching her brother? She and Reid had gone over her mom's statement, but he was right—incredibly vague, nothing that might help them. Her mother's note was more of the same. Vague and useless, all of it vague and useless. Everything her mom thought might be wrong.

What was real? What wasn't?

She forced her hands to relax; her knuckles ached from gripping the steering wheel, her eyeballs sore from straining to see the road behind her. What would her stalker name be? Peek-At-Chu? Not as elegant as The Night Stalker, but more in the spirit of who she was as a human.

Maggie shook her head, trying to ignore the random nonsense. Her brain always went a little haywire when things were hard, and—who was she kidding?—when they weren't. If there was a punishment for racing thoughts, she'd have been tortured already, maybe locked in a padded room with an irksome radio personality hellbent on explaining why feminism was *totally unfair* to men or—

The tires shrieked as she jerked the wheel to the right. She'd been so busy obsessing over who was driving behind her that she hadn't noticed the entrance to her father's neighborhood approaching.

Only inky darkness followed her into the subdivision. Her heart slowed. She hit the brakes and took the turn onto her father's road at a less breakneck pace. She shouldn't have told Reid that she was working late tonight—she'd intended to put in a few more hours, but she hadn't been able to focus. Were there still patrols driving past her office instead of her house?

She sighed. *Shit.* Between her mother's "he's after you" note and the mere possibility that someone had been following Aiden before he vanished, she clearly had reason to be concerned. Yet, the idea that her mother—her father—had known someone was watching Aiden but done nothing about it was ridiculous. And though she racked her brain, she could think of no reason for her mother to lie to the police.

Amendment: she could think of a million reasons for her mother to lie to the police, but not about someone watching Aiden. Not about that. And the police thought that her brother knew his killer. The police—or maybe just Reid—thought that her dead fiancé had something to do with her brother's murder. That Maggie's own attack was connected.

So much information to process. Too much.

Maggie took the final gentle curve that led to her father's home. How was this real life? Nothing fit, a million disjointed pieces swimming around in her brain, and she had no idea which of them would help her find her brother's killer. It had only been a day since she'd identified his bones—*a day*—but it suddenly felt critical that she know who had killed him now, tonight. Her lungs ached with the pressure of it. And her hands, once more fisted around the wheel.

The lights on the porch seemed darker than usual, fogged by the humid night, moths patterning the bricks with their shadowed wings. The porch lights were not actually dimmer, of course—it was her mood. Darker. Heavy. Any yahoo, even one without a psychology degree and a hearty knack for overexaggeration, would know that.

She slammed her car door and made her way toward the house accompanied by the wild cries of the whip-poor-wills, the birds keeping time to the metronomic slapping of her flats against the driveway. The damp air was thick in her lungs.

She turned, scanning the night behind her, but there were no other cars on the road, and the trees along the drive were too thin to hide a person. Perhaps that tricycle in the neighbor's yard was the real threat—had it once held a circus bear with a taste for psychologists?

Maggie climbed the porch steps, chuckling to herself. As it had been when she'd left, the porch was clear. No new gifts from Tristan, no flowers, no Weird Al concert passes, no plane tickets, no bracelets that cost more than her car. Nothing to add to the dozens of other gifts he'd given her over the past year, despite her telling him to knock it off. If she didn't have to work with him, she'd probably have gotten a restraining order.

Her keys jangled against the door. She shoved them into the lock, but—

The door cracked open with the pressure of her key against the deadbolt.

Her windpipe shrank, a tiny straw that made

her inhales whistle. Had she left the front door unlocked? Not only unlocked, but... open? You didn't have your home burned to the ground and a dead body dumped in your garage without leaning a little extra cautious. You didn't have your mother vanish, your brother murdered, and forgo locks. Unless you were a maniac.

Was she a maniac? Of course she wasn't.

Maggie squinted, thinking, listening to her whistling breath, maybe trying to convince herself that she was wrong. The lock itself looked intact, unlike the door lock at her mother's house.

She peered at the crack between the door and the jamb, the lamps inside casting a spear of yellow over her shoe. Whatever had happened with the lock, Maggie had not left her house lights on. She was positive.

Needles pricked along her spine. Should she call Reid? By the time he got here, the suspect could be gone. Who did she even think was inside? There was no sign of damage to the door; the intruder who had broken into her mother's house hadn't perfected his lock-picking overnight.

The wailing night birds screed at her. No

sounds came from inside the house. She couldn't stand here all night. Intruders had more than enough street smarts not to leave the entire house blazing. Plus, they'd have heard her drive up—they'd have run out the back. If someone had been inside, they were already gone.

Unless they're waiting for you, Maggie.

The scar on her scalp pulsed angrily, sharp like talons in the back of her brain. Aiden's killer would have no reason to go after the dead child's sister; if she knew something about the suspect's identity, she'd have come forward before now. If a domestic abuser was running around as she'd thought at her mother's house, they'd want information first and blood second, and she was confident in her ability to stall. She'd have her cell out, ready to phone the police, just in case. And if Kevin had killed Aiden, the way Reid seemed to think—

She almost laughed aloud. Kevin wasn't waiting inside her house. His bloated corpse had been cremated the week they'd pulled it from the river. What did she think, that he had faked his death, shoved some poor lookalike in the driver's seat just so he could screw with her after she'd turned down his proposal? Alex or Sammy had probably forgotten something—they both had spare keys, so did Imani. It would not be the first time she'd walked in to find Alex on her couch. Oh, and Imani had said she was coming by tonight, right? No, wait, she had to work late—she'd texted.

Maggie pulled out her cell—*9-1-1*. She left her finger hovering over the call button. Then she squared her shoulders, nudged the door with her elbow, and watched the crack in the door widen.

"Fire!" she called into the interior. *Fire? Seriously? They'd know if the place was burning down, ya nimrod.* "Free bacon!"

No response.

Maggie pressed her elbow harder against the door, widening the opening to person-sized. She stepped over the threshold, her stomach churning, surely a sign that she needed to eat more than that green smoothie; it had tasted more like sugar than spinach anyway.

"Hello?" she called again, slowly, carefully making her way through the foyer. The house remained silent. But the prickling along her spine refused to relent. Maybe a cold shower would help. *Or a few hours in a sex club?*

She marched into the living room, ignoring the breeze from the half-open front door, the giant bouquet still sitting on the kitchen counter, the paper take-out bags poking from the top of the garbage can. The diamond bracelet, still in the box Tristan had delivered it in, open on the countertop.

Maggie scanned the living room for signs of disturbance, but nothing was out of place. The convertible couch-bed she'd slept on last night had been turned back into a sofa, the wooden coffee table mostly clear save for a stack of clean napkins. Alex had left her sweater tossed over the arm of the couch, a tiny cylinder of vanilla lip balm tucked down beside the cushion. Maggie's stomach growled, her heart steadying. She'd finish checking the house, maybe shoot Reid a text to get the patrols over here, *just in case*. And then... she was going to eat the biggest bowl of ice cream she could manage without puking. Maybe she'd top it with leftover PopTarts.

She padded through the living room to the hall, ears perked, breath held tight in her lungs. Her cell rang, and she startled—*just a phone call, my god*. But she paused with her finger above the screen. Maggie stared down the hall. The cell buzzed again, again, again, then stopped.

Maggie remained frozen on the carpet, squinting down the hallway, the one place where there were no lights blazing. But though no glow of lamplight came from the far end near the bedrooms, there was... something. A shadow near the bathroom door.

The buzzing came again—the cell. On the floor now, Reid's name blinking against the dark carpet, though she didn't remember dropping it. Sweat dribbled down her back.

The figure near the bathroom stepped out. A hulking beast in the dark. Wide—bulky. Muscular, far stronger than she was. Muscles borne of weights, not yoga.

Maggie eased backward, her heart lodged in her throat, her lungs burning, her heels catching the carpet. Her elbow hit the wall, smarting, but Maggie paid it no mind, sidling left and back to the hall closet. Dad was a man of habit. He had always kept Aiden's baseball bat in the back. Always. She hadn't checked lately that it was still there, but...

She snatched at the knob. The door creaked open—just enough.

The coats were soft and dense.

The figure in the hall stepped nearer.

Maggie shoved her hand further into the blackness of the closet, searching—*Where is it, where is it?*

She couldn't breathe. *There!* Her fingers closed around the handle. The bat slid out with a hissed whisper.

Maggie raised it above her head as the figure closed the distance between them and lunged.

CHAPTER **FOURTEEN**

The shadow was a blur of movement and muscle, a dark ghost made of terror. And the smell... was that myrrh?

But she had no time to consider it. Maggie's lungs were encased in ice. She felt the bat rise a little higher, the tightness in her shoulders more pronounced as she thrust the wood down—

"Maggie! Hey, stop!"

That voice...

The bat fell to the floor with a clatter that made her jump; she stared at it, as if unable to accept that she'd been holding it. The person in the hall—she'd almost smashed their head in with a bat, but it was not an intruder, not the person who had killed her brother. Not a stranger.

"Are you trying to get yourself killed? What the hell are you doing in my house?" *I should have gotten a restraining order. I should have forced him to stop with the gifts before it got to the breaking-and-entering phase.* She stooped to retrieve her cell—thank goodness she hadn't dropped the bat on top of it.

Tristan raised his hands, palms up—*whoa*—as if trying to tame a wild ferret. "I didn't break in, if that's what you're thinking. The door was open, and I had to pee. Plus, Reid told me what happened with your mom, and when you didn't answer my knock, I was... worried." He pushed his sandy brown hair back from his forehead—on the long side of professional, a little too bad-boy to be taken seriously in an office, a little too much mischief in those emerald eyes. The same color as the boy who'd attacked her in that building—the only thing she remembered about him. How had she never noticed that before?

But why would she? Lots of people had green eyes, and Tristan certainly wasn't the one who had attacked her all those years ago.

Tristan glanced at the front door, and the moment he broke eye contact, the thoughts subsided, her heart slowed, her throat loosened. She hated that she needed his help, but she couldn't be choosy right now. What was he going to do, give her more unwanted presents, break into her place... *again*? "Speaking of my mother, I need you to poke around, see if you can find her. And I have a few other names for you to check on, too, provided you can keep it confidential—I need their whereabouts for the past twenty-four hours." The domestic abusers might be a moot point, but there were too many options, too many suspects. She needed to rule them out—for certain. Because though her mom might have run off on her own, Maggie still wanted to know who had broken that lock.

Tristan turned back. He blinked. "I can keep anything confidential. And as far as your mother, I already looked, at the technical side, anyway; that's what the Fernborn PD pays me the big bucks for." Half a smile, more cocky than friendly. "According to the records, the tether was offline for a few minutes yesterday evening, which can sometimes happen with a battery change. It blinked right back on and was still transmitting from the house, so it didn't send up any alarms." *Duh. It's in the closet.* "Those aren't easy to tamper with, so if she's not home, someone who knew what they were doing helped her take it off."

"Helped her," she echoed. So Mom could hide it with her things—with that note. Looked like Mom's new boyfriend was an electronics guy. For now, that's all she needed to know, right? Tristan might be able to get a handle on her mother's location later, but she didn't want to push it now if Mom was still in the country. It hadn't even been a day since she vanished.

"Are the other people you want me to look into suspects in this tether removal?" Tristan asked.

"They're suspects in a door lock removal. She had reason to take off the tether, but she wouldn't break her own lock."

Tristan's brow furrowed; he cocked his head. "Like... the deadbolt?"

Crap. She hadn't told Reid that part. "Yeah. And get me some dirt on Birman, too. He's been acting weird, and he's not on social media."

He shrugged. "Neither am I."

"Yeah, I know." Oops; she shouldn't have said that. Now he knew she'd looked.

"Your wish is my command." His mouth was still set in a cocky half-smile, much like Reid's when he knew something she didn't. *I guess they got that from their father.*

But Maggie felt none of the affection she tended to feel for Reid, none of the calm "partnership" vibes. She and Tristan were not a team. Tristan was... she glanced at the counter, the gifts. *Intrusive.* Maybe the door hadn't even been open.

But he's here, Maggie. He cares. He didn't really break in, any more than you broke into your mother's. And she still needed his help. They could keep it professional.

Tristan followed her gaze. The enormous bouquet was already wilting, the box of PopTarts half-hidden in the leafy boughs. "Pretty flowers," he said.

"You can have them back." *Yeah, very professional.*

He frowned, no longer convinced of his actions, or perhaps he hadn't considered a scenario where she wouldn't fall on her knees with gratitude. "I'm not here for..." Tristan shook his head, annoyed. "I thought you'd like them."

Maggie headed for the kitchen, too tired to get into the gifts—to tell him to stop, yet again. Her bones hurt, her stomach hurt. She was dizzy. She needed to eat something before she passed out, and she could smell the too-sweet strawberry filling of the PopTarts before she opened the package. Tristan watched her with the eyes of a greedy Doberman, but she wasn't sharing. Unless he wasn't looking at the food. The sentiment remained.

Tristan followed her to the kitchen but stopped short across the counter—beside his bracelet. "Listen, Maggie... I didn't come here about your mom or the gift. I'm here about Alex."

Alex? Maggie dropped the pastry and pushed her curls off of her suddenly damp forehead. Her pinky nail snagged near her ear. "What happened to Alex? Is she okay?" She tore her hand free with a tiny ripping sound and a sharp pain in both her finger and her head that radiated back to the scar, awakening a renewed bout of achy throbbing.

"Yeah, she..." He swallowed hard. "Sorry, I don't usually do this part." That... was true. Why was *he* the one here? Where was Reid? Oh, wait, Reid had called her. Just before her aborted at-bat. And... where was Tristan's car? "A few things aren't adding up," he said. "About the night your brother vanished."

Tristan set one palm against the counter and leaned closer, casual, but so near that she could smell his cologne. Spicy. Musky. Like Kevin's—

exactly like Kevin's. It was the kind of cologne that used to make her see Tristan's face in every anonymous sexual encounter.

The smoothie twisted in her guts; bile rose in her throat. She swallowed hard and shoved the thoughts aside as Tristan went on, "I've been looking into hospital records and police reports for the day your brother went missing. Reid wanted me to find someone with a stab wound to the face. Not sure why."

Me. Because of me. And he hadn't told Tristan. Interesting. "Did you find him?" And what did that have to do with Alex?

"I didn't find reports from the local hospitals for anyone with that injury. But..." He glanced down at the flowers—his flowers—then met her eyes once more. "I found an ER visit for Alex from the night your brother went missing."

Ah. Her mastectomy was probably throwing red flags because of the timing. Maggie shoved half of the PopTart into her mouth, chewed as unappealingly as she could manage, then said, "She had cancer. Had an operation the same week that Aiden went missing. She probably has a slew of—"

"Well, that's the thing that's strange. I've been tearing through her medical history—"

"Why would you be looking at Alex's medical history?"

Tristan shrugged. "Because it's weird that she had cancer and a mastectomy that young. Weird that she was in the ER that night. And Reid said to look at anything unusual from that time period. It's extra strange because your brother was killed with a huge-ass knife."

A huge-ass knife. She was missing the connection. "How did you even get into Alex's medical records?" Hacker or not, they should have been secure.

"Well... I didn't."

Good. It made her feel better that there were still some things that were sacred. She shoved the second PopTart into her mouth, remembered that this one was whole when the corner jammed into her soft palate, and settled for taking a bite. It smelled like sugar-berry, but it tasted like cardboard.

"I did get into the insurance records," he said, his gaze earnest. "You don't go to the ER for an emergency mastectomy. And while I wasn't able to see what medical codes were billed, I was able to see whether the deductibles were used. After that ER visit, Alex only had one other appointment, I'm assuming to remove the stitches or staples—general wound stuff. But outside of that, she hasn't had any follow-up care. None. Not then, not now. If she had cancer..."

Maggie paused, the pastry soggy on her tongue. She swallowed it down with a cough. "Tristan, what are you asking me?"

"I'm not really asking you anything." He shoved himself off the counter. "I'm telling you that Reid asked me to pick you up and drive you to the police station since he couldn't get here himself."

"The police station... why?"

"Your friend is in interrogation. She never had cancer. And Alex definitely knows more than she's saying about your brother's death."

CHAPTER FIFTEEN

Alex knows more *than she's saying about your brother's death.*

Maggie stared out Tristan's passenger side window, her arms crossed over her chest so firmly that her ribs hurt. But her thoughts were more painful still, electric and pressured, racing in circles that she couldn't seem to control.

If Alex never had cancer... how had she lost her breast? What had landed her in the emergency room? Had someone hurt her, too? Three attacks in one night? First Maggie, then her brother, and then... Alex?

Nothing made sense. It was like some asshole suddenly decided to go on a child-injuring rampage. Reid's words rang in her head: *Aiden knew the person who killed him.*

Maggie pried her arms loose and clasped her hands in her lap, but that was no better; her nails left little crescents of destruction along the backs of her knuckles.

"I'm sorry if I upset you by walking into your house," Tristan said, voice raised to be heard above the engine—a 1966 Pontiac GTO, one of many classic cars he owned. He'd parked up the road in a cul-de-sac where he thought it safer from door dings. As if she'd open her door right into his side panel—she used to own a DeLorean and had a healthy respect for the classics. "I swear, the front door was open, Maggie. And I'll figure out who broke into your mom's place, okay? I promise."

"Let's not talk," Maggie muttered. "But I do appreciate your help." It was his job, but... still.

To his credit, Tristan clamped his lips shut and remained quiet as they put distance between themselves and her father's home. They arrived at the precinct not near soon enough, and Maggie escaped the car without a backward glance, hoping he wouldn't follow—hoping he'd know better. He did; the GTO roared off into the night.

The police station was a bustling mess of

anxiety permeated by stale coffee. Reid was not at his desk, but Clark saw her enter—the detective who'd told Reid about her brother, who'd sent him over to the morgue to rescue her from Birman. Tall, muscular, and bald, he reminded her of Denzel Washington, but he was bigger and had kinder eyes. The type of man who might read poetry all night, which made him a little too... nice for her. She had considered setting Alex up with him before she'd met Kelsey, but that was before her friend was cancer-free. Now she wasn't sure what she was walking into—what additional childhood myths might be destroyed by the end of the night.

Clark led her down the back hallway to the closet-like observation room, connected to interrogation by a two-way mirror. Reid stood in front of the glass, his shoulders rigid, his arms crossed. Just seeing the tension in his bloodless knuckles made her own ache.

He glanced over as she entered, nodded his thanks to Clark, then turned her way. "Tristan found you, I take it."

"Yeah." She stepped to the glass beside him. "I told him to poke around my mother." *Among other things.*

Reid pressed his lips together, his jaw working. "According to Birman, your mom has been home all week—tether verified. Birman said that he figured she was avoiding the phone and the door because she didn't want to deal with the police."

He was a jerk, but Birman seemed more competent than that. "He's lying to you."

"I know."

She snapped her head in his direction; his eyes remained locked on the glass as he went on: "He's got a domestic abuse history, an ex with a restraining order filed six years ago. She's fine now, no issues with Birman since—no stalking complaints since the divorce. But I don't like it. And I heard today that this is going to be his last case. Old boy's finally retiring."

If Birman's ex was readily available and not missing, he'd have no reason to break into her mother's house looking for her. That wasn't the connection. And it was disconcerting how Reid was delivering the news to the glass—staring at Birman himself. "I told Tristan to look into him, too," she said. She waited for him to nod, then followed his gaze.

Alex looked tiny through the two-way mirror, her face drawn, purple bags beneath her eyes like she'd been punched. Birman sat in one of the chairs opposite her. Malone stood at the head of the table, towering over her friend. Maggie wondered if he still stank of mustard.

Alex hated mustard. The PopTart churned in Maggie's belly. She swallowed hard against the bile and the sickly sweet pastry that was trying to edge up her esophagus.

"Why were you in the hospital the night Aiden Connolly vanished?" Malone said, his flat face pained, his voice soft, vowels extra round. Like he hated that he had to do this, the same way he'd behaved in the hospital morgue. *Canadians, eh?*

"I had cancer," Alex said, her shoulders relaxing. Authoritative—more assertive than Malone. If Tristan was right, either she'd convinced herself that it was true, or it was an exceptionally well-rehearsed lie. That would make sense if she'd been practicing the ruse her whole life.

"Are you sure?" Birman snapped. His fisted hands felt more threatening now that she knew about the restraining order. His flannel shirt felt sorely out of place.

Alex turned slowly toward the other detective—the non-Canadian clown. "I think I'd remember whether I had cancer."

"Who was your oncologist, if you don't mind

me asking?" Malone said.

Alex stiffened, then shook her head. "I don't remember. It was a long time ago. I was only thirteen."

"But you surely have an oncologist now," Malone went on. "Even just a doc for annual follow-ups, to make sure that you're still cancer free, eh? We all know these kinds of things tend to recur, as unfortunate as that might be." And he really did look sorry; the muscles around his eyes indicated that he was being truthful. Very good at lying, or just very nice. Probably both.

Maggie leaned toward the glass, her forehead so close that she could feel the chill leeching off the surface. *Come on, Alex. Have an explanation. A* good *explanation.*

"I..." Alex dropped her gaze. Unlike Malone, every muscle in Alex's body was screaming *LIAR*. Maggie's heart sank deep into her sour belly. First her brother, then her mom, and now Alex? What the hell was going on?

Malone slid into the chair beside Birman and rested his hands on the table. "Someone attacked you. Didn't they?"

Alex nodded at her lap.

"Did you tell him?" Maggie whispered to Reid. "About... me? The building?"

Reid shook his head. "I didn't need to. Tristan looked into her because he didn't like the statistical anomaly—an extremely rare breast cancer surgery on a child the same night that your brother vanished. Once he found it was done in the emergency room—wildly unlikely for cancer—he was a dog with a bone. We can't use what Tristan found directly, but they brought her in under the pretense of asking whether she'd seen anyone strange in the ER that night."

"Who was he, Ms. Dahlgren?" Malone asked. When Alex said nothing, he went on: "Just tell us what happened. We don't think you hurt Aiden Connolly—we know he was three hours away while you were in the hospital."

No, Malone, you know that someone made a phone call. "Are they serious with that, or just trying to get her to talk? I mean, they found his notebook out there, but they can't be sure Aiden was with it."

"Birman says there was a surveillance video from a now-defunct grocery store a mile from the gas station that clearly shows your brother. That would explain why he's so certain Aiden was there. But I haven't seen it, and he can't seem to produce it. The line is that it got damaged or lost while in evidence these past twenty-four years."

She frowned. "Why would he lie about that? Is Birman... a suspect?" Either he was guilty and manipulating evidence, or he was innocent and had actually seen a video with her brother in Yarrow.

Reid kept his eyes on the glass. "I dug a little deeper on that phone call," he said, "the one claiming they saw your brother. I have records from the phone company that show it came from a payphone in Yarrow."

Her jaw dropped. The call was legit? Really legit? She dragged her eyes back to the glass as Malone went on, "Alex, we need to know what happened so we can piece together a timeline. And the sooner we know who hurt you, the sooner we can—"

"My brother." Alex's voice cracked.

Her *brother*? Maggie balked. "That's... impossible." She'd known Alex since middle school—she didn't have a brother.

"She never mentioned him?"

Maggie shook her head, mute. Alex raised her face, but the tremble in her lip made heat rise in Maggie's chest. Alex lied. All these years, Alex had lied to her. Why would she lie about the cancer, about her family?

Why didn't you ever tell her what happened to

you in that building?

"I was in the kitchen. Grandpa had bowling league." Sweat shone on Alex's forehead, the armpits of her blouse dark. "Dylan... he came in through the back door, raging, screaming—covered in blood. There was a huge gash in his cheek."

The world stilled, Maggie's lungs painfully tight, but this was good, wasn't it? One mystery solved. Alex had a brother, and he was the one who had attacked Maggie. But if he went home afterward, then he wasn't in Yarrow with her brother. Right? "At least we know I didn't kill the guy," she said, her words more barbed than intended.

"Yep. But I already talked to Tysdale about using their hounds; they'll be out sniffing the park building's foundation first thing. We don't want to disappoint them by calling it off."

Pressure on her hand made her glance down. Maggie hadn't realized that she'd reached for Reid, but she was leaning on him instead of the ledge beneath the window, clutching his forearm. He'd wrapped his hand over hers. And when she looked up, he was watching her, eyes liquid and sad—steady. Supportive. The fire in her chest eased. It was as if he was bleeding the strain from her body through the pads of his fingers, but her heart rate remained high, throbbing frantically in her temples.

They both turned back to the window when Malone said: "What happened to his cheek, Ms. Dahlgren?"

Alex shrugged, her face sickly pale in the fluorescents. "I figured that he got into another fight. That he got what he deserved." With this last sentence, her shoulders squared. She sniffed.

"Because he'd attacked people before," Birman said, and Maggie glared at him. *Oh, like you haven't, Mr. Restraining Order.*

Alex swallowed hard. She nodded. "He'd beaten me badly in the past—my grandfather too. And his father, I mean, my father, used to beat the shit out of my mom. Before she... vanished."

Maggie's brow furrowed.

"Didn't know that either?" Reid said. "Grandpa turned her father in for grand theft and armed robbery—said he pulled a gun and stole everything in his safe."

"I thought her mom was dead. And that her dad had left them when she was a baby." Her voice rang hollow. Had Alex ever told her the truth about anything? Maggie's eyes burned.

"So, Dylan came in through the back," Malone said. "I'm sorry to have to dredge up these painful memories, but we do need to know... What happened next?"

Alex's shoulders were trembling. Maggie squeezed Reid's arm tighter. Part of her wanted to burst into the room and throw her arms around her friend, tell her it'd all be okay, that they'd figure this out over tacos and a dumb movie. But another part of her wanted to punch Alex in the face. Yes, Maggie had her own sins, her own withholdings—she understood that trauma could make you hold back. But cancer? *Cancer, Alex?* She could have said she fell off a jungle gym or got hit by a car.

Maggie's throat was tight with heat, empathy or fury she couldn't tell. Forgiving a misguided moment of weakness was one thing, but it required asking for forgiveness, not being caught in a lie.

"I... I screamed," Alex said. "I screamed *so loud*, but I wasn't loud enough for the neighbors, I guess. And then he... he... grabbed a knife from the butcher block." Her eyes glittered, brimming with tears, though they did not spill down her cheeks. Alex never cried. "I tried to fight him off, but he jumped on my back. He bit me." She reached across her chest to tap a spot on her upper back. Maggie's breath caught. That spot she was pointing to... that was where her tattoo sat. The free-form, multicolored heart. Was it a cover-up, to hide the scar?

"Sounds like this guy has a pattern," Reid said, but his voice came to her as if he were talking underwater. All she could hear was Alex.

"He tore my shirt, and then he... stabbed at me with the knife. I think he wanted to stab me in the heart."

The same way Aiden had died. That was not a coincidence—could not be a coincidence. "Piquerism," she said quietly. "Stabbing or biting is the compulsion—the source of sexual gratification." And he'd been young then, only just beginning to like the way his teeth felt sinking into living flesh. He'd still been experimenting with his M.O.

Alex took a long shuddering breath, her arms wrapped around biceps—self-protection. "I twisted at the last minute," she went on, her voice so soft that Malone leaned forward to hear her, his face a mask of sympathy. "Instead of the knife going into my chest, the blade stabbed into my... And when he yanked his hand up..." She hiccuped, recovered, swallowed hard. "He ran, but I was so scared, I just... I just couldn't..." Her words disintegrated into a round of unintelligible whispers.

"Jesus Christ," Reid said.

"Why didn't you call the police?" Birman snapped, and in those words, Maggie heard the way he'd interrogated her the night Aiden vanished: *Where were you, Maggie, what happened to your wrist, Maggie, did you see your brother, were you mad at him?* Her hackles rose.

"He wanted to kill me," Alex said to her lap. "I just wanted to go to the hospital—I *needed* to go to the hospital. There was so much blood... I thought I was dying." She raised her head and met Malone's eyes, the safer, kinder of the two detectives. "I didn't want to *die*."

Malone nodded, his lips turned down. "So, you went right from the house to the hospital?" he asked.

Alex nodded. "I waited until I was sure that he was gone, and then I wrapped myself up and took my bike to the bowling alley. Grandpa was just getting out by then."

"Did your brother carry a Bowie knife?"

"I wouldn't know. He was in juvenile detention when we were younger, but he got out around the time my dad went to jail. My grandfather immediately sent him away to boarding school. I don't know the details. I never wanted to know anything about him."

"I can understand that," Malone said. "I'm sure I'd want him as far away as possible. But since he had no connections here... Do you have any idea what brought Dylan back to Fernborn?"

Alex shook her head. "No."

"Where is your brother now?" Birman asked.

Alex glanced his way, then immediately turned back to Malone. "I haven't seen him since the day Aiden vanished. That's the honest truth. If I had..." She shuddered.

"Speaking of that poor boy..." Malone pushed himself to his feet once more, leaving Birman alone across the table. "When you found out that a child had gone missing the same night you were attacked, did you think to tell anyone? It's not your fault, of course, but this might have helped with the case."

Alex frowned. "How? I didn't think that Dylan hurt Aiden. Dylan wasn't a pedophile, and he was with me when Aiden was taken, wasn't he?"

"That's what we're trying to figure out." Malone nodded. "As hard as this is, you're really helping us out here." Alex's shoulders relaxed, but this time, it felt like a ploy on Malone's part, the muscles around his eyes twitchy. He... knew something.

"I'm sure you thought about it a lot," Malone went on, and Birman leaned back in his chair, letting his partner lead. "You figured it wasn't Dylan since he was with you. But you lived right near those woods—they wove around on both sides of your street, and there's nothing behind your house." It was a straight shot to Tysdale from there, that's what he meant. "Was there anyone else you suspected at the time, even briefly? Maybe you saw someone out there while you were pedaling your way up the road?"

Alex bit her lip. The air caught in Maggie's lungs—hot. Reid's bicep tightened, and she glanced down; her fingernails were claws against his flesh. She loosened her grip and dropped her hand.

"It's okay," Malone said. "It's not like we can arrest someone based on a guess. But we'd really like to put this to rest. To give Maggie and her family some peace of mind."

Alex's lower lip trembled. "I... I thought it was Kevin."

Maggie stared, stunned, her back tightening.

Reid straightened, too. "Did you tell her about the attack? The building?"

Maggie shook her head. "No." And the building was the reason Reid had suspected Kevin. But now Alex...

What was she missing?

"Kevin Hill?" Birman asked now, planting his elbows on the table.

Alex nodded.

"Why him?" Malone cut in.

"I mean, he and Maggie were kinda a thing. And it was her brother who went missing."

"That was the first time Kevin and I had really hung out together," Maggie said. *Our first date—what a start to a relationship.* "That's not a reason for her to connect Kevin to Aiden's disappearance."

Birman seemed to have come to the same conclusion, because he growled, "Maggie Connolly was thirteen years old. Kevin Hill, only fifteen. They couldn't have been that much of an item." He leaned over his steepled hands toward Alex. "It would have been very hard for a boy of Kevin's stature to get Aiden through those woods to the well—he wasn't strong like your brother. Only a year older, but Dylan was tall and made of muscle."

Maggie swallowed hard. He was right. Dylan had been strong—so strong, broad-shouldered and muscle-dense, his fingers digging into her arms, his knee on her spine. But he'd also been injured. Apparently, he'd still had a lot of fight left in him, more than enough to mutilate Alex.

"Kevin lived up the road from you before your brother was sent away, didn't he?" Birman asked.

The room stilled. Yes, he had. Kevin had moved across town the year before he and Maggie became an item.

Alex's shoulders convulsed. She put her head in her hands. "Yes," she whispered.

"Why would it be Kevin above anyone else?" Birman went on. "What aren't you saying?"

Malone slipped back into his chair. "You know more than you're telling us." Almost the same thing Birman had said to Maggie.

The room was devoid of air, Maggie's pulse thready in her neck.

"Kevin was Dylan's best friend," Alex said, raising her face. "He was just as sick as Dylan. And I... I almost let my best friend marry him."

Her breath shuddered from her lungs in a long torturous gasp. She turned her eyes to the glass. "I'm so sorry, Maggie."

CHAPTER **SIXTEEN**

KEVIN WAS DYLAN'S FRIEND. The idea seemed impossible, ludicrous. But was it true?

Probably. Alex didn't have a reason to lie, but she certainly had reason to withhold it: self-protection. And protection of their friendship. Maybe she'd even thought Maggie would take Kevin's side—after all, to explain Kevin, she'd have to admit that she had a brother in the first place. She'd have to admit that she'd lied about the cancer. If Alex hadn't been coerced, Maggie never would have known, and that sat like a stone in her guts.

Had Birman known this whole time? Had he assumed Maggie knew? Even if he didn't know about the attack at the building, he might have pieced together enough to make Kevin look guilty—make him look like Dylan's partner in crime.

She walked through the halls of the police station and out into the parking lot with the hairs along her spine prickling, the unfamiliarity of every unknown officer in the hallway reminding her that her best friend was essentially a stranger. Even Reid's back as she followed him through the dark lot felt strange and unknowable. He was an enigma, an alien wearing a Reid suit, wearing Reid's brown hair, using Reid's voice to say: "Do you mind if I swing by my place?" He glanced over his shoulder. "The sitter texted, said she saw someone walking the block—that they passed the house twice. It's probably nothing, I might have put her on high alert unnecessarily, but..."

"Yeah, fine." Her words echoed over the asphalt and bounced against the metal bumpers of police cruisers.

"Tristan's at your mom's house, just so you know—talking to the neighbors since Jerry's doorbell cam didn't tell him anything." Reid shrugged. "I'm not yet sure how your mom managed to trick the tether or why Birman is lying to us about her being there, but... if there's something to find, Tristan will find it."

"I hope so." She wanted to know who'd broken in. Maggie climbed into Reid's Bronco with a vise crushing her sternum. The break-in, while important, didn't feel connected to the rest of this. Her mother had removed her tether, had run off with her boyfriend—she was fine, and either mistaken or covering her own ass with that note. She was also out of Maggie's life for good. If she'd escaped to some non-extradition country, she could not fly home to see her daughter. And if she was still in the United States, just calling Maggie was a risk.

And then, there was Alex.

The silence intensified as Reid started off into the night, the whispering of the tires their soundtrack, every murky side street hissing that she should have seen this coming, that she should have known her best friend was lying.

Alex could be forgiven for withholding the attack, for not discussing her brother and her fractured home life. She'd been a victim, too, and it was difficult to reconcile those feelings, even within your own head. Maybe Maggie could have forgiven the cancer lie, too... eventually. But Kevin. All this time, Alex had let her believe that Kevin was a good person. All this time, she'd known that Kevin and her psycho brother were besties.

It didn't mean that Kevin was a psychopath, too—he could have been taken in by Dylan's charms, done things he never would have otherwise. A victim in his own way. And that would certainly explain his strong reactions to what happened that day.

Had she mistaken intense guilt for trauma? They did present similarly, especially because trauma often came with a heavy dose of shame. But if he'd hurt her brother... *How did I miss this?* How stupid was she?

Kevin's best friend—that was the guy who'd taken a bite out of her head.

Betrayal blazed sharp inside her chest, the deception palatable, bitter on her tongue. Alex had refused to elaborate on what "just as sick as Dylan" really meant. Maggie could ask Alex herself, but not now.

Now, she had to think.

Reid's sigh rumbled through the car. "This is some bullshit."

Maggie dragged her gaze from the window. She'd been staring at the glass for fifteen minutes, and she hadn't seen a thing. "What?"

"You've already been through so much, and

now you have to add your best friend and your ex-fiancé on top of it? What the fuck?"

Reid rarely swore. She raised an eyebrow. "You sound angry. Would you like to process your emotions?"

"Pulling out the shrink talk, huh?" He smiled, but it was strained. "Sorry. I just... it's ridiculous. All of it." He relaxed his grip on the wheel and ran a hand through his hair. It spiked up on one side. "I'll go with you to tell Birman what happened in that building. I think it's time. Anything they can piece together from that night might help."

Maggie's mouth went dry; her stomach clenched. But she nodded. "Do you still think it was Kevin?"

He glanced her way. "Do you?"

"I don't know anything anymore. If he and Dylan were friends, Kevin definitely would have gone back to the building to check on him, like you said." But had Kevin killed her brother?

She turned to Reid and waited until he looked over. "I want to know what else you're thinking."

His brow furrowed, his expression pained. "About..."

"Anything. Everything. It's too much for me to process. I feel like I'm missing something, and you said yourself that I'm too close to be impartial." *I need answers, Reid. I need help.* And he suddenly felt like the best person to talk to. She trusted Sammy with her life, but he was too close to this, same as she was—both of them had known Kevin. And Reid... hadn't. He didn't always make the right calls, but he wasn't emotionally invested the way they were. He'd be less blind.

Reid swallowed hard and turned back to the road. "Are you sure you want to hash this out here? Today of all days?"

Today of all days? Because she had just identified her brother's body last night—had it really only been last night? Because her mother was missing and had left her a cryptic warning-slash-goodbye note? Because she'd just found out that one of her best friends had been lying to her for years, and that her almost-fiancé, a man she'd sincerely loved, was besties with a psychopath and might have murdered her brother?

"Yeah. Today is just perfect, Reid."

"Okay, here goes." He sucked in a breath as if steeling himself. "I think it's weird that Alex's brother returned to Fernborn the very same day that your brother vanished. That he conveniently showed up at the same building where you and

Kevin were throwing rocks at walls, or whatever you were doing."

Bricks, rocks, who cared? "The biggest issue is that he knew Kevin, though. That they were friends." And Kevin hadn't said a word when he saw Dylan on the floor. Hadn't reacted at all except to grab her and get her out.

Reid frowned, his jaw tight. Holding onto something—something major. Something that would... hurt.

"What is it? Just spit it out."

"Whose idea was it to go to that building, Maggie?"

"I..." *Kevin's. It was Kevin's.*

"It's coincidental that Kevin left just in time for Dylan to walk in."

"He just went up the road to the drugstore..." His meaning finally dawned on her. "You think they planned it? That Kevin brought me there so they could hurt me?" She hadn't known Kevin very well at that point, but the accusation felt very wrong. And he'd helped her out of there—protected her, patched her head. And after... all the years after. All the years she'd spent under his spell, loving him. Perhaps after what she'd done to Dylan, what had happened to Aiden, he'd realized the error of his ways. Maybe he'd gotten close to her and stayed close to her as a kind of... penance.

She shook her head as if to shake the thought from it—to shake the doubts aside. "Why me?" But Dylan wouldn't need a reason; for a sadistic psychopath, a better question was *why not?* "I'd only recently met Kevin, but even if they knew me, why Aiden? We have to assume the two are connected." It was illogical to think it coincidental now. Somehow, these events were all linked in a way she wasn't seeing.

The highway lights played across his face, flickers of bright white painting his already pale cheeks in the ghastly hues of the dead. "My best guess is that Aiden was collateral damage. You told me that Aiden wouldn't have walked by that building on his way home from the school. But he might have gone looking for you."

She frowned. "I told him to walk home on his own. That I wasn't going to be there."

"So he knew you weren't going to walk him home."

She nodded. "Yeah. I didn't want him to wait for me or call my parents." *I didn't want him to be scared.* That had worked out smashingly.

"What about the building? Could he have known that you were going there?"

"I'm not sure. I think I talked to Kevin about it on the phone the night before. He might have overheard, I guess." Or listened in. He did that sometimes. Little brothers, and all.

Reid sniffed.

"You don't think he was taken from the road or the woods," she said, her eyes on his face. "You think he was taken from the building."

"That's more likely than those boys targeting you separately, especially since you had no connection to them prior to that day—no reason for Kevin or Dylan to hold a grudge. You'd never met Dylan to piss him off, and with Kevin—"

"I said yes." *Until he asked me to marry him.*

He nodded and blinked at the road, as if unable to meet her gaze. "I think Kevin went back to that building after he dropped you off—if nothing else, he'd want to make sure that his friend was okay. And I walked the beat yesterday from building to high school, from middle school to the building. I made Clark walk from your dad's house to the building too. If he hustled, Kevin could have gotten back to the building soon after Aiden would have made it over from the school."

"And what was Kevin's motive?" Kevin—it was the name of a stranger. Had the caring though flawed man who had loved her been a killer at worst and an accomplice at best? It still seemed impossible, felt impossible. Was this the way Hannibal Lector's psychologist colleagues felt when they realized he'd been eating folks? Stupid as hell, sightless as bats, utterly blindsided?

"Maybe Kevin wasn't the one with motive. Dylan was the one who attacked you, and he wouldn't want another witness. He might have enlisted Kevin's help, asked him to convince Aiden to go with while Dylan patched himself up at home. While they figured out what to do next."

"So, Aiden waited with Kevin in the car outside Alex's place. Alex was home, Dylan was furious, unstable—he hurt her in a fit of rage. But after that... they couldn't have made it to Yarrow in time for the witness to see them. Even speeding, it would have been tight."

"Tight, but not impossible. And the witness didn't see who was with the boy, only Aiden himself. Kevin could have easily made it to Yarrow if he took Aiden in Dylan's car. And then..."

Right—and then. "So, Kevin went off to Yarrow with Aiden while Dylan was at Alex's. But at some point... maybe he realized that he couldn't hurt my brother." Her voice came out a pressured hiss, devoid of air. "That's why he came back here. Kevin couldn't finish what they'd started, so he came back to Fernborn so Dylan could..." Tears smarted in her eyes. *The man you loved your entire life helped to kill your bother and dumped him in the woods after the police cleared out.*

"Kevin wasn't a psychopath," she said, more for herself than for Reid.

"I know. He killed himself."

The words stabbed into her lungs, but... he was probably right. Again. She'd always wanted it to be an accident, but she'd suspected the worst. Sammy called that bridge "Dead Man's Dive," and it had never been lost on her that diving was an active event and not a mistake.

"Kevin had a lot of guilt about something," Reid went on. "And if I had been even tangentially involved in a child's death, then fell in love with his sister..." He sighed. "I hate this, I do. Maybe Kevin's death was just a drunken accident. I wish I had some logical reason to believe that the worst was impossible."

She shifted against the car door.

"I'm sorry, Maggie. I am."

"Me too." She stared into the night, a deep

hollow blackness like that which had hidden her brother for so long.

"I talked to the medical examiner earlier," Reid went on. "She's done with Aiden's... well. I'll get him transferred over to the funeral home so you can make arrangements. And I'll help with anything you need."

"Thanks, Reid. I appreciate it. I appreciate... everything." Her voice cracked on the last word. He reached over the console and squeezed her shoulder, just once, then replaced his hand on the wheel.

"Look under your seat." He hit his turn signal and hooked a right. "I was going to give it to you tomorrow, but I think you could use it now."

Maggie raised an eyebrow, but unbuckled her seatbelt and reached between her ankles. She felt around for a moment, searching, the rough carpet abrading her knuckles in a way that made her feel more alive—was she numb? Then... *ah*. She pulled the item into her lap: a wrapped package, the size of a small book.

She traced the pattern on the shiny blue wrapping paper—spiders. "Where did you get this paper? It's amazing."

"There is more to the gift, but I'm glad you like it. I had to send away for it months ago." He chuckled, but it was thin, guarded. Still a little sad.

Is that why he hadn't given her the present on her birthday? He was waiting for the paper? But if that were the case... "Why were you waiting until tomorrow?"

The light up the road went yellow, then red. He slowed to a stop. The crimson glow made him appear wickedly sunburned as he cocked his head her way. "Tomorrow's your birthday, isn't it?"

She frowned.

"It's... not." He sighed and slumped back against the seat. "When is it?"

"Yesterday."

"Well, shit. I mean, that sucks for a bunch of reasons, but..." The light changed, staining his flesh a green Hulk-like hue. He pressed gently on the gas. "I guess I should have known better than to trust Tristan, especially when it comes to you," he said to the windshield. "I'm so sorry. I didn't forget, obviously, I..." He shook his head. "Damn, I'm an idiot. Tristan probably got you something really nice."

Yeah, a bunch of diamonds, after I asked him a thousand times to stop with the elaborate gifts. This time, he almost got a bat to the face for his trouble. He should have stuck to the much more reasonable birthday flowers.

But Maggie said none of that; she dropped her gaze to the package. Multiple threads of thin black ribbon curled over the edges. Exactly eight strands of ribbon. It was perfect. She'd lost her pet traumatically, but she had spider pajamas, spider art, and she'd been clear with Reid that she still loved the little creatures. She'd probably get another tarantula once she could assure that he wouldn't befall the same fate as the last. Once she stopped treating Ezra.

She tugged the ribbons and watched them fall away. The paper tore. Inside...

Her heart stopped. *Aiden*. No, not him, but... a photo of him, sitting beside a tree—a tree that still remained in her father's backyard. She'd lost most of her pictures in the house fire, and they were the only items that she had really grieved. "How did you... where..." Maggie was not often speechless, but her mouth wasn't quite connecting to her brain.

"I know you've been upset about the pictures you lost last year. So, I enlisted the help of our forensic sketch artist. I borrowed the shot from your dad's place and asked for Sam's help, too. Just to make sure I got it right."

Maggie stared into her brother's eyes. This was the way she wanted to remember him: mouth smiling, eyes glittering, Aiden happy and healthy and alive. It was the most incredible gift she'd ever received. He'd given her a piece of her brother back.

Reid turned into his driveway, then turned to her and smiled. "Well, anyway... happy birthday. The timing is terrible, I know, but maybe it'll ease things just the tiniest—"

He never got to finish the sentence. She wrapped her hand behind his neck and raised her lips to his.

Reid inhaled sharply through his nose—*oh no, he's going to pull away, this is a mistake, what are you doing, Maggie?*—but then he sighed out a breath and leaned into her, tangling his fingers in her hair, his pinky tracing the scar on her head. She waited for the revulsion, for him to move his hand, but he only explored the inside of her mouth more fervently, massaging her tongue with his.

Her chest warmed with feeling, a familiar yet mysterious sensation, something that had lain dormant for so long that she wasn't sure what it was until he unbuckled his belt and leaned over the console. He pressed harder against the scar, drawing her to him, his other hand sliding over her knee. Affection, but not the kind borne of the caress of strangers. It was a deeper connection, the feeling of being known, of being *wanted* for something besides her flesh. He knew it all, all the important bits anyway, and her past did not bother him. The scar beneath her hair was not some inconsequential part of her—it was the reason she had wound up in this car.

She gasped as Reid broke their kiss. He leaped from the Bronco without another word, hustling around to the passenger side, haloed by the glow of passing headlights. He ripped her door open. Maggie blinked up at him. Then he reached for her, waiting for her to take his hand. Waiting for her to follow him—to say yes.

She was in his arms again in a second, her mouth on his, the gift still clutched in her left hand, Reid's gentle fingers on her lower back. Holding her. Telling her it was going to be okay.

But was it?

She tensed—*we shouldn't.* But she didn't say it aloud. Because for once, she didn't want control. She didn't want to be in charge of every single element of her experience. She wanted to be taken and cared for by someone who was absolutely, one hundred percent for sure not a psychopathic child killer.

Can you know that, Maggie? Can you really be sure?

She pushed the thought aside, and when he hauled her against him and slipped his hand down the front of her pants, the pain of the last twenty-four hours vanished into the night. *I could love him—maybe, one day, I could.*

It was the last thing she thought before her mind went perfectly, gloriously blank.

CHAPTER SEVENTEEN

He drove slowly down the street, his teeth aching, molars grinding. The detective's house faded in the rearview. But he could still see them there, Reid pulling her from the passenger seat, pressing her against the side of the car. The way the detective had taken Maggie's hand and led her to the porch.

He slowed to a crawl, scowling at the road, the trees casting the streetlights into globular patterns on the asphalt that looked like a virus beneath a microscope—toxic. Pestilent. He stopped. Far enough away that the detective could not see him from the house proper, but the headlights of the babysitter's car glared at him from the curb. The woman was leaving. It seemed that Reid was not expecting to drive Maggie home tonight.

His fingers clenched around the wheel. This was an unexpected complication. So long as they'd been together in that club, he'd been satiated, satisfied with the sweet anticipation of what their future might look like. But he had not imagined that she would suddenly jump into bed with a colleague—never imagined she'd sleep with a coworker at all. She was not that kind of woman, or she'd have gone at it with Owen years ago. No, Maggie kept her private life so far separate from her personal life that the two did not intersect.

When had that changed? And more critically, how had he missed it? At some point between her lover's drunken plunge off the bridge and her brother's bones being discovered, she had become more… flexible.

Perhaps it was the stress. It was stress that had led her to spending her nights in that club. No boyfriends, no other complications, just that dark basement. Just him in that green bracelet, the scent of her in his nose, her skin soft beneath his fingertips.

The babysitter was nearer now. He lifted his

foot from the brake, hit his turn signal and twisted the wheel to the right. Around the block, again, squinting in the rearview until the headlights of the sitter's Prius passed the intersection and vanished up the road.

He took another right, his chest filled with molten steel, then another. He'd seen enough. He'd seen more than enough. But he was drawn back to the detective's home as he might have been attracted to the scent of some noxious gas, seeking the source of his discomfort—needing to decide what it meant, what to do.

He watched the detective's street pass. He took the next right and parked just far enough from the stop sign to avoid being towed. The bungalow in front of him was blue with garish white shutters, as if someone had printed the colors in reverse. He could see the top of the detective's roof if he squinted—Reid had a brick fireplace, unlike most homes in the neighborhood. A tall chimney.

He reached up and tugged his hood low over his face, then climbed from the car, closing the door softly behind him. His feet made barely a sound as he ducked into the shadows behind the first home. The detective's cameras had only one blind spot, and to get beyond it, he'd need to zig-zag through the yards of the houses behind Reid's. This was fine—he'd done it before. But never while the detective was home.

Reid would be occupied tonight, though.

The fire in his chest raged anew; the night air reeked of iron and mud. He ducked around the corner of the last house—the old woman here was never awake past six—and slipped into the thick evergreen bushes, a double line of shrubbery to keep the riffraff out. Pointed leaves stabbed at his arms, scratched his legs, but even if she looked out her window now, it would be nearly impossible to see him inside the greenery, especially in his dark clothes. He was made of shadows.

He reached into the pocket of his sweatshirt and turned to Reid's little home, raising the binoculars to his eyes. The curtain in the bedroom window offered only a few inches of visibility, but he'd have recognized Maggie's curls anywhere, currently wrapped around the detective's fingers, his other hand on her ribs, and her breasts, her bare breasts, pressed against his chest...

Fury, hot in his guts. *Why are you doing this to us, Maggie?*

A crackling sound cut the night. He went

stock-still, eyes on the window, the air frozen in his lungs. The noise did not come again, but his hand... stinging. He glanced down. The outer casing on one side of the binoculars had cracked in his clenched palm.

Just as well. He could not watch anymore.

He'd made plans in the past—many plans. He'd executed each of them to perfection, waiting for the ideal moment. He had imagined that she would be raw and vulnerable after her brother's death, but he had thought she'd be too consumed by grief to accept a man into her heart, let alone into her bed. Had he missed his chance?

No. This thing with the detective was surely a distraction from her pain. An inconsequential moment of weakness.

He'd forgive her.

And once he was sure that she'd take him on, no couple would ever be as happy as they would. She would love him in a way no woman has ever loved a man before, and he would spend his life fulfilling her every need.

He just had to convince her—to show her how good they'd be together, how perfect.

No matter how long it took Maggie to accept him into her life as well as her bed, she was definitely worth the wait. But it was almost time to make his move. Time to close the distance between the rabbit and the fox. His pants grew tight around his groin.

He smiled. Yes. It was time to end the chase.

By any means necessary.

CHAPTER **EIGHTEEN**

Maggie woke to a blade of light piercing into her eyeball. But she always kept her curtains drawn. Had someone gotten into her house—her dad's house? And the sheets...they were softer than hers, weren't they? Fuzzier, like fleece or flannel.

She stretched, cracking one eye. And stilled.

The bedroom was not hers—she barely recognized it at all. But at least she knew why. She'd snuck in here in the dark, tiptoed past Ezra's room on the other side of the house, through the dining room to the master. The babysitter had tossed her a knowing glance as she collected her purse.

Reid had stood in the bedroom doorway, holding the door for her. She'd had her shirt off before she made it inside the room. And the rest of it, his hands on her back, the way he'd kissed her, the way their bodies had joined so perfectly, so completely that she'd felt the hollowness in her heart finally sealing as if he had created a bridge over a river of grief...

She did not want to consider what it meant. How when she'd finally fallen asleep in his arms, she had felt whole for the first time in over a year... nearly two.

Maggie blinked and rolled over, away from the blinding sun—toward Reid. Barely dawn, but the angle of the window was just right, or just wrong, depending on how you looked at it. The light didn't seem to bother Reid, who was now her... colleague with benefits? Lover in the nighttime? His eyes were still closed, his brown hair tousled against the pillow. One muscular shoulder poked above the sheets, highlighted by a brilliant tattoo of a cardinal; a strange art piece for a detective. She had not noticed it last night, though she had seen a much larger one on his back, shoulder blade to shoulder blade: Medusa, snakes that slithered up his spine, one viper sinking its deep fangs into his upper rib.

A man of many secrets, this Reid. But unlike the ones Alex had been keeping from her, the ones Kevin had kept from her, none of Reid's secrets felt unsafe. If Kevin had a secret tattoo, she'd have been fine. She could have handled the deception if Alex had merely been concealing an artistically lopsided heart.

Reid grumbled and his cardinal tensed then released. Her stomach clenched. *What have I done?* Nothing terrible, so long as they could keep it from affecting their professional relationship. While they did work together, it wasn't a therapist-patient thing. It wasn't against any ethical code that she knew of, only the old adage "don't shit where you eat" and...

It hadn't been shit. She blinked at the curve of his heavy lower lip, his square jaw so peaceful in sleep. The flesh of her thighs tingled where his mouth had been just hours before. No, it definitely hadn't been shit.

But she didn't want to hurt him. She and Kevin had broken up once for nearly two months —and she'd taken full advantage—but she had not considered those men once they'd left her bedroom. She'd never been with anyone else that she cared for. And her one-and-only real relationship... he might have killed her brother, or at least helped.

Betrayal burbled in her guts, hot and sharp, a

belly full of smoldering needles. She swallowed hard. While this might end up being a wonderful thing with Reid, it was also an additional complication. She still had a brother to bury. They still had a killer to catch, and—

Creeeeak!

She turned toward the door. Closed and locked, she'd watched Reid secure it last night. But they weren't alone in the house.

Oh no. Ezra. Apparently an orgasm—fine, three—made a woman forgetful. She should get out of here before the boy made his way to the kitchen for breakfast. He had finally started making progress in therapy, and she'd just slept with his foster father. And having a sexual relationship with a family member of a current client... *That* was sticky. Forgetful indeed.

She closed her eyes. *Dammit.* Perhaps she'd ask Owen to take the boy on. Would Ezra feel betrayed? Abandoned? Yeah, this was a bad idea. Such a bad idea.

And yet...

She blinked at Reid, his broad chest, the gentle curve of his muscular bicep. The tip of his tongue, barely visible between his teeth. Her belly warmed. Orgasms might make you forget complications, but they certainly made for delicious muscle memories and gave you a strong urge to repeat the process. The men who complained about not getting enough sex had not yet discovered that little tidbit—please a woman right, and she'll come back for more.

Maggie bit her lip. While a repeat performance would be an amazing way to wake up, there was no way she'd get out of the house before the child saw her. And that wasn't how she wanted him to find out. That would end badly, and in very short order.

Maggie slipped from the bed, the chill air kissing her bare flesh in all the places Reid had last night.

She found her pants near the foot of the bed, her shirt on the chair in the corner. Her underwear on the lamp. Socks, socks... no socks. Wait, one sock, hooked into the dresser drawer pulls. Maggie tucked her birthday gift beneath her arm.

She grabbed her shoes from the jamb beside the door and tiptoed through the dining area toward the exit. Plain, understated walls, but everywhere she looked was another painting in vivid colors, each more vibrant than the last. Maggie unlocked the deadbolt and slipped onto the porch, then eased the door shut behind her.

The sun was blinding. She squinted against

it, shoved her feet into her shoes, one sockless, one not. Then Maggie pulled her phone from her pocket and headed up the road. It wouldn't take long to order a car, and truth be told, she needed the fresh air. She needed to think. This emotional roller coaster was going to be tricky, but would it be good tricky or bad tricky? At least it seemed to be numbing the epic void that had exploded in her chest when she saw Aiden's corpse.

Her shoes made a sharp slapping sound as she made her way down the drive. Birds twittered from the nearby trees. But as she stepped onto the sidewalk, the hairs on her spine prickled so angrily it was almost painful. *I'm not alone.*

She turned slowly, muscles tight, fist clenched, but no one stood on the walk behind her. The parked cars on the road appeared empty. Reid's house was still dark, the bushes on either side of the porch glistening with early dew, the windows reflecting the sun. But...

Maggie squinted. In the far window, the drapes twitched. And as her eyes adjusted, a form took shape. Little shoulders. A small head. A child's face. Ezra stood just inside the glass, half hidden behind the gauzy curtains. He'd seen her —definitely.

Her phone buzzed. Was it Reid? She should

have left a note. She glanced at the cell: two text messages. Owen—he wouldn't be in the office this morning, had to meet with his attorney. Again. The second was from Tristan, but her skin was burning with the intensity of Ezra's gaze. *One thing at a time.*

She refocused on the window and raised a hand—*I should say hello, right? Or should I try to play it off like I'm arriving?* But the boy just stared, his mouth set in a grim line of agitation. Maggie slowly lowered her arm as Ezra vanished into the blackness of his room.

Shit.

Her phone buzzed again. And as she hustled away up the street, she finally read the second the text message:

"Do you know why your mom confessed to Aiden's murder?"

CHAPTER **NINETEEN**

TRISTAN DID NOT ANSWER the phone when she called, nor did he answer the second time. Or the fourth. By the time she climbed out of the Lyft at home, her heart was fluttering like a meth-addled bird against her rib cage, and her finger was sore from slamming the *End Call* button.

What kind of jerk would send a text like that and not follow up with an explanation? Had he found her mother? Was Mom in jail? Had she actually confessed to killing Aiden? That couldn't possibly be true. Reid answered on the first ring, but he had no idea what she was talking about; he said he'd call her once he got to the precinct—once he figured out what was happening.

Neither of them mentioned last night.

Her hair was still wet when she pulled into the office parking lot, reddish strands clinging to her blazer. Colder today than it had been earlier this week, a gasping breath of chill infusing the clouds with threads of bitter gray. Rain later, despite the brilliant way the morning had begun. And though her skin was damp along her shoulder blades, though she sensed the gooseflesh running up her spine, she could barely feel the prickling that usually accompanied it. Everywhere her hair touched, every tender place her purple blouse shimmied, she felt Reid's fingers. She felt his breath against the back of her neck.

But it was Tristan's voice that she heard inside her head: *Do you know why your mom confessed to Aiden's murder?*

No. She could not wrap her head around that sentence, could barely understand its meaning. Maybe Birman had given Tristan bogus info just to get her down there or to throw her off—to see if she'd call her missing mom so they could track her down. The latter made more sense than anything. And going to the precinct wouldn't give her information faster than Reid could acquire it.

Maggie took the stairs to the third floor, listening to the metronome of her booted footfalls against the metal treads. Sammy... she had to call

Sammy. She'd meant to call last night after she got home from interrogation—after she'd found out about Alex, about Kevin—but then Reid had happened. *Thrice.* And poor Owen didn't even know about Aiden yet, off dealing with his divorce drama.

She sighed. So many people to call, patients to see, funeral arrangements to make, and maybe tomorrow, a murder to solve. How was solving her brother's homicide last on the list? *Ha-ha, world, well played.*

Maggie shoved her key into the lock, half-expecting the door to creak open as the one at her house had last night. But it was secure. She busied herself flicking lights and unlocking doors and heating water for tea—forcing herself to breathe. She'd spent enough time locked in cells with murderers to know that tension tended to sharpen her focus. By the time she lowered herself into the chair behind her desk, she'd written off her mother's "confession." If her mom was in custody, Reid would have called. Hell, her mother would have contacted Reid personally before confessing to someone else. But that didn't stop her belly from churning, hot and oily and sick. It didn't stop death from leeching into her thoughts.

Her first client was a young man with six piercings in one eyebrow and three more in his lip. Anxiety, depression, and a history of sexual trauma. The session focused her attention, but also reminded her that Aiden might have been abused in more ways than they knew. If the killer did that to him... hopefully he'd been dead first.

Her second session was with a parolee—vehicular homicide. As he detailed his guilt, his horror at what he'd done, she heard Kevin on the nights he relapsed: *Things just feel too heavy*. And that last night, the night he'd proposed... perhaps that was his final plea for absolution, for forgiveness.

And she'd said no.

Was that what she'd been all those years? Was making her happy atonement for his part in her brother's murder?

Her last session was a new intake. Mr. Melon? She headed for the waiting room and turned the corner to find a man in a black T-shirt and a leather jacket. Not a new patient. She wasn't excited to see Malone, but better him than Nick Birman, whose entire personality was the embodiment of the term "swamp ass."

"You didn't have to make an appointment," she said, waving him into her office, but her words came out strangled. He was here about her mother, wasn't he? Tristan's text that her mother had confessed to Aiden's murder couldn't be a coincidence. Tristan still hadn't called her back, that jerk—if he wanted to be overbearing, now would be the time. But if it was about her mom...

Reid should have called.

She waited as he settled into his seat, then lowered herself with her fingers laced on the desktop. Studying him. His eyes were cast down as if playing at guilt, but his shoulders were as rigid as ever, his mouth set in a determined line. Something was definitely wrong, but she couldn't bring herself to ask what. At least he didn't smell of mustard—molasses today. Maybe brown sugar. Maple syrup.

When Maggie remained silent, he cleared his throat and said, "I just had a few follow-up questions."

She frowned. Follow-up questions? *Stop playing games and tell me what happened with my mother!* But she wanted him to lead; she wanted to hear the pitch so she could figure out what their goal was.

He slipped his cell from his pocket and turned the screen her way. "Does this man look familiar?"

A man, not her mom? Perhaps Birman had not involved his partner in his little "mom confessional" game. Her shoulders relaxed, but that relief vanished when she squinted at the phone. Before her brain had processed the face, her ribs clamped down, her heart shooting into her throat, and the scar on her head erupted into knifelike stabbing. She could not have built his face from memory, did not recall his sandy hair, but physical reactions could be as telling as words. She'd been wrong about his eyes, though —she'd thought them fully green, but they were hazel green in the photo. Close enough.

"Dylan—Alex's brother?" Kevin's best friend. Malone nodded. For him to be asking her about Dylan, perhaps they already knew he'd come after Maggie herself. If not, it was well past time to confess. He was trying to put together a profile of the killer, tracing Aiden's last hours, and anything she knew might help.

Her heart was still lodged in her throat, but she took a breath and forced out: "If you haven't pieced it together already, Alex's brother attacked me too. The day Aiden went missing. No sexual assault, but he bit me in the head, probably would have killed me if I hadn't stabbed him." It was out—it was finally out in the open. If Birman wanted to give her shit about her thirteen-year-old stabby self, so be it.

Malone's eyebrows hit his hairline. "We suspected, but... we'll need an official statement. You can come to the station—"

"I'll type it out and send it over."

Malone sniffed, appraising her, then nodded and pulled the phone back to his lap. "We have a consultant looking for Dylan, but he ran away from boarding school and fell off the grid before your brother vanished. No idea how he was making money, but my guess is that he used an old trick, and a rather low-tech one: Stole the identity of a dead person."

"Tristan's looking at that too?"

His eyes narrowed as if he had not expected her to know the names of the other consultants. But Malone recovered quickly. "Yeah, he is. Scouring databases or whatever he does. But your mother... apparently, she contacted Detective Birman and confessed to your brother's murder."

Her chest went hot—*there it is. I thought Canadians were better than that.* Maggie crossed her arms. "There is no way that my mother hurt Aiden."

"We know she didn't do it. Your mother was

here in Fernborn when your brother was in Yarrow with the killer. But your mother also wouldn't confess for no reason."

"She *didn't* confess. Birman has had it out for me since I was a kid. He's lying."

"Or she is. I saw the text message."

Her arms dropped along with her jaw. She planted her palms on the desktop as if to hold herself upright under the weight of sheer absurdity. "First of all... she confessed by *text*? Anyone could have sent that message. And on the ridiculously improbable chance that she did send it, why would she confess to something she obviously didn't do?"

"If we could find her, we'd ask her." His tone was low—dangerous.

The words hung in the air. They knew. They knew her mother was gone. Did they think Maggie would tell them where she was? Did they think she knew?

Malone's eyes bored into hers. "We're looking for her, tracing her cards, her last known contacts, talking to her husband, the usual. But as of last night, no one has any idea where she went. It seems she disabled her tether. Any way she's a wiz at electronic devices?"

She almost laughed. "No."

"There's a lot here that's not adding up, Doctor." His gaze did not waver. "And I could use your help, if that's okay."

His excessive chivalry was grating on her last nerve. "If it's okay? Can I say no?"

He blinked, then dropped his gaze to the phone's screen once more. "We found an article of clothing with the body—wrapped around him like a shroud," he said, thumbing through his pictures.

A shroud—a death shroud. Her stomach turned. Her hands left sticky palm prints on the wood.

"It'd be helpful to know if you noticed this item in Kevin's locker, or if Dylan was wearing it. It was several sizes too big for your brother, so we don't believe it belonged to him."

No, probably not. Wrapping a body was a show of guilt, which would fit her profile if Kevin was involved. "Killers who wrap their victims after death often do so as a sign of remorse. Was the insulation dust beneath the jacket or on top of it?"

He paused in his scrolling, finger frozen over the cell, and raised his face to hers. *Yes, Reid told me, get over it.* "The dust was on the outside, but there were only traces; it could have transferred from the killer's clothing when they moved him to the woods."

"Well, that doesn't help much, does it?"

Malone must have caught the pointed look in her eyes, because he said, "May I ask you to humor me? It took the techs hours to recreate with the dirt and decomposition, and I have to justify the expense." He extended the phone her way, the glossy screen reflecting the sunlight from the window at her back. She leaned in once more, squinting against the glare. A green sweat-shirt with a corded hood, the sleeves loose without elastic at the wrists. Blank except for a single emblem on the left corner of the chest, a golden bird with white-tipped wings.

"Do you recognize it?"

His voice faded in her ears. The noises of the room, the barely there hiss of air conditioning, the cars on the road outside, even the gentle throb of her own heart, all gone. Maggie's mouth was so dry that her inhales whistled painfully over her tongue.

It was not Kevin's shirt. It had not belonged to Aiden. Nor had Dylan been wearing it.

But she knew whose job had a logo like that. She knew exactly whose shirt it was. And it was someone she never would have guessed, the absolute last person she wanted to believe.

No way. No. But she was sure. She'd seen that sweatshirt a hundred times.

She couldn't breathe. Goddamnit, she couldn't *breathe.*

Malone's phone buzzed—Birman's name on the screen. The detective pulled it back before she could read the text, but Malone himself made quick work of it. "There's something else," he said, squinting at the message. "New development."

She waited, trying to force her lungs to work, trying to keep the dizziness at bay, but the detective seemed to be having equal trouble getting the words out. His eyes looked... sad. A bulldog kind of sad, pug-sad, and that was very sad indeed. "I don't have the details yet, but can you make yourself available to come to the station this evening?"

Answer him, Maggie. "I can," she croaked. "What's the issue?" *Or more accurately, what did that liar Birman say was the issue?*

"I hate to be the one—"

"For fuck's sake," she snapped.

Malone swallowed hard. "They found another body a few minutes ago. An older female."

The air vanished again. Maggie's chest clenched. Her eyes burned.

Birman might lie about a lot of things, but he wouldn't lie about that. The discovery of a body was easily and quickly verifiable. And there was only one reason they'd need her there.

They'd found her mother.

CHAPTER TWENTY

HER OFFICE WALLS felt closer since the detective's visit, the air laced with needling pressure. The sun through the windows was too bright.

"Is it my mom?" she'd asked Malone in a shaking voice, peppered him with questions for fifteen minutes, but he'd had no answers. Yes, they had found a body, yes, they were bringing it to the morgue, yes, later, she might need to come down. It might be her mom, it might not, and they couldn't verify anything until they got her out of the ground. Malone didn't even know where they'd found the corpse, so she couldn't go to the scene of the crime. All Malone knew, all Birman had said, was that they had "found a body, older female." He'd showed her the text the fifth time she asked, had called Birman, too, but the man hadn't responded, presumably dealing with the body itself. Which left Maggie alone with her thoughts.

She's dead? She can't be dead. She just ran away, she was with her boyfriend, she was *fine.*

Her mother being dead, even the possibility of it, was too big a blow to process. Maggie felt it only at the corners of her awareness like a fog creeping down a mountain. It would hit her eventually, but now... *You don't know anything yet, just don't think about it. Give yourself an extra day where she might still be alive, the way you tried to do for Sam and Alex.*

Right, because it was just that easy. One side of her brain was telling her not to think about a polar bear, and her mother was a polar bear, and all she could see was a dead freaking polar bear. Sammy was a bear, too, her best friend who was somehow involved in her brother's death. That was hard to swallow, and not in a weird cannibal way, though she wasn't sure this way was worse.

Maggie punched the redial button—ignoring three missed calls from Alex—and listened to it ring. Sammy's voicemail picked up, a robotic message telling her that he was unavailable. Again. Not so much as a ring on Tristan's line—

straight to voicemail, as it had been all damn day since he'd hit her with her mother's confession and immediately ghosted her. Reid's number was going to voicemail, too, likely because he was dealing with the fallout from this new body. Instead of being on the outside, Reid was probably being pulled in on the second homicide.

On her mother's homicide... maybe. But her mother being dead didn't make *sense*.

She understood throwing suspicion on her mom with an absolutely batshit texted confession. Who better to frame for a crime than someone already suspicious, already on the wrong side of the law? When she'd vanished the other day, everyone who knew her assumed that she'd run off to avoid arrest—to live free on some island like she'd wanted to for months. Sending that text message was icing on the cake, just another charge for an already condemned woman.

But her mother's death by homicide—if this new body was, in fact, a homicide or her mother—threw suspicion elsewhere. It was stupid to kill her. And if her mother was dead, really dead, Reid would know—Reid would have called her. Birman was screwing with her.

Yeah, that, or your mother's dead, Maggie. Not wanting it to be true doesn't make it false.

Nor did ignoring that sweatshirt.

With each breath forced into her too-small lungs came the brutal reality that Aiden could have borrowed the shirt, he could have found it in the school hallway, but it was not as simple as that. Sammy's words were playing on a loop in her brain: *Not even his clothes, like a hoodie to preserve his... modesty?* She could hear his voice as clearly as if he were in the room with her.

Sammy had *known*. He'd known they'd find the sweatshirt with Aiden's corpse.

But she could not believe that Sam had murdered her brother. She wouldn't. Was someone setting him up? She felt like she was trying to play Solitaire with half the deck—who the hell had the rest of the cards?

Maggie tore the phone from her ear and pulled up Imani's number. The ring tone was the same as Sammy's, but the voicemail message was Imani's clear alto: "Hey! You've reached Imani. Leave a message, or text me if you expect a response."

Her friendly voice only tugged the prickling hairs along Maggie's backbone into rigid spines of anxiety. Imani might be in court—she might be busy with the kids. But that both she and

Sammy were indisposed, that the logo on that sweatshirt had been so damn clear....

Maggie waited for the beep, her knuckles aching around the cell. "Hey, Imani, I really need to talk to you. Or to Sammy. Please call me."

She hung up, sent a text message that said almost exactly the same thing, then threw the cell onto her desk. Her hands shook. It had only been twenty minutes since she'd started calling around, but it felt like an eternity.

Maggie jerked her fingers through her hair. She didn't have any more sessions scheduled today, but the thought of leaving the office made that chasm in her chest tear open once more—hot and hollow and filled with teeth. Reid might have made her forget about that grief briefly, but now it was compounding, every new piece of information pulling the jagged edges open farther still. Her brother dead. Her mom, maybe dead. Should she go to the station? But if they didn't know it was Sammy's shirt, she might be cornered, asked more questions. She wanted to talk to him before she wound up in interrogation herself, and not one of Malone's "sorry to ask you" kind of interrogations. The Birman swamp-clown kind.

She snatched up the phone and tried Sammy's number again. This time, the regular voicemail message did not answer, but another one: "We're sorry, the voice mailbox you're trying to reach is full."

She glanced at the clock. Nearly two. Thirty minutes since the detective had left, thirty years inside her head.

How was she supposed to decide what to do next? Her thoughts were a garbled mess. Sammy's shirt had been wrapped around her brother's dead body. Alex had lied to her. She'd slept with her detective friend, the one person she trusted who was removed enough to offer perspective, and even he wasn't answering his cell. Her dad was dying, albeit slowly, she had a funeral to plan, she hadn't even told her business partner about Aiden's corpse, wasn't even sure her mother knew about Aiden, and Tristan kept giving her obscenely expensive gifts, was ignoring her calls hours after he texted: *Do you know why your mom confessed to Aiden's murder?* She was losing it.

The phone buzzed, and she fumbled it from the desktop. Alex. Again. She silenced the call. It was all too much.

It was only a matter of time before the police traced that logo—it belonged to the graphic design company that Sammy's father founded. He'd sold it when he retired, but they'd figure out, and quickly, whose kid had been wearing it. Tristan should have been able to trace the logo in minutes.

Actually… it was strange that they hadn't traced the logo first. Then again, maybe they had.

Shit. Of course they'd traced it to Sammy's father.

Maggie leaned back in her chair. More than likely, they knew who the logo belonged to before Malone came to see her. He had just wanted to see if she would lie to him about it. And… her mother confessed. Whether the confession was fake or not, in Malone's head, in Birman's mind, her mother would certainly confess to protect her. Mom would have lied to protect Sammy, too —he'd been like her own son, especially after Aiden vanished.

Malone had come here because they thought she was involved—somehow—even if her only crime was protecting someone she cared about. She'd fallen right into the trap Malone had set with his sad pug face.

How long did she have before they picked her up? How long did Sammy have? If she was in the mood to take bets, she'd have put money on

Malone heading to pick Sammy up for questioning as soon as he left here. Or on Birman taking Sam into custody while Malone talked to her, so she and Sam didn't have a chance to talk to one another. It's what Reid would have done. Hell, she would have suggested it.

The bobblehead on her desk nodded—Bert. From Kevin. It had been staring at her all morning, and she hadn't even noticed.

A low achy stabbing bloomed in her guts. She swept Bert into the drawer and slammed it shut.

Her phone buzzed again. Not Alex this time. Not Sammy either. *Imani.*

She jerked the phone to her ear so hard it smarted against her temple.

"Maggie." The word burst from the phone. "They took Sam to the station. They think..." A sharp intake of breath. "Well, I think..."

Maggie waited for her to continue, and when she didn't, Maggie grabbed her keys. She'd been right—Birman had been on his way to Sammy's when Malone had been with her. And she should go down to the precinct anyway. What kind of monster wouldn't show up if they thought their own mother might be dead? It might be a trap... but she didn't think so. And if she had to identify her mother's remains, she'd rather do it with Imani at her side.

"Did they take him from his office?"

"No, he called off work today. But I don't think he was sick—he wasn't home." Her voice cracked on the last word, and that tiny hitch told Maggie more than she wanted to know.

Sammy never called in to work. He had avoided the office for a reason. He had done it because he knew they'd come for him, the same way he'd known that his sweatshirt had been wrapped around Aiden's corpse.

CHAPTER
TWENTY-ONE

THE STATION FELT different when she was on the defensive. Although Maggie wasn't the one under suspicion, the fact that Malone had gone to her office to try to trip her up, to keep her from talking to Sammy, made her feel like she was walking into a wasp's nest where every stinging insect held a "wanted" poster with her face on it.

Imani met her in the lobby, stiff-shouldered and tight-lipped. The chartreuse silk of her blouse didn't have a wrinkle on it, nor did her skirt, but Imani's face was a mask of barely contained panic. She was struggling to hold it together the same way Maggie was.

Ask about Sammy, not about your mom. Don't

think about polar bears or mothers or corpses. Give yourself ten more minutes.

"Is Detective Birman interviewing him?" Maggie forced out.

"Interrogating—officially. But it's not Birman. Some Canadian." She wrapped her arms around Maggie and held tight. Shaking. She smelled like lemons, deodorant, and the sharp musk of fear. "I don't like him," she said into Maggie's hair.

"Me either." But Malone had been with her when Sammy was picked up. If not Birman, who had taken Sam in? Either way, the fact that they were "officially interrogating" him meant they'd identified the sweatshirt. You didn't pull a lawyer into interrogation unless you could compel them to answer—unless you had evidence.

"Where are the kids?" Maggie asked.

"They're going to the neighbor's after school."

"Good." Kendra and Justin would be better off with friends than sitting around the house worried about their dad.

Think about Sammy, Mags, about his kids, anything to avoid thinking about the polar bear. Good job. But wait... your mom might be dead. Maggie's stomach rolled.

Imani released her. "I don't know what to do," she sighed out. "Sammy refused an attorney. And I can't imagine that Sam would have hurt your brother—I just can't. But since they found Aiden's body, he's been acting... strangely. Is this why? Because he assumed they'd think he was involved?"

It seemed that Imani knew less than she did. "I wish I could answer that. All I know for sure is that they have evidence that ties him to the crime." When Imani's eyes widened, she went on, "But even if the worst is true, they can't throw him in jail for something he did at thirteen. Your children won't lose their father." *How do I feel about that?* Did she want him to go to prison? Thirteen-year-olds made stupid mistakes, but this one was too big to write off as a childhood error in judgment. She wanted whoever had killed Aiden to be punished—harshly. But did she believe Sammy was a killer? No, and yet... the shirt.

She couldn't think—damnit, she couldn't freaking *think*.

Imani's eyes hardened to chips of obsidian. The air in the brightly lit hallway dropped ten degrees. It smelled of iron. Of blood. "He didn't do this, Maggie. He couldn't have."

Maggie swallowed hard. She hoped Imani was right, that there was another explanation. But that hope didn't *feel* right. Nothing felt right anymore. *Nothing.*

Don't think about the polar bear. Don't think about your mom. She blinked down the hallway—bright lights, desks in the bullpen, a bustling flatfoot, a suited detective with a folder. *Don't think.*

Imani was still watching her, waiting, head cocked, but Maggie's thoughts were tangled, pure chaos. What was she supposed to be telling her?

"Maggie, what—"

"They found Aiden's body two days ago" —*polar bear*—"and I feel like I haven't had a single moment"—*Mom, no, not my mother*—"to breathe let alone think." *Dead, my mother is dead.* Her voice shook; her fingers were trembling, too, her skin hot—the pressure of a dam on the verge of breaking. And when Imani grabbed her hand, the words she'd been avoiding exploded from her in a rush. "Malone told me that they found a body. It might be my mom." Her eyes burned, and this time she blinked and felt wet heat sliding down her cheeks.

Imani's jaw dropped. "Oh, Maggie." She stepped closer and gathered Maggie in her arms once more, much the way Sammy had the other night. How'd they both get so good at hugs? "There has to be someone we can ask, right? To know for sure? Maybe..." She pulled back a little, nodded, and Maggie turned to follow her gaze.

Reid. The man she'd spent the night with was striding up the hall, oblivious to a flatfoot who jumped back to avoid getting bulldozed. He looked exhausted, the bags beneath his eyes bruised and puffy. But he'd slept last night—she'd watched him.

Reid stopped in front of them, his gaze locked on her, and before she could say a word about her mother, he spit out: "Did you know?"

She frowned. About her mom? No, that wouldn't make him angry, and his lips were set in a bloodless line. He was asking... about the sweatshirt.

The sweatshirt. That he clearly knew about. And that meant...

Heat rose in her throat. He'd known that Malone was coming to talk to her, and he hadn't warned her. And as soon as Malone told him that she'd stonewalled... he knew she'd lied. Why even answer?

The silence stretched. Imani stiffened. Maggie turned to her instead. "Malone came to the office this afternoon. He showed me a photo—a recreation of Sammy's sweatshirt. It was found with Aiden's body."

Imani blinked. "And you didn't tell them it was his." Not a question.

Maggie shook her head. Imani squeezed Maggie's hand, still clutched in her own. Maggie had chosen a side. It was the truth—the law—or Sammy, and she'd picked Sammy.

Reid clearly knew it, too, his hard gaze matched by the tension in his jaw. Was it strange that she hadn't even considered telling the truth? She wanted to believe she'd lied because she knew beyond any doubt that Sammy was innocent, which meant someone was setting him up—she didn't want to help them. But she suspected it had been a reflex. She was so overwhelmed trying to convince herself that her mother wasn't dead that her brain had reverted to tried-and-true habits. When in doubt, always protect the ones you love. And there was more than enough doubt here—she needed to talk to Sam before she answered a single question. About anything.

She blinked at Reid. It might have been in her head, but she could hear the grinding of his teeth, the shrieking of his molars. "They're asking

Sammy about the other body too," he said. "They might hold him until tomorrow."

Imani sucked in a sharp breath, but Maggie did not look over. Her gaze was locked on Reid as if trying to decipher whether her mother was dead in the set of his lips.

"Is it my mom?" she blurted.

"Is what your—"

"The body."

Reid's brow furrowed—genuine confusion. "Of course not."

Why of course not? Her brother was gone, why not her mom? But any retort was locked in her throat, her words choked with emotion. Imani clutched her hand tighter.

"Remember when I said I'd run around the building site with cadaver dogs?"

Maggie stared. *Dogs?* She could barely think. The relief coursing through her veins was so hot, so all-consuming, that it made her thoughts feel thick—muddy. Her mom... she wasn't dead. She was missing, but she wasn't a corpse.

Probably.

She forced herself to nod, and Reid went on: "When they started howling, I assumed it would be bloody clothes, something that Dylan or Kevin buried while they were waiting for the search party to clear the woods." His nostrils flared. "I was wrong. The body was hidden deep against the outside of the original foundation. Too deep for anyone to have done it by hand. My guess is that she was dumped around the time the developers began prospecting, digging around the foundation to see if it was stable. The killer could have dumped the body in and shoveled enough dirt on top to hide her."

Maggie vaguely remembered that—watching the bulldozers after school. Once the developers were done, bulldozers filled everything back in, then left it through the demolition the following year.

She frowned, considering the timeline. "So this body was from the year before Aiden died?"

He nodded. "Not too many people in the city went missing that year. But there was one name that stuck out. A locket on the body verified my suspicions."

"Is there a reason you're dragging this out?" Imani snapped. "Just say it." Maggie wanted to throw her arms around her friend, at least buy her a taco for her terse reply. *Took the words right out of my mouth.*

Reid glanced Imani's way, but did not elaborate. Maggie raised an eyebrow. "Come on, Reid. Who is it?"

"Alex's mother."

She and Imani exchanged a glance. Alex's... mother?

"I thought she died of cancer," Imani said.

Maggie nodded agreement. Cancer. Freakin' cancer. She'd forgotten that. It had made the story about Alex's breast that much easier to believe—"shit genes," Alex had called them. And they'd never asked Alex where her mom was buried. Until today, Alex's mother was just another long-gone family member. Like Aiden. A person they didn't discuss because it hurt.

Reid ran a hand through his hair. It spiked above his ear. "I just talked to Alex—cut her loose a few minutes before you got here." He shot her a pointed look, as if she might run out to the parking lot and catch her.

But that was the last thing on Maggie's mind. The building. Alex's mom. And Dylan himself, off the grid before Aiden's death... That was the connection, wasn't it?

"That's why Dylan was at the building that day," she said. "He was going to move the body because he thought that they'd find her when they tore it down. He didn't realize they were keeping the foundation." Which meant... Dylan had killed Alex's mother—his own mother.

Reid nodded. "That's the going theory. Dylan went to that building to move his mother's body and wound up attacking you instead. The wound to the face slowed him down enough that he couldn't complete his goal, but it didn't fully incapacitate him. Birman thinks he was still there when your brother showed up looking for you; another witness he wasn't ready to deal with. So, he enlisted his best friend's help with Aiden while he raced home to get cash from his grandfather's safe—to disappear. That one is Alex's guess. She said the safe was disturbed when she got back from the hospital."

But as Reid had said, Dylan would not have wanted a witness. "If moving the body was the goal, why would Kevin bring me there? If Kevin knew Dylan that well, he probably knew the body existed." Maybe even participated in her death, the way he had with Aiden. Maggie's hand was cold; Imani had let go and was leaning against the wall, staring, wide-eyed, at Maggie. Oh... she hadn't known about Maggie's attack. A lot of information to process. *Welcome to the club.*

"Dylan might have asked Kevin to bring you.

Maybe Dylan had a grudge against your family that Kevin was unaware of."

"Why would Dylan hate my family?" But none of them knew the answer to that question. Instead of bothering with a response, Reid just shrugged.

"It looks like you have all the answers you need," Maggie said. "All the motive you need in Dylan, no matter what started it." She glanced Imani's way, but Imani was already pushing herself off the wall, finishing Maggie's thought: "And none of it involves my husband."

Reid turned to Imani. "You're probably right, but Sammy was with Alex the night Aiden died. He was the one who took her to the hospital. And with that shirt, we have a direct link between Sam and Alex's family."

Maggie shook her head. "No, that can't be right. Alex and Sammy met through me, and I didn't meet Alex until a week or two after Aiden vanished. They didn't know one another the night my brother was taken."

"I don't have all the answers, Maggie. And I can't do this right now; I have to go get Ezra. I should have left already, but after the park, I had to..." His eyes tightened, but it wasn't sorrow this time. Guilt? About...

Damn. He'd been the one to pick up Sammy. Not Birman. "Where is old Clown Face?"

He shrugged. "No one seems to know. He turned his cell off."

Well, that was incredibly suspicious. Her mother confessed in a text sent to Birman's phone, and he vanished before he had to produce the evidence?

Reid turned to leave, but she lurched forward and caught his arm. "Reid, wait—"

He turned back, and all the things she wanted to say caught on her tongue. Her mother, the false confession, Birman, Sammy—*I'm sorry for sneaking out of your house, you smell like strength and calm and sex*—but instead she said, "Where are you going? We can hash through this, look at–"

"There was an incident at Ezra's school. He got into it with another kid. And I can't..." He swallowed hard and sighed. "I just need to pick him up. Then I'll be able to think again."

Her heart dropped into her belly. No wonder he was extra tense. The boy acting out just hours after he'd seen her leave the house was a bad sign.

Reid glanced at the ceiling, avoiding her gaze. "I'll call you. Might need an emergency session."

Her back tensed. For the kid? Right, for the kid. Worried or not, it felt like a slap in the face. They were all going through some shit, and dead-brother-missing-mom-arrested-friend should trump schoolyard fisticuffs. She released his arm, and Reid turned on his heel, leaving her in the hallway with her questions, with her pain.

Just as well.

If her track record was any indication, she'd be better off alone.

CHAPTER
TWENTY-TWO

SHE AND IMANI huddled in the back corner of the lobby with their heads together. Posing questions. Brainstorming. Occasionally staring blankly at the walls because some queries had no good answers.

Did Dylan hate Maggie's family?

They couldn't think of a reason.

Why would Dylan kill Alex's mother?

Maybe Dylan thought she was going to turn his abusive father in or had plans to send Dylan himself away. The grandfather certainly did, and had managed both soon after Alex's mother was gone.

Did Kevin help Dylan kidnap Aiden?

It fit the timeline. And if it was between Kevin

and Sammy, both Maggie and Imani were willing to believe Kevin the accomplice, even if they didn't yet understand how the sweatshirt fit.

Was Maggie's mom okay?

Probably. There was more evidence to suggest that she was fine than there was to suggest that she'd been taken or hurt. Tampering with a tether was a tedious process; one move, and she could have alerted police if she was being kidnapped. Imani believed they'd get postcards from the Maldives. And so did Maggie.

But as they watched the sun cross the afternoon to kiss the edge of evening, the conversation dwindled into uneasy silence. This wasn't just about the shirt. Malone had something else on Sammy, and neither Maggie nor Imani knew what. Reid wasn't around to ask, probably didn't know since he was out dealing with the school and his foster son, and Tristan...

He hadn't called her back since sending her that text about her mother confessing to Aiden's murder. The next time she saw him, she was going to kick him square in the baby maker.

"We should call Alex," Imani said. "Maybe she knows something we don't."

"Even if she did, she'd somehow blame it on cancer."

Imani blinked at her. The silence stretched.

Maggie broke eye contact first and sighed, leaning her head back against the wall, the plaster pressing into her scar. "You're right. But I should go talk to her in person." She should stop at the funeral home, too, sign the paperwork so they could reduce her baby brother to ash.

Imani raised an eyebrow. "You want to do it in person because you're a human lie detector, right? You want to watch her while you ask her questions?"

Maggie closed her eyes a beat longer than a blink, then said, "Again, you're right. As usual." Her stomach growled, but her abdomen was tight, bile burning the base of her esophagus. Her skin was itchy, the walls of the precinct closer than they'd been earlier—they were going in circles here. She needed to do something useful, or she might explode.

"Go, Mags," Imani said, reading her mind. "Talk to Alex. Get some food, too, will you?"

Yeah. I will. I might puke it up, but I will. She still had questions for Sammy, but she wanted to ask them while looking him in the eye, the same way she wanted to question—*interrogate*—Alex. But the police were busy asking their own questions in that little room. Right now, they were the ones keeping her from answers.

Maggie pushed herself to her feet. "I'll call after I talk to her. And if you need me, I'll be back here in a heartbeat." But the weight of that promise felt extra heavy; her emotional reservoir had been sucked dry. Should she call Owen to sit with Imani? But Owen and Imani had never been particularly close, and he was deep in his own divorce bullshit, didn't even know about Aiden yet—one more conversation she had to have, one more awful thing she had to do. In this moment, their group had been reduced to two, both distraught and stressed and overwhelmed. It wasn't freaking fair.

Imani stood and wrapped Maggie in a brief but fierce hug. "I'll call if anything changes here." But her promise felt as hollow as Maggie's own.

Maggie left the station with her chest still tight. She'd start with Aiden's remains; it was concrete, something she could check off. Dealing with Alex felt like a mountain, and she was fresh out of climbing equipment. And food—she needed food.

The late sun glared at her as she crossed the parking lot. She squinted, half blind. Were there still officers watching out for her, patrolling her house? Maggie realized that she had no idea. She wasn't sure she cared.

"Maggie!"

Maggie jumped, heart hammering against her ribs. The sun was so bright that she hadn't even seen the Bug, but there was Alex, climbing from the Volkswagen. And... she wasn't alone. In the passenger seat, a man with light hair and broad shoulders was blowing smoke out the side window. Was that Kelsey, the guy she'd been out with all of twice? She'd brought a date to an interrogation?

Maggie's shoulders stiffened as Alex approached, but this was advantageous. Mountain or not, it was one less stop.

"Maggie, I'm so sorry. I didn't—"

"How could you not tell me?" she snapped. Not particularly well-mannered, but it cut to the quick of her rage.

"Dylan said that if I told anyone, he'd kill me."

Maggie had the sudden urge to look at her tattoo; to see if the scar on her back matched Maggie's own—*twinsies.* "He almost killed you anyway," Maggie fired back.

"He definitely killed my mother."

"You didn't turn him in for that either." It was

a low blow, and unlikely that Alex had even known for certain, but the fury was sharp as railroad spikes in her temples.

Alex threw her hands in the air. "I didn't *know*. Not for sure. She seemed so... happy the week before she left. She told me not to worry, that everything would be okay. Almost like she knew—"

"She knew that your brother was going to kill her? Or... your father?" Alex's dad had been still free when her mother vanished, so it could have been either of them. Or both.

"Honestly, I thought she ran away—my father used to hit her. But when Dad got locked up, and she still didn't come back, I knew something was wrong. And that night... Dylan admitted it. Said he was going to kill me the way he'd killed our mom." Her breath was coming too fast—panting. "They're going to talk to my dad in prison, but he won't admit anything. He has a few more years, and then he's back on the street, and then..." She choked on her words. "Please, Maggie. Please forgive me. I love you, and I didn't mean to hurt you. I swear."

"Did Sammy kill my brother?" She knew the answer, but she wanted to watch Alex's face.

If Maggie had said such a thing to anyone

else, they would have been surprised. But Alex's eyes did not widen in shock. Instead, she swallowed hard—guilty. "No. Sammy didn't do anything to Aiden."

"How did his shirt get around Aiden's body?"

"I don't know. Maybe Kevin took it from your house."

"Why are you still lying to me?"

Alex's jaw dropped. "What do you—"

She stepped forward, fists clenched. "I know you were with Sammy in the emergency room the night that Aiden vanished. I know you didn't kill him because Aiden was in Yarrow while you were getting stitched up. But something happened with your brother and Sammy. There's some connection that I'm missing. Because Sammy's sweatshirt somehow ended up in my brother's grave."

Alex went stock-still, and for a moment the only sound was the whooshing of blood in Maggie's ears and the distant ping and clatter of car doors slamming. "Okay, just... listen. You're right. I saw Sammy on the street that night. I was covered in blood, and he had a sweatshirt wrapped around his waist. But I don't remember it being there later after he biked me to the hospital."

Biked her to the hospital. It was a very

Sammy thing to do. "So you think he lost the shirt, Dylan found it and—"

"I don't know. It's a guess, but a good one. And I really need you to believe me."

The words rang true, but wanting to be believed was the goal of any liar. "What I think doesn't matter, not now." The police had all the evidence they needed on Alex's brother. And Sammy had no motive to hurt Aiden. None at all. Plus, he was alibied up the wazoo.

Maggie met Alex's eyes—glassy, but no tears. "I didn't know you and Sam met before we became friends."

"I mean, we only barely did. After that night, we didn't talk again until... you know. Your place." Her eyelid twitched, the muscle in her forehead contracting so slightly that it might have gone unnoticed... for someone else. *She's lying.* But Maggie didn't believe she was lying about speaking to Sammy. Why Sammy wouldn't tell her about the bloody mystery girl and the hospital, she had no idea, but that was a question for him to answer. Alex had withheld something else. Suddenly, everything about the weeks after Aiden's disappearance, about meeting Alex in the bathroom, Alex knowing Kevin, Maggie's relationship with him... it all felt a little too convenient.

Her guts twisted, an acidic stew of bile and fury. "You tried to get close to me on purpose," Maggie hissed—a pressured whisper was all she could manage. Her windpipe was too small. "You didn't accidentally meet me at school. You used me to see if I knew your brother was guilty. If I knew about Kevin and Dylan, if I thought they'd hurt Aiden—if I knew Dylan had hurt you. You wanted to know what Sammy told me."

Alex shook her head, frantic—panicked. "That doesn't mean I didn't care about you. We were friends. We... *are* friends. I just wanted to know what you knew. I wanted to make sure that you stayed safe. What if Dylan had come back?"

"What if he did? You certainly weren't worried enough to tell the police." Maggie's face was wet; her chest, too. Was she crying? Yes, she was, tears of rage as much as grief. "You knew who killed my brother. All this time, you knew that Kevin and Dylan were a tag-teaming murder machine. And you just let me wonder. Let me suffer."

Alex stepped nearer; Maggie stepped back. "I had no evidence about your brother or about my mom. Telling the truth about my attack felt more dangerous than keeping quiet—the worst that would happen is he'd end up at juvenile hall again, but he'd be out in a year. And Dylan had vanished before. I figured he would again, so long as I didn't give him a reason to... you know. Hurt me. I *couldn't* give him a reason to come back here." Her lip trembled. "The greatest trick the devil ever played was convincing people that he didn't exist."

What a weird saying, especially in this context. "That's why Sammy didn't come forward about your attack. You told him that if he did, I'd be in danger. That the person who hurt you had maybe taken Aiden and might come back for me?" It made a certain amount of sense—Sammy was the protective sort, and thirteen-year-olds weren't known for thinking things all the way through.

Alex blinked then nodded, eyes widening as if she didn't believe Maggie had made that connection. Or was she surprised at the accusation? This time, Maggie could not tell, and that did nothing to cement her trust in Alex's intentions—not then, and certainly not now.

"Did Sammy know about Kevin?" He couldn't possibly have known. If protection was the goal, there was no way in hell he would have let Kevin hang around her without coming clean.

As expected, Alex shook her head. "No. And Kevin was sick, but he was a follower, not a leader. I thought he might be okay so long as Dylan stayed gone. From the way he acted after that, it was like you had... fixed him. You molded him into something better."

Was she calling Kevin a pushover—a submissive? *No, she's calling him not a murderer.* But bringing a child back to be killed, if that's how it went down, was as bad as doing it yourself.

"Instead of telling me, you let him into our lives. Into my life." Maggie took a single, measured step forward, her fists clenched at her sides. So close she could smell Alex's coconut shampoo. "That's the part I can't get past, Alex," she whispered. "You let me almost marry the best friend of the man who attacked me—who cut you in half. For years, I slept beside a man who at the very least participated in killing my brother. Every time I told him I loved him, every time I..." Her breath caught in her lungs. She turned away and started for her car once more. "I have to go, Alex."

"But, Maggie—" Alex called after her.

"Go inside," Maggie said to the asphalt.

"Imani has questions, too, and it'd be better for her to hear all of this directly from you. You need to help Sammy."

"I did what I could, but I don't have the answers they... n... n... need."

You don't? But the way she said it... Alex had fooled her when they were children, carried those lies for twenty years, but that last bit sounded genuine, shaking voice and all. Alex had never cried talking about her cancer.

Maggie turned back. Mascara streaked Alex's cheeks. "Answers about what?" she asked.

Alex's gaze flitted to the station at Maggie's back as if checking that they weren't being observed, then lowered her voice. "Like... there was a duffel bag with my mother's body. Malone said it was Sammy's, buried with her, but that doesn't make sense. My brother wouldn't have had access to Sammy's old baseball bag."

The bloody sun glinted in her peripheral, and this time, Maggie stared into the glare, letting the striations focus her. The year before Aiden vanished. A bag—a baseball bag. She... remembered it.

Maggie closed her eyes against the sun. Smears of light wiggled behind her eyelids, then solidified into her mother's face, that sly smile with her right eye crinkled just a little more than her left—the way she looked when she was doing something righteous but sneaky. "What was in the bag?" Her voice rang hollow.

"Clothes."

"Sammy's?"

"My mother's." Her voice cracked on the last word.

Maggie opened her eyes. "Your mom had a bag full of her own clothes?"

Alex nodded. "Yeah."

Her heart stuttered, a too-fast staccato. There was definitely an explanation for that. A perfectly logical one. And Maggie couldn't believe she hadn't thought of it before.

She knew exactly where that bag had come from. She knew exactly why Dylan would have wanted to hurt her family.

"My mother... she knew yours. Didn't she?"

Alex bit her lip. Which was answer enough.

Damn. No wonder her mother had vanished.

CHAPTER **TWENTY-THREE**

SHE DROVE to the funeral home with her guts twisted into a solid knot, her brain a stupid lump inside her skull.

How did I miss this? Aside from the more recent development of distributing guns to domestic violence victims, her mother had another, less illegal, passion project: she helped abused women disappear. Maggie had always thought she'd started after Aiden went missing—after she went a little nuts. Wasn't that what her mother had told her? Now, it seemed that this timeline was incorrect.

The clincher was that duffel bag. Her mother had always been working on some charity drive or another—something that sane people did instead of hiding humans or passing out handguns. Sammy's parents often donated items they were no longer using, and Sammy had played baseball for exactly one week before realizing he was a *Dungeons & Dragons* kid. The duffel still looked new when it had gone into the pile.

Her mother had tried to hide Alex's mom. She'd made Dylan hate their family, had tripped him into going after her own child. It felt flimsy, but it was logical if you were an abusive psycho being raised by another abusive psycho, and Dylan might have had revenge on the brain after his mother was gone and his father was locked up. She wasn't sure if he'd tracked his mother down and murdered her, though it did seem that he enlisted Kevin's help to bring Maggie to that building—to hurt her family the way he'd been hurt. But things hadn't gone to plan. Whether he'd sought Aiden out or it had been an unfortunate coincidence that Aiden wound up at that building, her mom had set off a chain of events that had gotten Maggie attacked and Aiden killed.

No wonder her mother had wanted to forget about Aiden; why she'd wanted Maggie to move on. She'd known—or at least suspected—that he was already dead from the beginning because she knew why someone would want to hurt him. And the guilt... yeah, that would eat at a mother.

She eased off the freeway. The slash of bloody sky seeping through her windshield made her feel stained. Maggie still didn't understand the confession, didn't know if it was some weird game Birman was playing. She had no idea why her mom would vanish instead of sticking around to protect Maggie, why she'd suspect that Dylan would return after Aiden's bones were discovered—she had to know about Aiden, somehow. And why not call Maggie directly instead of leaving that note?

Protection maybe, though not for her daughter—her mother didn't know Alex's mom was dead, that she no longer had to hide her whereabouts. Would she run to avoid that interrogation? Did she assume Reid would protect Maggie herself? Maggie could not make sense of her mother's behavior when she was working from a playbook that Maggie was not privy to. And though her mother had not been found near the foundation of that building, she could still be dead. Unlikely, but...

He's coming for you. I'm sorry. If she suspected Dylan, she should have come out and said it. Even if she thought Alex's mother was still alive, Maggie had to be in more danger than she would be. Maggie wasn't in hiding.

Maggie parked in the back of the funeral home lot, her hands shaking, her chest tight. An officer slid into the space behind her—no unmarked this time, a cruiser with flashers and everything. Reid's guy? She'd forgotten all about the escort, hadn't noticed it on the way, which didn't say much about her powers of observation. To be expected in her state of mind, but she didn't love knowing that she was blind.

The dusty air inside the building made her sneeze. Bone dust? No, certainly not. Just the smell of old things. Antique furniture in the foyer, industrial-grade low-pile carpet that might have been thirty years old, cushions faded by thousands of butts. Through a set of double doors to her right, caskets gleamed from every corner of the showroom, the carpet a sea of brownish burgundy that felt prematurely muddy when the coffins would soon be fully encased in dirt.

Maggie approached a child-sized casket with white satin pillows and navy accents for the most discerning sea-faring ten-year-old. What would her mother like when the time came? She wanted to be buried, had already purchased the cemetery plot beside Aiden's empty one.

"Good evening."

Maggie turned.

The funeral home director was a short woman with a friendly face and thighs thick enough to inspire a sequel to Sir Mix-a-Lot's first smash hit. Her eyes widened when she saw Maggie. Cleo Pratt. Maggie's mother had represented her husband in some traffic violation case back when she was still an attorney.

"Oh, Maggie," she said, approaching. "When I got the call, I thought it was about your father, but..."

Her father had made her drive him here soon after his Alzheimer's diagnosis, said he'd wanted to pick out his "party favors." They'd gone with cremation and a potluck: jalapeño poppers and deli meat and Greek salad. It was a solid plan, and one that took the burden of decision-making off of her. But this...

Maggie's guts clenched; her eyes burned. She inhaled slowly. *I cannot break down right now.* She had to finish this—get it done so she could check it off the list and move on to things like catching the asshole who'd killed her brother and maybe finding her mother so she could tell her off. Mom had reasons, fine, but it was a real jerk move to vanish like that. It was cruel to make Maggie be here alone.

The funeral home director was still watching her.

"I just wanted to sign the papers," Maggie forced out. "Get the cremation... set up."

The woman's brow furrowed. "I spoke to your mother on the telephone, and she already faxed over the paperwork. Has something changed since then?"

Her breath caught. *Her mother faxed the—* "When?" And who still had a fax machine? It was probably from the same time period as the carpet. Maybe they had a record player around here, too.

"The day the remains came in," Cleo said. "Last night, I believe? She said that she would like to have a service at his home as soon as possible. We're set to cremate him tonight."

Maggie frowned. At *his* home? Maybe at her mother's home. Or Cleo misspoke. *Or you're just overthinking every godforsaken thing like you always do, Maggie, so you don't have to consider that your mother isn't dead or kidnapped, she has access to telephones and fax-machine technology, and she's just avoiding* you. At least Mom already knew about Aiden's body. One less conversation Maggie had to have.

Cleo cocked her head and went on, "However, your mother did not specify what kind of urn she might prefer. Do you happen to know?"

Maggie swallowed down the acid in her throat, said, "We don't need an urn. A box is fine. I'll come pick the ashes up... tomorrow morning?"

"Anytime after noon." Cleo tucked a swath of thick dark hair behind her ear and nodded. Why did her chest hurt so damn bad? It felt as if her belly were twisting in ribbons of thorny vines.

"And if you should decide you need our services, I'm certain that we can accommodate whatever schedule—"

"Can I see him?" Maggie had not realized her intent to ask the question until she heard the words fall from her lips. But she suddenly wanted nothing more.

Cleo winced. "Well, he isn't prepared for—"

"I already saw the bones," she said. "I had to identify his body. But I'd really like to be near him one more time before you reduce him to a smoldering pile of dust."

Cleo paled; she bit her lip. *Too soon?* She was the queen of "too soon" lately. But Cleo made no comment; the bereaved customer was always right. What a job she had, always seeing people on the worst days of their lives. Or the best, she supposed, if you were burying an asshole. Birman's family would probably have a party.

"I... of course. Just give me a moment to set things up for you."

You can take longer than a moment. I'm sure he won't mind. "Cleo?"

She turned.

"Thank you. I appreciate it."

The woman flashed her a tight smile, then vanished through the far door. The moment she was gone, Maggie released a pent-up breath, the exhalation hissing through the room, bouncing off satin and cotton and wood, the silver handles that looked to have been polished moments before she walked in. There was strange beauty in the way the caskets were pieced together, the smooth curves of woodgrain like waves, the satin a cloud. If you were lucky, they'd close the lid before the service, muting the excruciatingly long speeches, your loved ones watching one another, trying to see who was saddest. Then the final march to a cold cemetery. And then... alone for eternity.

A cough at her back.

Cleo stood in the archway. "Follow me." A little brusque, not that Maggie blamed her; she deserved it. She probably deserved a kick to the ovary. Or the kidney. Somewhere it would hurt.

Maggie followed her down a hallway with wallpaper not unlike that in her father's home—gilded flowers and embossed vines, exceptionally busy, a balm against the quiet of the dead. The double door at the end of the hall led to the preparation room. Bigger than the single room in the Tysdale morgue, but still only one table.

Cleo stopped just inside the door and waved her in—waved at the stainless steel. She'd laid white satin over the top. Had Maggie seen the same kind of cloth in one of the caskets? But none of the caskets in the showroom held a box.

Aiden's body, reduced to a cube of cardboard.

Cleo softly bowed out of the room, and Maggie approached, each step easing the tension between her shoulders. For days, she'd been struggling with the who and the what. Which of her friends was guilty, who wasn't. Nearly every one of her relationships had been compromised in the last two days, some by her own design.

This wasn't complicated. This was her brother. The goodbyes were the final step, the wondering over. Tomorrow, she'd be left to deal with the grief.

Maggie reached her hand into the box. She wasn't sure if it was the medical examiner or the funeral home director, but the bones had been scrubbed of particles—yellowed, but clean.

She traced the ridge of his brow. When they were small, they'd played "the floor is lava" every opportunity they had. Once, he'd smashed his head on the hardwood doing a headlong leap over the magma-soaked coffee table, and she'd begged him to stop crying, not to tell their parents. There was no trace of such an injury now. The missing teeth were disconcerting, more pronounced without his lips to hide the gap. The police had taken his spacer.

Maggie wanted it back. She wanted his clothes back, too. She suddenly wanted to hold and touch and cherish every scrap that had been with him when he died. She wanted to say goodbye to his shoes, to his fingernails, to the buttons on his pants. Those were the things he had touched as he let go of this world. The things he'd been clutching when he should have been clutching her hand. What essence might she absorb from hugging his jacket one more time?

Her eyes burned, her throat tight. She was being ridiculous. *That's how you get to be a hoarder, Maggie.* And yet she could not shake the sensation of things undone and unfinished. Of things missed.

She drew her finger lower over the hollow of the cheek, then the long bone of his jaw. Smooth, like his face, like his skin. So many times she'd sat beside his headstone in the cemetery, the heady scent of wildflowers in her nose. Now, she imagined she was smelling his last breath, encased in the calcium. She could smell the earth though it no longer existed.

So many things no longer existed. Two days ago, she'd had two childhood friends that she loved more than anything—Maggie had no idea what she might be able to forgive in the coming months, but letting her almost marry a murderer would not be top on her "let it go" list. Then there was her mother, hiding of her own free will, but she couldn't come back without getting arrested. And Reid...

Had she lost him too? Ezra was acting out, so obviously they'd made an error there. But it was more than that. He hadn't called to warn her about Malone, to follow up on her mom's confession, or to tell her about Sammy. If she hadn't gone to the precinct, maybe she wouldn't even know about Alex's mom. And she was keeping things from him even now—she hadn't called him after she'd talked to Alex.

They'd slept together, but they still didn't trust each other. That was not a good sign.

Maggie stared into the box, into the hollows of the skull as if trying to meet her brother's gaze. Aiden was gone, but she had these bones. And the responsibility for disposing of them—for getting rid of her brother.

"Bye, Aid." Her voice shook. "I still love you. And I swear, I will find the person who did this."

"Maggie?" A low voice at her back.

She jumped, the bones clattering, and whipped around. Had she just slapped her dead brother? But she did not have time to consider it—did not *want* to consider it.

Owen stood in the doorway, fingers laced in front of his belly, one eyebrow slightly raised. Tall and broad-shouldered, muscles hidden behind tweed and khaki, but he felt bigger in the small room. "I drove by your place, but you weren't there, and then... I just figured."

Figured. That I'd be here with Aiden. She stepped closer. "How did you know? I mean, I meant to tell you, but—"

He shrugged sheepishly. "The paper."

The... paper? Oh. They'd done a news story on Aiden? But of course they had. It just hadn't occurred to her because she didn't watch the local news or read the local paper.

"Owen, I'm so sorry," she said, closing the distance between them. "I was going to tell you, but I only saw you that one day, and then you were with the attorney—"

"Maggie, for god's sake. It's not like you kept it from me on purpose. If I hadn't been dealing with Katie and the divorce..." His eyes drifted to the table, to the box—her brother—and back. "Don't apologize for not telling me. You didn't do anything wrong. I only wish I'd known sooner so I could have helped."

"But... I thought you had to deal with your lawyer today." She frowned. "And then you have dinner with your kids, right?" What day was it?

He shook his head. "No. I mean, yes, that was the plan. And I did meet with the lawyer. And then Katie's boyfriend-slash-lawyer." He smiled briefly, but it was a sad one, laced with regret. "I let Katie take the kids for the next two weeks. I didn't want to be the bad guy or make Katie look like a monster. Even if she sort of is, it's not good for the girls to see us at each other's throats. California should be... fun." Owen flinched, then swallowed hard. "Anyway, this week, I'm all yours. Whatever you need, I'm here."

Her lip trembled. Her face went hot. Owen had always been more traditional, straight-laced, but he had a huge heart. And Owen was the only person who could offer an ear and a shoulder without her feeling like she was taking advantage. Plus, Owen had no connections to her childhood or to Aiden. No child who might kill her pet for revenge or ruin what might have been a good relationship. She could not handle any more surprises.

Tomorrow, she had to solve a murder. Tomorrow, she needed to find her mother. But tonight... she just wanted to cry.

Maggie let the first lines of tears trickle down her face, but when Owen reached for her, her breath hitched—the dam broke. She collapsed into sobs. Owen wrapped her in his arms, the tweed of his jacket itchy against her damp cheek.

"It's okay, Maggie. I've got you. We'll figure this out."

She clung to him, wetting his shirt, releasing

days of pent-up emotion. Aiden's bones watched from the table, Cleo probably listening to her snort and weep from the next room. Maggie didn't care. Not one bit. None of this was fucking *fair*.

She wasn't sure how long she cried, but eventually, her breath came more normally. Her eyes stopped leaking. Owen squeezed her tighter, but he didn't say a word. He didn't need to.

"Katie is out of her mind for leaving you." She sniffed. Her stomach rumbled; she'd forgotten to get food.

"I tried to tell her that." He chuckled, his baritone vibrating her eardrum. "But there's no accounting for taste."

"True enough. She doesn't like me either."

"Eh, she'd be jealous of my mother if the woman was still alive. I think she was sleeping with her boyfriend before we split, so she saw cheating everywhere, even in the most faithful of husbands."

Maggie pulled back, wiping her face with her sleeve. "Well, she's a bitch, Owen. You'll find someone better."

He shrugged. "Maybe. We'll have your mom set me up the way she's always trying to do for you."

Ah yes... her mother's disappearance wasn't in the paper. Maggie forced one corner of her lip into a passable smile, though Mom wouldn't be setting him up—might never talk to Maggie again outside of the occasional postcard from the Maldives. But... huh. He was right. She always tried to talk Maggie into dating more, as if a relationship was the end-all be-all of human existence. And she'd married Jerry after a few months. Her mother wasn't one for being alone.

Owen cocked his head. "Maggie? What is it?"

But Maggie just wiped her face again, her thoughts spinning. Her mother had run off, but she wouldn't run off by herself—Maggie had already considered that. She had also considered that Mom's mysterious boyfriend had helped her to remove the tether. And it had to be someone who knew what they were doing. Someone who had... tampered with it before?

She cast another look at Aiden's bones, but the cardboard felt too dull, the sheen of his skull too slick, too oily. Bile rose in her gorge. She snapped her eyes away.

"Now that my mom's alive, I have a stop I need to make," Maggie said slowly. She had nothing more than a strong suspicion, but she needed verification. "Want to get some food?"

"Now that your mom's... alive?" Owen blinked. "Was she not alive at some point?"

She looped her arm around his elbow, swallowing against the sickness in her belly. "We have a lot to go over, Owen. And we might as well do it over dinner."

CHAPTER
TWENTY-FOUR

THE THAI RESTAURANT where her mother violated her tether was nearly an hour from Fernborn. Owen followed her in his new coupe, Reid's police escort not far behind. Now that his kids were living with their mother half the time, Owen was leaning a little mid-life crisis-y. And she was fully supportive. He deserved all the sports cars he could handle.

They sat in a corner booth, spring rolls and noodles and pepper sauces spread out on the table. Her stomach had settled in the car after a box of stale crackers and a bottle of water, but her heart was still beating too quickly, her temples sore.

Maggie took tentative bites of chicken. Dark

fabric covered the chairs, the tables a honeyed wood like that in the coffeehouse she and Reid frequented. Carved art pieces graced the walls. A giant Buddha fountain sat dead center.

Why were you here, Mom?

Maggie had never quite believed that her mother was willing to risk jail for Thai food—no meal was that good. And she hadn't accidentally wandered outside the tether's boundary. She'd claimed there was a short in it, and that had been verified, but the tether had likely malfunctioned because someone had tampered with it the way they had this week. A trial run, perhaps? But still... why this place? It was an unnecessary risk.

She watched the room, the slump-shouldered way the waiter carried himself—dealing with some form of emotional pain, maybe grief over a lost relationship. But he was too young to be her mother's boyfriend, and if her mother had come here, the person she was meeting wasn't affiliated with the restaurant. Don't shit where you eat, and all that.

Who were you with, Mom?

Maggie didn't want to go full-on interrogation mode, but perhaps someone who worked here could enlighten them; she'd already flashed her mom's picture at a busboy on the way back from the bathroom. No dice. But there were four servers on staff tonight, and though it had been three months, her mom tended to take up space. One of them should remember her.

Another waitress strode by, smiley—all teeth—with a high voice and the demeanor of someone who'd just won the lottery. Maggie squinted, then averted her gaze when the woman glanced her way and grinned.

Owen was chewing, but he swallowed when she met his eyes and said, "So, are you going to tell me why we're here?"

All week, she'd been avoiding it—avoiding him in one way or another. And he'd more than earned an explanation, even if he'd followed her here without one. Hell, he deserved one *because* he'd followed her here on faith.

She lowered her chopsticks and filled Owen in, all the details surrounding her brother's death, her mother's disappearance, her attack. Told him about Alex, about Sammy—Dylan and his best friend, Kevin. He listened carefully, his eyes growing wider with each new revelation.

"I feel like I'm losing all the people I love. Except you, of course," she amended when he cocked his head. "And Imani."

Owen sat back against the booth—stunned,

but not overwhelmed by the information the way she was. "Maggie, you're allowed to be angry, allowed to have questions, and are obviously entitled to answers—you *need* those answers to heal. You need to know what happened that night, top to bottom, in and out. It might be simple, that Alex's brother took Sam's sweatshirt off the road while Sam was with her at the hospital. I doubt he'd be stupid enough to use his own shirt if he'd hurt Aiden. And no, you and Alex might not make it past the things she withheld. But for now, can we acknowledge that it wouldn't hurt so much if you didn't care?"

"Straight into shrink mode, huh?"

"I know you think I'm a bleeding heart." The lamplight painted orange highlights in his blond hair. "Listen, I understand wanting to assign blame—wanting to know now. Unfortunately, we can't be sure of anything yet. And if they do prove that Kevin was involved, I certainly wouldn't forgive him, but you don't have to. He's gone. The only person that needs forgiving in that relationship is you." He crossed his arms and shot her a pointed look.

Her jaw dropped. *Me?* "I didn't do anything wrong."

"If—and it's a big if—Kevin had something

to do with Aiden's death..." He shrugged. "You pride yourself on being able to read people, and you missed this enormous thing in the man you loved. We *all* missed it." He leaned forward and planted his elbows on the table, then shoved a bite of spring roll into his mouth. "If it helps," he said around the roll, "I'm furious at Kevin on your behalf just for lying about knowing Alex's psycho brother." He swallowed, his nostrils flaring, blue eyes blazing—anger laced with a hint of feral excitement. If Kevin was here now, she had no doubt that reliable, pacifist Owen would punch him in the jaw.

She stabbed a piece of chicken, but her tongue was dry. She forced it down. Maybe this was why she'd refused Kevin's marriage proposal. Had she known, somewhere deep, that he wasn't who he said he was? But, no. If she'd suspected, she wouldn't have been with him at all.

Her guts clenched, the noodles on her plate gelatinous looking, slippery like intestines. She coughed, covered it with a sip of water before she choked her fool self and wound up in the ground next to Aiden. This wasn't about her, not right now. She was here about her mom. But what did she expect to see, a man in a trench coat passing out brochures with a title like "How to Escape Your Tether"? A guy with a shirt that said "I Help MILFs Vanish"? A boyfriend wouldn't have to come all the way out here. Even meeting someone about a fake passport here would be idiotic. Outside the tether's boundary, you were asking for the cops to come storming in, blowing your cover and your plan.

It was stupid for her mother to come here. Her mother was a lot of things, but stupid wasn't among them. So why? "Why did she do it, Owen?"

His brow furrowed. "Alex?"

"My mom. Why this place?" She shook her head. "I'm missing something; I need your shrink eyes to tell me what I can't see."

Owen smiled. "You can count on me. I feel a little scandalous just thinking about this clandestine mission." He waggled his eyebrows.

She almost laughed. If questions were scandalous, she was basically a demon in a priest suit, but she'd let him have it. "We're officially partners in crime, Owen." She cut her eyes at the approaching waitress—black turtleneck, black jeans, chopsticks holding her hair back. Bubblegum pink lips.

He plunked a new spring roll onto his plate,

his gaze on the waitress. "You lead. You know your mother better than I do."

Do I? But she nodded.

"Hey there." The waitress's brown eyes sparkled, but the dark circles beneath hinted that she was working a double. Or she was having trouble sleeping. "What else can I get you?"

"Actually, my mother told me that you guys have this amazing dessert." The faux cheerfulness was sandpaper in her throat, her voice laced with nihilistic friendliness. "But I can't for the life of me remember what it was."

The waitress pursed her lips in a way that made it look like she was blowing a bubble. "Do you know what it had in it?"

Maggie shook her head. "I'm not sure she told me." *Careful, Maggie, the staff is your last chance before you have to bring Tristan in on this.* And she really wasn't in the mood to talk to him. They were supposed to be working together, but it had been hours since he'd sent that cryptic text about her mom's confession, and he still hadn't called her back. Yes, she'd gotten the info from Malone, but it felt like a tease, punishment for not liking his gifts. It felt... vindictive.

She turned her phone to the waitress—her mom's smiling face. Would she ever see it in person again? "Do you know her? I know, this is so weird, but it's killing me that I can't remember." *Get it? Killing me?*

The woman squinted at the phone. "Hmm. She looks familiar, but I didn't wait on her. I'm not sure she had more than drinks. She kinda... stormed out." She winced.

Stormed out? A fight with someone then. Had Maggie been wrong about meeting the boyfriend here? It seemed dumb, unnecessary if they were screwing back in Fernborn, but... "Do you know who waited her table?"

"Bobby? But he's not here today."

Maggie's heart sank. That would have been too easy. She exchanged a glance with Owen, but his eyes looked as defeated as she felt.

"Maybe you can text your brother," Owen said slowly. "Wasn't he with her?"

Thank goodness he's here—shrink power.

Maggie turned back in time to see the waitress frown. "Actually... I don't think so. Is your brother a lot older, a real lumberjack type?"

Her lungs constricted, the air sharper, colder. A lumberjack type. *Of course it's him.* "Was he wearing plaid?" she forced out. "Kinda looks like the Joker without the makeup?"

The waitress bit her bubble-gum lip, but smiled. "Yeah."

That was all the verification Maggie needed. Those plaid shirts had been his style since they'd met, the day he'd interrogated her about Aiden's disappearance. He'd been the one to miraculously receive a texted confession from her mother.

Stupid butt-faced, clown-mouthed, restraining-order-having Nick Birman. He'd been here with her mom—he was her mother's boyfriend. And now he was trying to frame her mother for Aiden's murder.

CHAPTER TWENTY-FIVE

MAGGIE LEFT the restaurant with a pit in her belly, the spicy food churning and rolling and twisting as much as her brain.

Her mother and the detective. Birman and her mom were... together. Was that true? And if so, had they been together during the investigation into her brother's disappearance? Had Mom been dating him while she was divorcing her father, throughout her marriage to Jerry? It would make sense for Birman to be the man who'd released that tether.

But he had a restraining order history. Mom wouldn't date a domestic abuser, would she?

Maggie barely made it out of the parking lot

before snatching up the cell and hitting the speakerphone button.

Tristan answered on the first ring. "I was just about to call y—"

"What the hell with that text this morning?" The words burst out of her. Her fingers tightened on the steering wheel. That wasn't why she'd called him, but it had been a scant dozen hours, and that rage had clearly not settled; the sound of his voice made her face burn. *Do you know why your mom confessed to Aiden's murder?* Screw you, Tristan.

"Just so I know, is that slight better or worse than me sending you flowers on your birthday?"

I knew it was about those damn gifts. Jerk. The flowers weren't the issue, and he knew it. Diamonds, plane tickets, concert passes, those weren't the same as birthday flowers, and she'd asked him to stop giving her any gifts at all—he was purposefully disrespecting that boundary. For a rich guy like Tristan, maybe diamonds and flowers were all the same, just a drop in the bucket. The silence stretched.

Finally, he sighed. "My cell broke—smashed it on your mother's driveway. I didn't have your contact or anyone else's saved in my brain, and then I got going on a lead and didn't have time to snag a new one until now. I figured Reid would tell you."

A likely excuse. But despite her fury, they had more important things to worry about. She took a breath to steady her voice and said, "Finding my mother will make us even. She's banging Birman."

"Yup, I know. That's what I was going to tell you. Birman is the one who broke into her house. And yours. I've got him on highway cameras driving away from both scenes."

"He probably went to both homes looking for her," Maggie said, frowning. Mom had to have broken things off if he was telling people she'd confessed to Aiden's murder—if he'd had to break into her house. But then who had removed her tether?

And... *He's coming for you. I'm sorry.* Did she think Birman would try to hurt Maggie to get back at her mom? Maybe. They had other suspects in Aiden's death—Dylan, Kevin—evidence that she wasn't involved, but that hadn't stopped Birman from treating her like a criminal. Hell, maybe Mom was running from the detective himself. Maybe her disappearance had nothing to do with Aiden, outside of being terrible timing. The thought of Birman laying a hand on her mother made her belly solidify into a ball of molten steel.

"Is Birman with her now?" she asked.

"Birman's gone. He's skipping out on work, left Malone to interrogate Sammy on his own. Your mom is still missing, too, but I can't tell if they're together. No cell signals on the numbers that we know about."

But if Mom was running, exploiting the network she'd used to protect so many other abused women, she wouldn't have her cell. Could someone in that network remove a tether? Would they? That part felt... off.

"He never should have been on this case," Maggie said. "It's a conflict of interest." She hit the turn signal and slid around a Camry that was going five miles an hour over the speed limit. She'd already left Owen in the dust.

"Yeah, I'm with you. And I found something more interesting. Three months ago, the week your mom violated her tether, Birman bought cruise tickets for him and a woman who looks suspiciously like your mother."

She frowned at the highway. A... lookalike? "I don't get it." But then she did.

"They don't take fingerprints to get on a cruise ship. If your ID is valid, if it looks like you, off you go—not hard to procure for a guy like Birman."

"You mean for a cop."

"Yeah. Longer term, they probably planned to get trickier with identity theft. They were scheduled to leave the night she was arrested. If she'd gone with him instead of going home, she'd have made it out."

"She was running away. She met him at the restaurant to go on that trip." And for whatever reason, she'd fought with him, stormed out. She'd... come back.

"There's more."

"Do tell."

"I found your guy."

The subject change made her feel like someone had slapped her upside the head—dizzying. She eased into the right lane and slowed. "What guy?"

"The psycho who bit you. Alex's brother." He paused, perhaps for dramatic effect, perhaps because he was pulling the information to make sure he got it right. "The night your brother died, an older teen was brought into the emergency room in Cerora via ambulance. He arrived at nine and was there through the night. Facial wounds that match what you described."

"But... Cerora is two hours out." And the opposite direction of Yarrow. Was Tristan wrong? He was never wrong. "Did he use his name?"

"Well, no, he didn't use any name. No license on him, either; a passing motorist found him in a ditch off the interstate. Smashed his stolen car into a tree, but they didn't run the plates until the next morning. By then, he was gone."

"But... if Dylan was in a hospital in Cerora at nine, he wasn't the one who hurt my brother. There's no way he attacked Alex and was still around to kill Aiden when Kevin returned from Yarrow." *Dylan could not have killed Aiden.* The voice echoed in her head on repeat. He was in the hospital while someone had been driving her brother back to Fernborn. How was this possible?

Behind her, a horn honked, and she glanced in her rearview, then at her speed. Ten miles an hour below. She pressed the gas, her brain nowhere near this stretch of road. Kevin killing Aiden was horrific, yes, but it was a long trek through the woods. Dylan was a big guy—it would have been possible for him to carry Aiden. But not Kevin. Not alone.

Someone else was with him. Someone else helped Kevin to dispose of Aiden's body. Maybe there was merit to Reid's off-the-cuff remark about throwing him over the back of a bike. If Kevin had a bike.

"Maggie? You there?" When she grunted her presence—*mm-hmm*—he went on: "Got one more thing. Better news. A teenager with the same build as Dylan was found three weeks later in Ohio. Decomposition had done a number on him, so identification was tricky. He was listed as John Doe—that's why we couldn't find Dylan's name on any death records. But with that distinctive facial wound, I'd say we've got our guy. Found a shirt with the body, too, must have had it on him in the car to staunch the bleeding. Alex identified it as hers twenty minutes ago."

"He... died?"

"Yup. Didn't stick around to get the care he needed, sepsis probably did him in quick. No other wounds on the body."

Just that wound to the face. The wound she'd put there.

The world tightened around her. *I killed him.* Alex's brother was dead. But it was of little relief—too much still didn't fit. Aiden had been in Yarrow while Alex and Sammy were in the emergency room, but someone had wrapped his tiny body in Sammy's shirt. Had it really all been Kevin?

"I still need you to find my mother, Tristan."

"I've been trying, but she's so far off the grid—"

"She called the funeral home, faxed them the paperwork for Aiden's cremation."

"Oh, shit. Okay, that'll only take a few minutes." A pause. "Did you say a fax? Who the hell still uses—"

"Tristan, please."

"Hang on one sec..." In the background, keys tapped. He must be at home. Reid said he had a heck of a setup. "Okay, it was a scanned email thing, actually, and it came from... huh."

"What?"

"The DA's office," he said. The horn behind her honked again, but this time, she did not respond by pressing the gas. Her foot was numb.

"I can't guarantee it was Sammy," Tristan went on, "but... it does look like his cell number called the funeral home earlier that morning. Would he have let your mom call from his phone?"

Imani had told her that Sammy called in to work. But he wasn't home. Had he been with her mother? Had he found her and not told Maggie?

Maybe Birman had gone into the district attorney's office—could he have sent that fax on her mother's behalf? But the call, the call from Sam's cell phone... that had happened in the morning, well before he'd gone into interrogation. Unless it had been stolen, Sam would've had the cell on him.

Her eyelids were coated in sandpaper. Her heart was ten sizes too small, vibrating in her chest. What part had her friends played here? How was her mother involved? What about Birman? What in the world had happened that night?

And why couldn't anyone seem to tell her the truth?

"Tristan I... I need to think about this, okay? And in the meantime, just look for my mom and Birman." She had some questions, and as Owen said, she was entitled to answers.

This time, the silence lasted so long, she thought he'd hung up until he coughed. "You want me to keep this fax thing on the down-low?"

"Please."

Another pause. "Okay. And then you'll owe me, right? Maybe I can take two camping trips: one with my brother and one with you. I promise not to send you flowers ever again."

She'd almost forgotten about the camping

trip. Maggie had tried to force them to make up, but good intentions sometimes backfired. She should have seen that coming.

He was still waiting for an answer. And she didn't have the energy to fight him, not tonight. He might be abrasive and overbearing, but at least he told her exactly what he wanted.

"It won't be a camping trip," she said with a sigh. "But yeah. I'll owe you."

CHAPTER **TWENTY-SIX**

MAGGIE DROVE HOME on the lookout for strange cars. Familiar cars, too—Alex's Bug, Imani's Fusion, Sammy's Jeep, even Jerry's Toyota. But Owen's car never caught up even after she'd slowed while talking to Tristan, and she arrived back at her father's house with no visitors and no followers except Reid's very obvious patrol. No additional calls or texts either, no information from anyone she loved or anyone she didn't. Whatever her mother was doing, whatever Sammy was hiding, it was clearly not on the up-and-up—something was going on. Something so critical it was worth risking jail time. Sammy wouldn't be arrested for what he'd done at thirteen, but he'd certainly be in trouble for helping her convict mother skirt the law.

Should she call Imani? And tell her what? That she thought Sammy was hiding something but had no clue what it might be? That Sam and her mom were in cahoots? That Birman and her mom might be in cahoots? Did people still say cahoots?

Cruel is what this was. Worry and questions without a single way to alleviate the anxiety. Speculation was all she had until the people she loved decided to stop lying to her.

By the time Maggie locked the front door, blocking the patrol car in the street, the thoughts had eased into a muddy mess, gloppy and thick and slow. Her belly was full. Her bones were heavy. Her head hurt. When was the last time she'd slept? It had only been two days since Aiden's body was found, but from the state of her sandpaper eyelids, it might have been weeks.

Maggie kicked off her slacks and fell into bed, her cell phone still clutched in her fist, half expecting it to light up with a call from her mom, something from Reid, maybe Sammy. But the dark screen only glared.

Her heart squeezed—too fast, too hard. The shadows thickened. When the room's corners began to shimmer, each highlight from the wavering moon drawing to mind the shiny ends of Aiden's arm bones, she climbed from the mattress and flicked the hallway light. It glared into her eyeballs, but it eased the moonlight into a muted haze—made her brother's bones vanish from the shadows.

THE CELL WAS near her knee when she awoke. Alex had texted her—*Maggie, I'm sorry about Kevin, I really am*—but that was not a battle she needed to have right now. She did not have the bandwidth to forgive, not this week. She did not have the capacity to care whether Alex was sorry that she'd blown up Maggie's life by letting her *almost* marry a killer.

Maggie swung her legs to the floor, grabbed a pair of shorts, and padded up the hall to the kitchen. She was too tired to shower, too tired to brush her teeth. Too tired to eat. So she did none of those.

The countertop was covered in petals. She hadn't put the flowers in water, maybe as a passive-aggressive dig at Tristan and his overzealous gift-giving. Maggie swept the bouquet into her arms and fumbled the garage door open, then the mechanical aluminum door that led to the outside. The cement floor was chilly against her bare toes and rough when she made it to the driveway proper. She dumped the whole mess into the garbage bin with a sigh. The flowers stared at her, the buds like eyes. Accusatory.

I killed a man. It had been justified, but it made her uneasy all the same, perhaps because it didn't bother her the way she thought it should.

Maggie flipped the lid closed and headed for the house, trying to shake the thought, but it stuck like a soggy gum ball in her gray matter. She felt like a dandelion pod whipped about by the wind. Every time she turned around, it was something else twisting her up. Her brother's death. Her mother vanishing. Alex's lies. Sammy doing god knew what. Kevin... Kevin. Even the flowers felt like a dig—something she hadn't asked for, nay, had specifically asked for the opposite, and... there they were.

She had no control. Over anything.

Maggie kicked the garage door shut at her back and swept the remnants of the bouquet into the trashcan. The velvet box containing the diamond bracelet was still open on the counter, the jewelry glittering. She snapped it shut.

But her gaze lingered on the gift beside it: the framed picture of Aiden. Maggie lifted it, tracing her brother's face, trying not to see his bare skull in her mind's eye. Reid had captured Aiden's smile, a difficult, nearly impossible, gift to procure—to do right. And he'd recreated her brother's face *so* perfectly.

Maggie wasn't sure how long she stood there, staring at her brother, her eyes burning, but the doorbell dragged her from her stupor. She glanced at the clock on the stove. Eight. She'd had no calls. No texts. But Tristan might deliver her mother to her door the way he had those flowers. What better way to keep it on the down-low than to sneak her mom into her house?

Maggie hustled to the door and peered through the peephole, but it wasn't Tristan. Reid stood on the porch, his arm raised to wave off the patrol in the road. Apparently, he was going to do the Maggie-babysitting today. She should probably feel something about that, but her brain still felt fuzzy. Her chest was numb.

The door opened slowly. He met her eyes then glanced at her hands, and she followed his gaze to... his gift. Aiden's picture, still clutched in her fingers.

She stepped back and nodded him in. "So,

how's it going? Beautiful weather we're having. You seen those Steelers?" *Wow, Maggie, way to pull out all the worst party conversations at once.*

He shook his head as he closed the door behind him. "You just can't help yourself, can you?"

"That's why you love me, right? Or like me, I mean." *Shit.* She had not imagined things could get more awkward, but there they were.

"You got me." He nodded with a tight smile. "Are you going to be in the office this week?"

"No, I've already rescheduled my patients." Or, rather, Owen said he would, before she left the restaurant last night.

The silence stretched. But he didn't have to tell her why he was asking. Reid wasn't here for her or for Aiden or for her mother. He was here about Ezra.

Her shoulders tightened; her jaw too. It shouldn't bother her—he was a foster father, of course he'd be worried about his child. Yet, it *did* bother her. Her brother's body had been found two days ago, her friends were being called in for questioning, her own mother was missing, and he was worried about some schoolyard dustup?

Irritation prickled in her chest, but she managed: "How is Ezra?"

"Not great." He dropped his gaze to the floor.

"He punched another child at school, broke his nose. And he won't talk to me. At all. He's doing the same thing he did after... well, after his dad died."

After he killed his father, you mean. But selective mutism was significant. Ezra was more fragile than she'd hoped—more volatile, unstable enough that she didn't want to make major changes to his routine. For now, she'd treat him. And over the next six months, they'd work on transitioning him out, into the care of another psychologist. Owen wouldn't want to, didn't want anything to do with the police department or the courts, but he'd see the child if she asked him.

Maggie waited until Reid raised his face, then said, "Did he tell you he saw me leaving yesterday morning?"

He winced. "Shit." It was a loaded word. She had already crossed an ethical line by treating Ezra and sleeping with his foster father, but more complications would surely arise if they tried to maintain their professional and personal relationship in equal measure. "I don't think we should see one another, Reid."

He frowned, his eyes tight. "We don't have to do this now."

"But I'm right. It was a mistake."

Reid stared, but said nothing. His lips clenched, his teeth grinding, the muscles in his jaw ropy and tense.

Maggie turned and headed for the kitchen. She slid the picture onto the counter beside the jewelry box. She'd said all she needed to say about the two of them. And they still had a crime to solve. Had he really only come here about the boy?

She turned, intent on heading back to the foyer, but Reid had followed her, standing so close that she could smell his soap—citrusy. His eyes were locked on hers, his fingers so close to her hip that she could almost feel them touching her, pulling her nearer. Her heart ratcheted into overdrive.

"Why did you come here, Reid?" Her voice was a whisper, but it was the right question.

He blinked. Then Reid took a step back, swallowing hard as if eating his feelings, forcing down the things he wanted to say. The silence was deafening. Finally, he looked away—at the counter. The pressure in her chest eased.

"Alex's mother was beaten to death," he said to Aiden's picture. "Broken leg, broken ribs, skull fracture. We can't prove much with DNA; it degrades, and she was in the dirt for a long time. We'll question Alex's father, but my guess is that he'll blame Dylan, especially once he realizes that the boy is already dead."

And because Alex said that Dylan admitted to killing their mother. But there was only one way he'd know that Dylan was dead. "Tristan called you, huh?"

"He did." A pause. "You sound surprised."

I am. Reid turned his face to her once more, leaning his palm against the counter, his pinky finger inches from the bracelet. Did he know Tristan had given it to her? No, of course not. How would he?

"Maggie?"

She dragged her gaze from his hand. "Sorry. But yeah, I'm a little surprised. Tristan's not always the most forthcoming." *Look who's talking?*

"Except with you."

She blinked at him. It was true, but she wasn't sure how to respond. And just last night she'd specifically asked Tristan to hold information back from the police department—from his brother. Despite her best intentions and forced camping trips, Maggie was clearly not helping them to heal their relationship.

"There is something bothering me that I'm

hoping you can help me explain." The implication was clear: *You can help me explain, but I'm not sure if you will.* "Alex said that once Dylan left, she patched herself up to walk to the bowling alley. She met Sammy in the street instead, and he biked her down to the hospital. We have her admission paperwork."

She met his eyes and waited. When he remained silent, she said: "Is there a question in there?"

"From your account of events, the timeline we've pieced together, Dylan had to have left for Cerora almost immediately after attacking Alex. Which means he didn't kill Aiden, or at least didn't bury him in that well."

He knows—he knows Kevin did it, and that someone else helped him. But did he know who? "Right. Aiden was with Kevin in Yarrow."

"Well, maybe."

She balked. Maybe?

"I've been by your mother's place. Her husband's back in town, and he hasn't seen her in days. But you're her daughter." He met her eyes. "Where is she, Maggie?"

With her detective boyfriend in the Maldives. Or running from her detective boyfriend to the Maldives. Either way, probably the Maldives. "I don't know."

"But you know why I'm asking. The duffel found with Alex's mother had clothes in it. In one of the waterproof pouches, they found a business card—your mom's business card from her law firm." He pushed himself off the counter and stepped closer. "She tried to get Alex's mother out. Didn't she?"

Her shoulders slumped. "Probably."

"So why is she hiding now?"

"I don't know."

"Your father seems to think it's because of you."

She stiffened. Her fists clenched. "You talked to my dad? Without me?" And more than that, he was lucid enough to give Reid information?

"I did. I was kind and careful, Maggie. We've done that dance before. I didn't say anything about Aiden. All he told me was that you didn't do it—that he never thought it was you."

Almost the same thing he'd said to Maggie herself. At least Dad was consistent—he had always been on her side.

"I think your mom..." He paused, swallowed hard. "I think she believes you were involved in Aiden's death. I know you didn't hurt him," Reid interjected when she tried to interrupt, "it's just a hunch based on what your father said and her actions this week. But..." He lowered his voice. "Whatever your mother thinks happened, she has a reason for it. I need to speak to her so we can figure it out. A lot went on that night, but none of you are being forthright, which makes you all look guilty."

Ask Sammy, then—he clearly knew something, had seen her mother just yesterday. But she couldn't form the snarky comeback, couldn't hear anything except the echo of Reid's words: *Your mom believes you were involved.*

Was that true, really true? But why? She could barely think, snippets of thoughts flitting through her brain too fast to catch. Kevin was dead—the only one with an opportunity to kidnap Aiden while Dylan was on the road to Cerora, while Sammy and Alex were in the ER. Sammy couldn't have been with Aiden in Yarrow, but he could have met up with Kevin after he dropped Alex at the hospital, and there was that shirt...

Reid was watching her, appraising her with a shrewd gaze that made her feel naked. "You're holding back, but I'm not sure why."

"It's not that I'm holding back"—*yes, it is*—"I just don't know what I can add. You already know Kevin killed Aiden." *Even if someone else did help him move the body.* "You know it wasn't me."

"Right. And we ruled out Sammy and Alex because they have alibis. But what if they didn't?" She blinked, momentarily stunned, and Reid went on: "What do you think your mother would have done if she thought you were guilty?"

"You already know what she would have done. If you're right, if my dad is right, she literally did it." Wandered around the house, got moody, left her husband, got reckless and arrested, cheated on her new husband, screwed around with a clown-faced detective—

"Why would Kevin have taken Aiden three hours out and three hours back, Maggie? Panic, fine, but there are plenty of woods between Yarrow and Fernborn—he didn't have to go that far. Even if he felt guilty enough to bring Aiden's body back, I can't see your brother staying calm for three and a half hours. All someone needed was that notebook to make it look like Aiden had been there, a description of the boy, and a connection in Yarrow to make a phone call."

The phone call. *A fake phone call.* Realization dawned with a ferocity that stole her breath. "You don't think that Aiden was ever in Yarrow.

We went over this shit thirty times, you convinced me that he was there, and now—"

Reid shook his head. "I wasn't trying to convince you. The evidence pointed to it. The call *definitely* came from Yarrow. And it's highly unlikely that Dylan or Kevin had a connection there who'd be willing to cover for them. But *your mother* might have known someone in the area—maybe another abused woman like Alex's mom, someone who owed her and would never risk outing themselves. As it stands right now, I don't think Aiden ever left this town. I think your mother believed you were involved, and that she protected you by giving you an alibi. She left that note to tell you that she knew what you did, and to warn you that the police might know too—that they were coming for you. It also explains why she'd confess."

"Maybe it was Birman. He's dating my mom, you know." Or... was. And he'd been shifty as hell, breaking into houses, lying and whatnot.

"I don't think he had anything to do with your brother's disappearance. I think he agreed to help your mom. I don't know what he thought back then, but now, Birman claiming there's a missing video of your brother at some conveniently closed grocery store... he's covering for you too. Whether they lay the murder on Alex's dead brother or on your mom, they can hightail it to some island knowing you're in the clear."

That plan actually did sound like something her mother would cook up. And if that was the case, no one was after her except the police. Her mother had warned her about them, but not because they were going to hurt her. She wasn't in danger. Dylan the head-biter was dead. And she didn't know enough about Aiden's actual killer to be a threat. Even the break-ins might have been a ruse, something to throw the police off if they ever needed to shift suspicion.

Maggie stared at Reid, his sorrowful eyes—he was right. If her mother believed that Maggie was in that deep, her last surviving child... she would have done anything she could to help. Mom had surely noticed the bloody towels from Maggie's head. And she'd never said a word.

But there was a huge problem with all of that: Maggie was innocent.

Her mother had protected someone else.

She'd given the real killer an alibi.

"Where would she go, Maggie? Where do you think she's hiding?"

Mom wasn't hiding—that was too simple a word. She was going to vanish the way she'd tried to help Alex's mother vanish. If they didn't find her soon, Maggie would never see her again; she'd never get answers. And she was positive that time was running out. Because Mom had taken a risk to send those orders to the funeral home. They had a cemetery plot, but she'd settled for an urn.

Mom knew she wouldn't have time to bury him.

"Is there anything else you need to tell me, Reid?" Maggie tried to keep her voice even, but her blood was vibrating, her muscles tight—she needed to get out of there.

He blinked. And shook his head.

Maggie broke eye contact and gestured to the door. "I have some work to do, so if you don't mind..." An abrupt send-off, like the one he'd given her at the police station, but she couldn't seem to muster politeness.

Reid frowned. "Maggie, where are you going? You can't just—"

She squared her shoulders, resolute. "Take care of your own family, Reid. And let me deal with mine."

CHAPTER TWENTY-SEVEN

REID STOOD on the porch until she closed the door in his face, his amber eyes tight with concern. She locked the knob. And the deadbolt.

Mom gave the killer an alibi.

The words ran through her head over and over and over as she hauled on a pair of jeans and a T-shirt. She tied on her Dr. Martens just in case. The sky was heavy gray, lanced through with ribbons of charcoal made all the darker by the occasional flash of electricity. The place she was going might be rife with mud by the time she arrived. But she had no choice. There was no more time.

She'd had an idea where her mother would be after speaking to Reid, and she was more certain by the time she climbed into her Sebring. A quick call to the funeral home had confirmed her suspicion—Aiden's ashes had already been picked up, not half an hour after they'd been processed. And her mother had told the mortuary where she'd be spreading them when she'd called: *a service at his home*. The only home Aiden had now was the gravesite. Had that been another hint for Maggie? She could hope.

Maggie checked her rearview as she pulled from the driveway, watching for Reid's Bronco or another police car, marked or unmarked, but no one followed her out of the neighborhood. She'd expected Reid to come after her, thought she'd have to take a few sharp turns and a detour through an underground parking lot, but the road behind her remained clear. Sex hadn't purchased her timely information about the case, but it apparently allowed for a certain amount of clandestine illegal mom-hiding activity. Good to know.

Yet, her eyes kept flicking to the highway behind her. Again, just in case. Because the words that had run through her brain while she dressed were still assaulting her, echoing in her head, reminding her that Mom had given the killer an alibi. The killer could be anyone.

Her mother making that call explained everything and nothing. Sammy and Alex no longer had alibis, but they also didn't have motives. Dylan did, and Kevin's involvement, being Dylan's best friend, still made sense. But if they hadn't needed to convince Aiden to get in the car, maybe Kevin didn't have anything to do with the murder itself. Perhaps Aiden came to the building looking for her, as Reid had suggested, and Dylan stabbed him in the heart before he had time to register what was happening. No suffering—a single, deadly thrust, and it was over.

But for Dylan to get to that Cerora emergency room, he was on the road when Aiden was dumped. He couldn't have made it that far into the woods and back out in time to be found by a passing motorist. And the body dump had to have happened that night unless they moved him twice—the building was gone the next day. And so was Dylan.

So, Kevin had helped him hide the body. How could he have done that alone? A wheelbarrow wouldn't fit along those forest paths—too unwieldy to be useful. And Kevin didn't have other friends back then, not that she knew of. If you were best buddies with a psycho, you probably avoided jealousy where you could.

She pulled into the cemetery lot, shocked that

she'd made it—she couldn't remember the drive at all. The sky was darker now, misted fog coating her windshield with a sheen of damp, the wind gusting in occasional bursts that sent up skittering tornadoes of leaves. Not another car sat in the lot. Her mother didn't have a vehicle, but she'd expected to see Birman here, driving whatever clowny lumberjacks drove—a clown car. And... nothing.

Her chest tightened as she hustled up the path, rubbing gooseflesh from her arms. Hills rolled away on both sides, the gravel crunching beneath her feet, the sky sinking toward her like foggy pillows intent to smother. Quiet, save the breeze. Too quiet.

Maybe she was wrong. Maybe her mother had taken Aiden's ashes with her, was on a plane already. Maybe she'd spread his remains on her fancy non-extradition island—in her new home.

But Maggie's breath caught as she crested the hill that led to her brother's plot. Her mother was here—*I was right*. But her relief in that was short-lived, giving rise to fury and grief in equal measure, a heat that tightened her lungs. While she might get answers—necessary answers—this would still be goodbye. They wouldn't have long, not if her mother intended to escape Fernborn...

or the country. And Maggie had no intention of stopping her, hadn't even considered it. Was that weird? Perhaps not; she'd already lost too much, and her own loyalty had never been an issue. Unlike Alex's.

Mom stood beside the grave, facing the headstone, her back to Maggie, long green dress billowing in the pre-storm breeze. As Maggie grew nearer, she could see the shiny blue urn clutched in her hands. Apparently, cardboard had not been good enough.

"Mom?" She could barely force the word out. She suddenly had no idea where to begin.

"I'm glad you made it." Her mother's shoulders straightened, but she did not turn. "How's Sammy? I heard they had him in holding."

"I'm not sure. Where's your restraining-order boyfriend?" But there was no heat behind it. Her voice just sounded tired.

A pause. "He'll be back shortly. He's a good man—that order was just a misunderstanding. But none of that matters right now." Her mother reached into the urn. She came out with a handful of ashes, and the wind took them, swirling Aiden's body into the atmosphere. The tightness around Maggie's ribs intensified. Mom was right: Birman didn't matter, the past didn't matter, and as far as her mother's love life, the woman could take care of herself.

But that dust was all that was left of her brother—there, then gone. And it didn't feel like closure. She hadn't felt better after touching his skull at the mortuary. Would she feel better after this? Unlikely.

Mom watched the dust vanish, her gaze on her fingers. "How's Alex?"

Alex. Her eyes stung; her face burned. Maggie brought her fingers to her cheek—wet. What a bizarre funeral-interrogation hybrid. Should she yell, start firing questions, or just cry and say a few nice words about her brother? Instead, she muttered, "I wouldn't know about Alex."

"Why not?"

Because she lied about having cancer. Because Kevin and her brother were besties and she didn't tell me. Because you can't be friends if you keep that many secrets—can't be family either. What was the point in justifying any of that now? Some things were too far gone to fix, and they had enough to discuss in whatever spare moments they had here. They were wasting time, but Maggie couldn't seem to get her head together. Her words were stuck in her windpipe as if trying to drag out the last face-to-face conversation she and her mother might ever have.

Maggie cleared her throat and said, "Alex's mother was murdered." It wasn't exactly an answer to her mother's question, but it was close enough.

Her mom finally turned her way. Her face was haggard, the circles under her lower lids so dark that she might have believed that asshole Birman had punched her if not for the spiderwebs of red through her bloodshot eyes—the tears dripping off her chin. And when she met Maggie's gaze, Maggie remembered: *She thinks I did this. She thinks I killed my brother.*

Her mother shook her head. "Well, that's a damn shame. It happens sometimes, but... you hope for the best."

That's all you have to say? Maggie stepped closer, so close that the air felt gritty, though she could see no dust on the breeze. "Is that why you left Alex in that house with her abusive father? Hoping for the best?" Maggie spat the words with more intensity than intended. *Do you think I'm a killer, Mom? Do you think I murdered your son?*

Her mother lowered the urn—*my brother*—to her hip, and Maggie could almost see Aiden there as he'd been when they were small, clinging to her mom as she watered the flowers. Her lungs burned; her hands shook. She had too many emotions zinging through her blood. Confusion. The tender ache of goodbyes. A wickedly sharp kind of love. Gratitude—her mom had tried to save her—and rage that she'd believed Maggie capable of killing Aiden in the first place. And above all, the sadness, poisoning her veins with a vital anguish that made it hard to catch her breath.

"Alex's mother had a plan to have Alex's father locked away. She only intended to be gone a few months—weeks if they could manage it." Her mother wiped dew from her forehead, misted water from the clouds.

"And after? When her mother didn't come back?"

Mom frowned. "You told me the girl had cancer. I thought her grandfather having custody might have allowed for insurance to cover her medical bills. But by then, it was none of my business. Her father had already been locked away. Alex wasn't in danger. Her mother wasn't in danger either, so far as I knew. My part was done."

And if she had alerted the police to the fact that the woman hadn't come home when expected, she might have outed the entire operation—exposed other abuse victims to discovery.

"It's all about damage control with you." Maggie's voice was a harsh croak, and it vibrated with sandpaper edges through her throat. "Is that why you had someone make that call from Yarrow?"

Her mother stared. The wind howled around them, but the silence was louder still, screaming in her ears.

"Did you drop Aiden's notebook too?"

Her mother finally lowered her head and blinked at the earth. She nodded, but did not raise her eyes from the grass, her fingers claws around the urn—holding onto Aiden as if she might clutch him back from death. "I got it done. That's all that matters."

Heat—fire in her belly. "You gave the real killer an alibi. That's what you got done. Because I didn't do it, and I can't fucking believe that you thought I had, and why didn't you just ask me, we could have figured it out together instead of assuming the absolute worst of me, and I can't..." The words raced from her lips as fast as those running through her brain. *I can't.* It wasn't a full sentence, but it felt complete. *I can't. I can't do any of this anymore. I can't.*

Her mother raised her face, her blue eyes pleading—desperate. "I'm sorry, Maggie. I am. And I never thought you killed him vindictively. I thought that he died in some tragic accident, and that you were too ashamed to tell us. In hindsight, it was insane, doing what I did. If you had hurt Aiden... we could have moved. Could have done any number of things to ensure you were okay in the aftermath. But I wasn't right in the head, not that day, and not for a long time. All I could think of that evening was that I had lost my son, but I still had one child to protect. I *still* have one child to protect."

But something she'd just said raised the hairs on Maggie's back. *That he died.*

"Did you know he was dead, Mom? For sure?"

She nodded. Her eyes filled. "I'm sorry that I blamed you, Maggie. Your dad was right. You didn't have it in you."

"I stabbed a guy in the face once." *Awww snap, Mom, take that.* Was that really what she wanted to say right now?

Her mother blinked. "What? When?"

"The night Aiden went missing. Alex's brother, Dylan, the same person who attacked her and took her breast." Maggie stared into her mother's eyes, trying to remember being small, trying to remember being comforted by her, but all she saw was pain, a heartbreak so biting, so acute that it reached from her gaze to rip at Maggie's insides. *You thought I was a murderer.*

Tears rolled down her cheeks, mingling with the cool mist that clung to her flesh like early dew. "There *was* a threat in Alex's home, Mom. But I was wrong too. I almost married Dylan's best friend."

"Dylan?" Her mother scoffed. "He didn't know Kevin."

Maggie wiped her eyes—tacky. "Dylan *did* know Kevin. Alex admitted it. They were best friends."

Her mom's brow furrowed. "How? The boy was away at boarding school."

"They lived up the road. Even if he just came home for holidays—"

"Sammy lived up the road too. Do you think he knew Dylan?" She shook her head, incredulous. "You really think I would have let you marry him, dear? That I would have allowed you to link your life to the best friend of a psychopath?" Her gaze was hard, resolute—certain.

Her mother stepped closer and reached for Maggie's arm. Grit on her fingers. *Aiden* on her fingers. She squeezed. "I promise you, Kevin never met Dylan in his life."

Maggie closed her eyes against the wind, against her mother's gaze. In her head, she heard the questions she and Reid had been asking since they'd found her brother's bones: *Why would Kevin take you to the place Dylan would be?* Reid had thought it part of a revenge plot. But if Kevin didn't know Dylan, then her and Kevin being at that building was just an accident—a coincidence. Kevin was... innocent.

And that was a terrible realization. Because it meant that Kevin had no reason to help Dylan. He wasn't the one who had dumped Aiden's body. Someone else had tossed her brother down that well—someone her mother had talked to. Someone mom would have believed if they'd said Maggie had done it.

There was still one very important question to ask. It felt heavier than the pregnant sky. "How did you know that Aiden was dead, Mom? Why were you so sure?" Her voice came out a whisper.

Her mother met her eyes. Then she stepped away and turned back to the headstone. "You should ask Sammy."

Sammy. Maggie gasped, choking on her tears, her airway far too small. Her mother flipped the urn over. Dust flew, wafting against her mother's dress, settling on the grass, powdering the top of the headstone. "Stop screwing me around, Mom. You owe me more than that. You owe me an explanation."

"I know. But it's not my explanation to give. Sam wants to tell you himself."

"I don't give a shit what Sam wants!"

Her mother turned to her, eyes brimming with tears—real sorrow, maybe regret at the way things had turned out. "We're out of time. Do you want to say anything, dear? Before I have to leave?"

Maggie's fury shuddered and settled deep in her belly where it burned like a hot knife. This wasn't just about saying goodbye to Aiden. Her mother's boyfriend would be back in a few minutes, and then they'd be gone. Even before Aiden's bones were discovered, her mother had been planning to leave Maggie behind. And there was no way back from that now. No way she could stay.

Goodbye, Mom. But the words caught in her throat. She couldn't say them aloud, could only wheeze at the dust swirling through the air. Maggie shook her head.

Tears slid down her mother's cheeks, and in

them Maggie saw their lives—her mom cheering while her father taught her to ride a bike, her mother dancing in the kitchen, breakfasts together where she harassed Maggie about her love life, all those years in tiny pearlized drops. It was too late to make more memories.

It was always too late.

Her throat was hot, her airway blocked—she couldn't look at her mother's face any longer, every fallen tear ripping the jagged hole in her chest wider. Maggie dropped her gaze to the headstone instead, blinking to clear her vision. Aiden's name swam. She blinked harder. And as her mother lowered the urn to the earth, Maggie saw it.

She stepped closer in slow motion, peering at the gray rock, Aiden's name on the front. But on the top was a smudge of something darker.

A heart, one side bigger than the other, drawn in red.

Marked in blood.

CHAPTER
TWENTY-EIGHT

Everyone has seen a little thumbprint heart. Children made them in elementary art class, finger-painted aberrations that good parents dutifully hung on the fridge. But no child had been out wielding their subpar paintbrush skills at the cemetery. And the lopsided nature of it...

Ask Sammy. Her mother's words whispered in her head, but that little heart blinked in her mind's eye. Sammy didn't draw that heart—that wasn't Sammy's thing. It was Alex's. They were both involved, and she had no idea how.

Had they killed Aiden together? Why would they? But the evidence pointed to her two best friends. Her two best friends who suddenly didn't have alibis for the time Aiden was killed and dumped in the woods.

Wasn't that what the heart was? A confession? An apology?

Maggie drove to Alex's house with fire under her wheels, the pedal to the floor, dialing Alex's cell over and over. Every ring went unanswered. She'd been calling Maggie for days, and now... the phone was off.

She was too late—always too late. Would she find her friend hanging in the closet? If Kevin was innocent, his dive off the Fernborn bridge might have been a drunken accident, but she didn't need to lose Alex because she'd refused to pick up the phone.

Alex's car wasn't in her driveway. No one answered her knock, just the blustery wind, tiny raindrops flicking against her face. Maggie returned to her Sebring with a pit in her stomach. She was still furious, absolutely panicked at what she might discover about their involvement. But the prospect of not knowing was more horrifying still.

Where would Alex go? The police station? No, it was too late for that. Alex hadn't even been able to tell her the truth when Sammy was in interrogation. This wasn't a police matter, not anymore.

She'd gone to the gravesite to say goodbye—to apologize. But it hadn't given Alex the closure she'd needed anymore than the cemetery had helped Maggie herself. Even watching those ashes flit around on the breeze had offered no solace. Aiden was gone—his bones were dust, wafting around the atmosphere, and everything from his death to her long-suffering grief to the pit in her belly still felt wildly unsettled.

Maggie headed out of Alex's neighborhood, fast but less speed-demon-y than before. This was a personal endgame. This was about finishing something that had started twenty-four years ago.

Alex would go back to where it had begun.

The middle school looked smaller than it ever had, the high school, too, every building in Fernborn tiny and insignificant as she passed. Others might reminisce about their childhoods with some amount of affectionate whimsy, but all she felt was empty. Every year had taken something new from her. Growing up here had been about loss.

Rain was spitting in earnest against her

windshield by the time she made it to the residential streets, maneuvering through the neighborhood where Sam and Alex used to live. Alex's childhood home had backed up to the forest, her front yard another swath of woods, the trees that snaked through the center of town—the way Aiden would have walked home.

Alex's car was not parked on the road in front of the house where she'd grown up. Wind chimes clinked from the postage-stamp front porch, agitated by the wind. But Maggie wasn't alone—while Alex's car was not here, Sam's was. Had they come here together?

What was she supposed to make of that?

Maggie slowed to a stop behind Sammy's Jeep and stepped into the road, raindrops stinging her bare arms. As she approached, a woman peered through Alex's old window, frowned, then vanished again behind the gauzy curtains.

But no matter. The lot beside Alex's was empty—there had never been a house on it, just a field of ryegrass. She went that way, skirting Alex's childhood property, and ducked inside the tree line.

Maggie wasn't sure exactly where the well

was, but she imagined she'd find it via crime tape, rotten dirt, a path marked by the footprints of officers and hand carts—a hand cart. Was that how they'd gotten Aiden's body back here? She made her way forward, squinting. The canopy above was blocking much of the needling rain, but the wind felt colder here, raising gooseflesh on her feverish skin. As expected, she picked up the worn path fairly quickly; not normal rocky ground, but heavily tread mud.

She jogged as fast as she dared over the uneven terrain, lost in thought. Kevin hadn't known Dylan. She and Kevin had just been in the wrong place at the wrong time—they'd wandered into that building on the same day a psycho had come to move his mother's body. Dylan had run off, intent on disappearing with money from Alex's grandfather's safe, probably assuming that Maggie would call the police. It was a mess, but he hadn't hated her and her family, perhaps hadn't even known that her mother had helped his to escape. It wasn't her mom's fault. It wasn't Maggie's either.

But her brother. What the hell had happened to Aiden? *What did you do Alex?* She should maybe feel more threatened, but she didn't believe that

Alex would hurt her. And if Alex did come after her, Maggie outweighed her by at least twenty pounds—she could take that little pixie of a woman. And Sam—

A branch snapped with a bright *crack!* behind her. *Immediately* behind her, so close that she could suddenly feel the heat of their body.

Maggie whirled, fist balled, and swung. Her knuckles connected with enough force that pain exploded though her forearm and into her elbow.

"Shit!" Sammy yelled, staggering backward.

"Oh, I... sorry," she muttered, realized who she was talking to, then balled her other fist. "No, wait, I'm not sorry. What the fuck with... everything?"

"I'll explain, just don't hit me again," he said, rubbing his jaw. "Even if I did deserve it."

"Did you kill him?"

"What?" His eyes widened. "No, Mags, of course I—"

"Then why the hell are you here?" Her fists were still clenched at her sides. He'd come here, same as she did. Because he knew. And her mother—*You should ask Sammy.* "What did you do?" she hissed. Did she want to know? No, she absolutely didn't. But she *had* to know. She had to know whether the person she trusted most in this world had murdered her brother and lied to her about it their entire lives.

"I didn't know it was Aiden," Sammy said, his eyes glassy. "By the time I showed up, he was already dead. I never saw the body. I was out riding my bike and found Alex all beat up in the road. I biked her to the ER, they called her grandfather, and I waited while they gave her some pain meds. Then I left and went to your house."

"My house?" She frowned. Her chest ached. "Why?"

"Alex asked me to talk to your mom." Rain dribbled over his forehead and into his eye. He blinked it away. She hoped it hurt. A lot.

"Why would she ask you to talk to the mother of a kid she'd killed?" Maggie turned to the path and started off again. She needed to know, but the sorrow in his gaze was stabbing at her lungs, and her muscles were itchy, her heart throbbing in her temples. And though Sammy had clearly done *something*, he wasn't a murderer. She believed him; he had shown up after the fact.

"I think she was trying to confess," Sam said, hustling after her. "But I thought she'd hurt Dylan, because Alex was mumbling stuff about *her* brother, you know? Said that she killed him, maybe hid him somewhere, I can't be sure to this day what she said. I was distraught, all that blood, and they drugged her up good at the hospital too—she was complaining that her socks made her toes feel too friendly before she passed out. We weren't exactly firing on all cylinders."

"Fair enough, she's a maniac on pain meds." She'd climbed out a window after her wisdom teeth surgery. "But—"

"She also told me that your mom had helped hers; that if they started investigating, then her father was going to kill her mother."

Ah... Because at that time, her father was only on trial, and they didn't have a body—Alex would have hoped her mom was alive. And if Alex thought her mom was in hiding, that she might be outed by a police investigation...

"I was so confused," Sammy went on, his voice shaking as much with emotional pain as with exertion. Maggie didn't remember consciously deciding to run, but she was jogging around underbrush, skirting potholes left by policeman's boots or whatever kind of forensic equipment they'd trekked out here. "Everything happened so fast. I think she might have been delirious with blood loss, but I was pretty crazy with nerves. And my parents were in Sarasota, remember? My grandma was home, but... I mean, I was much closer to your mom. I figured she'd know what to do."

"In Sarasota for business," Maggie panted. Her lungs ached. "I do remember. But, Sammy, this is a lot to choke down."

"That's what she said."

She glanced back at him. "Wow."

"Too soon, fine. But to the point: I told your mom my friend had killed someone. And that I wasn't sure what to do."

"And... my mom just said she'd take care of it?" Her shirt was wet, clinging to her skin.

"She'd already seen whatever injuries you had by then. She must have thought that I was protecting *you*. At the time, you were my only friend that she knew about—I had only met Alex that night. And, again, I don't think she knew it was Aiden, not yet. I didn't either. At that time, I hadn't seen you, and I had no idea that Aiden was missing."

And once Mom realized that her son was missing, she'd put it together. She'd tried to help the one child she had left.

Maggie slowed at a fork in the road, the pattering of rain against the leaves louder now, though she couldn't feel the storm on her already soaked skin. To the left, the path looked normal, full of sparse grass and stones. Undisturbed—unhelpful. The rutted earth edged right, the trail there denser, hooded with low-hanging branches. Maggie headed that way, ducking under the vines and into the shadows.

She chanced a look over her shoulder. Sam was squinting at the path, too. He'd never seen the body—he hadn't dumped Aiden. He didn't know where to go either.

"I'm so sorry, Maggie," he said, swatting a branch from his face. "It never occurred to me that your mom would think it was you. She knew Alex's mother, her dad—that's what Alex said. I thought that she'd figure it had to do with them. I thought I told her enough. But my brain was kinda... fried by panic or something. And by the time I realized what had happened, Alex had screwed me over. She told me she'd wrapped him a sweatshirt she found in the road. I was missing mine. She accidentally framed me—the only Black kid in Fernborn, the guy who'd biked her to the hospital. Figures."

Maggie shook her head and slowed to skirt a large patch of picker vines. "She used your shirt to wrap the body?"

"Yeah, she's a real criminal mastermind."

"Just run, Sammy."

"What if I'd rather you punched me again?" he wheezed.

We can do both. She stopped on the side of the path, pulled her hand back and socked him as hard as she could in the shoulder. Once again, her knuckles brightened with pain, her elbow sharp and angry. She squeezed her throbbing fingers in the other hand. "Shit, are you made of metal?"

"I'll let you kick me in the balls later. Imani doesn't want more kids anyway."

"Fine," she said, straightening, then started up the path once more.

"Fine," he repeated. "But not a 'this is over' fine, right?"

She shook her head, eyes on the forlorn woods, the dripping canopy. "No. This is definitely not over." Maybe it would never be over. No, Sammy hadn't buried anyone. He hadn't killed anyone. He'd tried to protect her, had told her mother. Things had gotten out of control, and by the time he'd figured it out, he couldn't walk it back without hurting Alex, without risking Maggie's own mother's future—fabricating evidence, faking phone calls, was illegal.

But he should have told her anyway. He should have fucking told her.

The path curved, a gentle c-shape with an extra hook at the end, and as they rounded the last turn, they both stopped. A giant tree stood on their way, completely blocking the trail.

"What now?" Sam asked.

Maggie was already squinting at the earth, the branches of the downed tree clattering, the wind howling, the rain tappity-tapping against the underbrush. But over all that, another sound...

Maggie turned to their left, her head cocked. A deer? No, too whiny, too sharp. Keening. Sam had heard it too; he was already rushing off-road, into the deeper woods, following the thin line cut by the downed tree and widened by the Tysdale Police Department.

"Alex!" Maggie called. No reply. But within minutes she could see the crime tape, whipping in the breeze like the tails of a kite. Maggie sped her pace, sweat trickling down her back along with the rain, following Sammy. At least the officers had battered down the dirt—forged a path straight to the well.

Sammy skidded to a stop, and Maggie smashed into him, her face planted against his shoulder blade—smarting. "Damnit!" She stepped right, rubbing her nose, and peered around his arm.

Alex stood at the edge of the well, her eyes cast down into the dark. "I'm sorry," she said, so low that her words might have been mistaken for the breeze.

"I'm mostly angry that you made me jog," Maggie said, stepping nearer. "*Jog*, Alex. Now back up, would you?" *Don't go over the edge. Don't die here like Aiden. We've all lost enough.*

"Yeah, I don't run unless something's chasing me," Sammy said.

"He *was* chasing me." Alex turned puffy eyes to Maggie. But she did not back away from the well. "I grabbed a knife and ran into the woods. There was this huge hollowed-out stump I used to hide in when my parents were fighting—no one had ever found me there. I have no idea how long I hid, but I was dizzy, puking; I thought I was dying. And it was so quiet. Dark, too, by then. So, I climbed out, thinking I could get to the hospital, but then I heard him coming. I didn't have time to get back into the stump. He tried to grab me, and—"

Her voice cracked, her breath panting from her lungs, convulsing so hard that Maggie was worried she might tumble into the hole. The toes of her shoes hung over the stony edge. "I think he just wanted to tap my shoulder, to make sure I was okay, you know? And I just... reacted. The whole time, he didn't say anything—not one word. And he was so... s... small." She inhaled a long wheezing breath, and Maggie's own lungs seized. "I shoved him inside the old oak—the one where I was hiding. Then I ran for the road."

And Sammy had biked her to the hospital. The insulation trace had likely transferred onto Alex's clothes when Dylan attacked her.

Alex swallowed hard. Her shoulders went still, her face a dull mask. Maggie wasn't sure if this sudden calm was a good thing; suicidal people were sometimes happiest right before they jumped. And there was a small part of her that wanted Alex to jump—the part that was, even now, watching her little brother, her worried little brother, approaching an injured girl in the woods. He'd wanted to help her. And she'd fucking murdered him.

"All night long, I remember thinking that I didn't want him to be cold," Alex whispered. Maggie's eyes stung. "But he was so close to the house—too close. I used a furniture dolly. Took me an entire day to get him to the well. I pulled half my stitches." Maggie could barely hear her over the gusting wind. "I tried to make it go away. I just wanted it to go away."

Sam crossed his arms, his face stricken. Maggie stepped nearer, her hands up as if she could telekinetically push Alex back from the edge. "You should have told me." *You shouldn't have killed him.*

Alex sniffed, her blond hair plastered against her ears. "It wasn't that easy. You and I didn't know each other then. And if I told anyone about Aiden, I had to tell them about my breast, about Dylan. I didn't want authorities looking for my mom, but I also thought that the police would bring Dylan back to Fernborn. He'd always wanted to disappear—he had money from the safe. I hoped he'd go away for good, because if he came back..." Tears and rain dripped off her chin. "I wasn't going to make it out alive. Not again."

"Why not just get him arrested?" Maggie asked.

"I *tried that.*" She looked at the ground—at the dark, dark well. "My mom did, too. He always got out of it. Always had a reason, an alibi. And he was only sixteen then, so it's not like he'd go to jail. Juvenile hall at best, and then he'd get out at eighteen and kill me in my sleep." Her lip trembled. She stared at the hole. "At least this way, I had a chance."

"You have a lot more than a chance." Maggie stepped carefully forward, closing the distance between them—one on each side of the well. "Dylan's dead." *Like my brother. Like Kevin, who I loved—you made me believe he was a murderer.*

Alex shook her head violently, but did not raise her face. "You can't know that."

"Tristan can," Maggie blurted, but her brain wouldn't settle, the thoughts running through her head like the rain down on her face—*you lied, you lied to me all these years.*

"He *can't*," she insisted. Alex finally looked up, her blue eyes sharp—bloodshot, but certain. "I identified that shirt, the one found with his body, but Dylan is smart. So goddamn smart, Maggie. And vicious as hell. He could be in Fernborn right now, and we'd never know."

It sounded paranoid, but Maggie understood her perspective—self-protection. Outside of her grandfather, the men in Alex's family were monsters. Her mother had tried to vanish, left her only daughter to stay alive, and had failed. Alex had barely made it out, and she'd lost body parts to do it. And Aiden... he'd just wanted to help her.

If Alex toppled into the well now, her brother's death was for nothing.

Her thoughts calmed, but her throat remained stranglehold tight. "We need your testimony to get Sammy out of trouble," Maggie forced out. "They have his sweatshirt in evidence. And once they find out that my mother was the one who called in that tip from Yarrow—"

Alex gasped. She stumbled, and Maggie's heart ratcheted into overdrive, but she could not get to Alex from the opposite side of the well—she was going to watch her die. Sammy lurched forward.

Alex righted herself just in time. She stepped back from the edge and met Maggie's eyes. "Your mom... *what*?"

Her heart—holy crap, her heart. Like a squirrel during nut season. "We have a lot to talk about. But Sammy doesn't have an alibi anymore. He looks guiltier than ever." Maggie felt tears, hot on her cheeks. "Please, help me do the right thing. And let's not do it near this well."

"Well... that's a deep thought," Sammy said.

Alex frowned at him. "Shut up, Sammy," she and Maggie said together.

Those three words were by no means the perfect way to say goodbye, but there was no denying that they felt like final gasping breaths, even if she couldn't quite define *what* was ending. The forest had teeth, and her heart was a jagged hole, horrific and awful and brutal and edged in twenty years worth of pain.

But the farewell was real. It was right.

Sometimes that's all you could ask for.

EPILOGUE

THE HAZY LIGHT made his eyes ache and reduced the participants in the main room to ghostly shadows. Music throbbed in his ears and pulsed in his abdomen. It smelled of caramel and Kevin's cologne.

He always wore cologne that might remind her of the people she cared about. She was deeply connected to her friends, and still pined for the man she'd lost.

But it was time she got a replacement. A *real* replacement.

It was almost time to make his move.

Her other lovers were out of her life now, all of them blips on her romantic radar, there, then gone. Kevin, for obvious reasons. Reid, too—the detective had not enjoyed a repeat performance since the night he'd taken her so brazenly to his home. Perhaps it was because of the boy.

He smiled. He'd thrown a stone at Ezra's window just before Maggie left the house. He'd made sure the child had seen her.

Sometimes he just had to set up the dominoes and watch them fall.

That's what he was doing tonight. Watching. Waiting. Confident that he'd set everything up perfectly. All the tension over the last year, and she was finally, *finally*, back in the club. She'd come back to *him*. And he intended to make sure that she never left him again.

Maggie's tall boots glistened, wet-looking in the candlelight as she scanned the room, the couples on the back couch, the voyeurs in the corners. She had been one of them once, just watching, imagining. For months, she came to this club to watch. And then, she'd let another man touch her. Then another. And eventually... him.

That's why she was here, now—for him. Playing hard to get, staring across the darkened floor at the other humans on offer, merely warm bodies to pass the night. Teasing him. Testing him. Dragging him to new heights by pretending that she might choose another.

He stifled his grin, trying not to appear too eager. Tonight was his. Once she met his gaze, once she invited him over, he would make his move. He would reveal himself to her. And he would make her his in life, beyond the walls of this darkened club.

Maggie raised her hand suddenly and pointed to the man standing in the center of the room. Bigger than those she usually called on when she came here, with stocky muscles and chest hair and an earring in his nipple. Tattoos ran in a colorful sleeve over his left arm, a mass of writhing serpents, three of them poking from the eyes of a black and red skull. Green bracelet on his wrist.

He blinked, at first unsure what he was seeing, but then realization dawned with horrible clarity. *No.*

The tattooed man approached Maggie, a smile touching his lips below his leather mask, his jaw bare.

He reached for his own mask, touching his chin. Leather shielded his entire face. There was an opening over his mouth, but the parts that might hint at his identity, even the shape of his jaw... covered. All covered. As they always were.

Tension prickled along his spine as the tattooed man drew nearer to Maggie. He scanned the room, squinting, frantically trying to figure a way around it. A distraction, perhaps, and the man would step back and allow Maggie to see him—only him. A couple sat wrapped in one another's arms in a huge leather chair; no bottom on that chair, he knew that for a fact. They were not looking his way. Nor were the two men leaning against the wall, curating their appetites for the evening. Could he use the candles, light one of them on fire? No, she'd see him engaging in any mischief. So, what was there to do? What could he do?

He had to do *something*.

The tattooed man was closer still. Watching Maggie. Watching his love.

Maggie smiled, tossing her flaming hair over her shoulder, and... *ah*. She turned his way. Their eyes locked, and his heart soared. She'd seen him—she'd finally seen him. Now she would shoo the tattooed man from her orbit and come to him, invite him to approach.

His shoulders relaxed, his belly sick with tension, but it eased the longer she held his gaze.

What had he been worried about? She had just been teasing him, that much was clear now. She did not pull her gaze from his, though she already knew his bracelet was green, knew every curve of his body even in the dimness, the rigid planes of his abdomen, the way his hair smelled like Kevin—exactly like Kevin. Did she imagine that was in her head? Or did she realize that he cultivated the scent on purpose, to make her happy, to make her comfortable? To make her love him?

He smiled at her. But he still had to wait for her to invite him over. She had the red bracelet. He had the green. That was how she wanted it—how she liked it.

And he had every intention of making her happy.

He took a step forward, his shoulders tight—he could not help it. Her eyes were beckoning him, calling him from the shadows.

She turned away.

His heart stopped.

Maggie turned back to the tattooed man, still sidling nearer. Still smiling. And then... she was smiling too. Not at him. At the *other* man. At the man with the tattoos.

Fire bloomed in his guts, an inferno that

reached into his chest, broiling his neck. *No*. This could not be happening.

The tattooed man came within arm's distance. She pointed to the door at the back of the room: the private playroom. The tattooed man turned and headed for the door, following her directions.

Maggie followed him silently through the hazy room, the candles flickering off the bare back of the man she'd chosen, a come-hither flutter of light.

No, no, no.

Maggie stepped over the threshold and looked back. He stood, stunned, mere feet from the door, his heart a lump of molten stone. Had he run across the room? He hadn't noticed, but he was here now, in front of the door, staring. Shaking.

Maggie cocked her head, her red curls falling over her arm.

His lungs clenched, the air useless. This wasn't supposed to happen. This was all wrong.

But wrong or not, it was happening. Maggie closed the door in slow motion, and as the crack vanished, he nodded to her. *I'll forgive you, Maggie.* He'd forgiven her for Kevin, for Reid, and he'd forgive her for this. That tattooed man could never give her what she wanted.

He could. He knew everything about her—her favorite foods, her favorite recording artists. Her favorite flowers.

He would win her back. He just needed the perfect gift.

The playroom door pulsed with shadows. He imagined the tattooed man inside, tethered to the bed with restraints that should have been his. Rage clawed at his insides, his blood boiling. He backed away and headed for the exit.

He could not lose his cool, not when he had so much time invested. And it was obvious to him now that none of his previous gifts had properly shown his affection—he hadn't thought big enough. They proved how well he knew her, but they had not demonstrated the lengths he was willing to go to. They showed his fondness, but not his commitment.

What was the perfect valentine?

A smile spread slowly across his face.

Perhaps the tattooed man's heart would do.

Your next book is waiting! Continue Maggie's

story with *The Dead Don't Worry* (read on for a sneak peek, then snag your copy on MeghanOFlynn.com)!

"*DARK PLACES* MEETS *YOU*... HEART-POUNDING, CHILLING, AND HAUNTING, PACKED WITH ELECTRIFYING PLOT TWISTS. AN ADDICTIVE MUST-READ."

~BESTSELLING AUTHOR EMERALD O'BRIEN

THE DEAD DON'T WORRY

MIND GAMES #4

How do you catch a serial killer who knows you better than you know yourself? An addictive psychological crime thriller for fans of *Dark Places*.

GET THE *DEAD DON'T WORRY* ON MEGHANOFLYNN.COM!

THE DEAD DON'T WORRY: A Mind Games Novel

CHAPTER 1
REID

THE STAIRS WERE a gateway to hell, not that you could tell from the outside. Simple enough, the ridged metal treads pinging like bells against his shoes, the cement walls chipped, the paint pock-marked like acne scars—imperfect, though not inherently dangerous. But Reid could feel the danger in his bones, smell it in the air, in the metallic tingle on the back of his tongue. Whatever he was walking into was not going to be pretty. Beauty was for artists, not homicide detectives.

The darkness at the bottom of the stairwell was thick and foggy, humidity that matched the July air. There were few abandoned buildings in this section of town, but the warehouse on the upper floor had most recently been occupied by a packaging company—wall-to-wall tinder. It had been no shock when a fire destroyed the south-facing side, and no company, not even the packagers who had called this place home, had returned to claim the rubble. Upstairs, heavy cardboard, moldering and still soaked in mineral-rich firehose water, made the warm air fog up like the jungle.

But down here... *it shouldn't be so dark down here.* The forensics team was already on the scene, the door propped open with a triangular hunk of wood. For a split second, Reid imagined that he was in the wrong place, that he had been lured here for some unknown-to-him reason. A deadly reason. But he could hear the others beyond the dark doorway, the shuffling of shoes, the low murmur of officers' voices, the clinking of instruments. It was a distinctive cacophony that made up a crime scene. The mere presence of a corpse dampened the voices of the living, eating at souls as reliably as rats eating a victim's flesh.

God, he hoped there weren't rats.

Reid reached the bottom of the stairwell. As if anticipating his presence, a light blinked on somewhere beyond the open door. The sodium glow blared against the wall at his right, then swung away as they adjusted the neck, presumably to focus on the scene and not Reid's burly ass ducking through the opening in his suit and pocket square—always neater than he had to be. Reid needed that neatness like an anchor in a storm. He needed to be physically put together when the rest of the world was a bloody mess.

But... huh. Blank floors, completely clear of debris—unexpected. Had the killer cleaned up? If so, his diligence had stopped at the floor. The cement walls were streaked with grime, striations of black and brown like uneven prison bars, runoff from the waterlogged paper products above. The spotlight was currently trained on the far corner of the room. Though Reid could not see the victim just yet, he could smell the death above the mildew and the thick dust that attached itself to his throat like ash.

He took a breath and closed his eyes for a beat longer than a blink, trying to see the room as the killer would have. The techs vanished. The light dimmed. The buzzing air went silent.

Reid opened his eyes and approached, the walls pressing closer with each step, the ill-aimed spotlight making the back wall gleam in such a way that it cast the victim in shadow. All Reid could see was a vague outline, an amorphous shape seated on the floor—an inanimate object, devoid of substance or hopes or dreams. As his eyes adjusted, he could make out her hands, wrists tied above her head, the rope looped around a thick metal ceiling pipe, the frayed edges prickly in the wan gray light from the far window. Her arms moved, jerking as she struggled against the binds. He could hear the timbre of her final screams—hear her begging him to let her go.

"Damnit!" one of the techs said, fiddling with the spotlight, and the victim's voice went silent as the rest of the room came rushing back at him. Now it was just the clinking of the light stand, the voice of the tech to his left, dusting the ground for prints. As he closed the distance between himself and the dead woman, a bulky shape beside the body rose like an apparition, then stepped into the glow cast by the blocky basement windows.

"What took you so long, Hanlon?"

Clark Lavigne was a bulldozer of a man, Black with a bald head and a ready smile. With a degree in French literature, he was the last person Reid might expect to become a cop, but Reid had seen him in action—no one should cross him. No one smart. Reid sure wouldn't.

Clark was still waiting for an answer, his thick eyebrows drawn in concern, and with good reason. Reid had been stuck in a meeting for his son's—well, foster son's—summer school program. Yet another *incident*, each bloodier than the last. From fists to fingernails to, this time, a pencil. The boy needed a new school—one without other kids, if you believed the principal. "I had a meeting," Reid said.

"Ah." It was a loaded word, heavy. Clark had warned him against taking the boy in—Ezra had some psychopathic tendencies. Even Maggie, his psychologist partner, had cautioned that the road to healing would be long, and might not go the way he wanted. It seemed she was right. She usually was. But no one else was lining up to take the child—it was Reid or a group home, probably juvenile detention... or worse.

When Reid didn't respond, Clark went on: "A couple of kids found her on their way home from school. They were screwing around, busting windows. They won't do that again."

"Or they'll do it even more, looking for that rush." Ezra certainly would.

Clark blinked at him. They both turned as the light shifted again, finally illuminating the vic as if she were onstage for her big debut. The amorphous shapes solidified into form and color and...

Clark stiffened. Reid stared, his heart stuttering, his windpipe clamping down, so tight he could not force a breath. *Oh no. Oh no, no, no.*

The victim's red hair glittered like fire. But she wasn't just any victim. He'd thought her hair was like dragon's breath on more than one occasion, most recently when it was spread over his pillow. He had hoped for a repeat performance once his son got used to the idea, but...

It was too late.

His lungs blazed, broiling with red-hot coals, his chest tight and painful. Reid stepped forward, moved by inertia instead of will, the world dragging him into her orbit. Her wrists were tied with nylon rope, as he'd noted before, but now he could see the wounds along the bottom of her upper arms. An angry zig-zag had been gouged deep into one armpit like the killer had played *Zorro* through the bristly hairs. Deeper wounds in her belly. Bruises covered her forearms and her pale legs, exposed beneath her jean shorts. She had been abused before she was killed —savagely.

But the shorts... Maggie didn't own jean shorts, did she? He'd never seen her in jeans at all. Or shorts, for that matter.

Reid slipped to the other side of the body, his heart thundering in his ears, drowning out the techs. He kneeled, trying to see her face. Her head hung limply to the side, her curly hair covering the hollow of her cheek, hiding her eye.

Reid reached out with one gloved hand and gently peeled her red hair from her sticky temple, holding the congealed mess out like a curtain.

"Shit," Clark said.

Reid swallowed hard, but did not look away. Her cheek was a mess of dried blood and swollen tissue, the flesh severed clear through the muscle, the wound so deep that the sides peeled back like lips to expose her pale white cheekbone. And her eyes...

They stared at him, glassy and wide—blue. Not brown.

His shoulders relaxed. His lungs loosened. Reid sucked a metallic breath into his lungs. *Not Maggie. Thank god, it's not Maggie.* But his chest remained tight. This woman was still someone's baby, someone's wife, someone's friend. And what the killer had done to her...

He frowned, locking himself in her dead gaze. He could see her eyes, but it was not because her eyelids were open. Thin even cuts ran along the flesh just below each eyebrow ridge. And based on the amount of blood that streaked her cheeks, she'd still been alive when he'd done it. She'd been breathing when he sliced off her eyelids—when he mutilated her.

"You know who she looks like, don't you?" Clark said. "Her hair, her build..."

Reid couldn't pull his eyes away, nor did he need to answer. The resemblance to Maggie was striking. Any fool could see it. That didn't feel like a coincidence.

Nor did this warehouse feel like the end.

Reid blinked at the victim's bloody cheeks, the flesh carved from her bones, the deep penetrating lacerations in her abdomen. The suspect had taken his time. He'd enjoyed every minute of listening to this poor woman scream.

The fine hairs along Reid's neck prickled. No, this wasn't over. This was a game to their killer.

And it was only just beginning.

GET THE *DEAD DON'T WORRY* ON MEGHANOFLYNN.COM!

"*DARK PLACES* MEETS *YOU*... HEART-POUNDING, CHILLING, AND HAUNTING, PACKED WITH ELECTRIFYING PLOT TWISTS. AN ADDICTIVE MUST-READ."

~BESTSELLING AUTHOR EMERALD O'BRIEN

WICKED SHARP

A BORN BAD NOVEL

"A white-knuckle thrill ride. O'Flynn is a master storyteller" (*USA Today Bestselling Author Paul Austin Ardoin*): When Poppy Pratt sets out on a trip to the Tennessee mountains with her serial killer father, she's just happy to escape their daily charade — but after a series of unlucky events leads them to a couple's secluded home, she discovers they're much too similar to her deadly dad... Perfect for fans of *Dexter*.

GET *WICKED SHARP* ON MEGHANOFLYNN.COM!

WICKED SHARP: A Born Bad Novel
CHAPTER 1

I HAVE a drawing that I keep tucked inside an old doll house—well, a house for fairies. My father always insisted upon the whimsical, albeit in small amounts. It's little quirks like that which make you real to people. Which make you safe. Everyone has some weird thing they cling to in times of stress, whether it's listening to a favorite song or snuggling up in a comfortable blanket or talking to the sky as if it might respond. I had the fairies.

And that little fairy house, now blackened by soot and flame, is as good a place as any to keep the things that should be gone. I haven't looked at the drawing since the day I brought it home, can't even remember stealing it, but I can describe every jagged line by heart.

The crude slashes of black that make up the stick figure's arms, the page torn where the scribbled lines meet—shredded by the pressure of the crayon's point. The sadness of the smallest figure.

The horrific, monstrous smile on the father, dead center in the middle of the page.

Looking back, it should have been a warning —I should have known, I should have run. The child who drew it was no longer there to tell me what happened by the time I stumbled into that house. The boy knew too much, that was obvious from the picture.

Children have a way of knowing things that adults don't—a heightened sense of self-preservation that we slowly lose over time as we convince ourselves that the prickling along the backs of our necks is nothing to worry about. Children are too vulnerable not to be ruled by emotion—they're hardwired to identify threats with razor's-edge precision. Unfortunately, they have a limited capacity to describe the perils they uncover. They can't explain why their teacher is scary or what makes them duck into the house if they see the neighbor peeking at them from behind the blinds. They cry. They wet their pants.

They draw pictures of monsters under the bed to process what they can't articulate.

Luckily, most children never find out that the monsters under their bed are real.

I never had that luxury. But even as a child, I was comforted that my father was a bigger, stronger monster than anything outside could ever be. He would protect me. I knew that to be a fact the way other people know the sky is blue or that their racist Uncle Earl is going to fuck up Thanksgiving. Monster or not, he was my world. And I adored him in the way only a daughter can.

I know that's strange to say—to love a man even if you see what terrors lurk beneath. My therapist says it's normal, but she's prone to sugarcoating. Or maybe she's so good at positive thinking that she's grown blind to real evil.

I'm not sure what she'd say about the drawing in the fairy house. I'm not sure what she'd think about me if I told her that I understood why my father did what he did, not because I thought it was justified, but because I understood him. I'm an expert when it comes to the motivation of the creatures underneath the bed.

And I guess that's why I live where I do, hidden in the New Hampshire wilderness as if I can keep every piece of the past beyond the border of the property—as if a fence might keep the lurking dark from creeping in through the cracks. And there are always cracks, no matter how hard you try to plug them. Humanity is a perilous condition rife with self-inflicted torment and psychological vulnerabilities, the what-ifs and maybes contained only by paper-thin flesh, any inch of which is soft enough to puncture if your blade is sharp.

I knew that before I found the picture, of course, but something in those jagged lines of crayon drove it home, or dug it in a little deeper. Something changed that week in the mountains. Something foundational, perhaps the first glimmer of certainty that I'd one day need an escape plan. But though I like to think I was trying to save myself from day one, it's hard to tell through the haze of memory. There are always holes. Cracks.

I don't spend a lot of time reminiscing; I'm not especially nostalgic. I think I lost that little piece of myself first. But I'll never forget the way the sky roiled with electricity, the greenish tinge that threaded through the clouds and seemed to slide down my throat and into my lungs. I can feel the vibration in the air from the birds rising on frantically beating wings. The smell of damp earth and rotting pine will never leave me.

Yes, it was the storm that kept it memorable; it was the mountains.

It was the woman.

It was the blood.

GET *WICKED SHARP* ON MEGHANOFLYNN.COM!

"FULL OF COMPLEX, ENGAGING CHARACTERS AND EVOCATIVE DETAIL, *WICKED SHARP* IS A WHITE-KNUCKLE THRILL RIDE. O'FLYNN IS A MASTER STORYTELLER."

~Paul Austin Ardoin, USA Today Bestselling Author

SHADOW'S KEEP

When a child is found mauled to death in the woods, the medical examiner says it was a dog attack — but deputy sheriff William Shannahan believes the killer was human. To solve the case, he must turn to his girlfriend, Cassie Parker, who knows more than she's letting on... A compulsively readable thriller in the vein of Gillian Flynn, Carolyn Arnold, and Karin Slaughter, *Shadow's Keep* is a mind-bending exploration of obsession, desperation, and how far we'll go to protect those we love.

GET *SHADOW'S KEEP* ON MEGHANOFLYNN.COM!

SHADOW'S KEEP
CHAPTER 1

FOR WILLIAM SHANNAHAN, six-thirty on Tuesday, the third of August, was "the moment." Life was full of those moments, his mother had always told him, experiences that prevented you from going back to who you were before, tiny decisions that changed you forever.

And that morning, the moment came and went, though he didn't recognize it, nor would he ever have wished to recall that morning again for as long as he lived. But he would never, from that day on, be able to forget it.

He left his Mississippi farmhouse a little after six, dressed in running shorts and an old T-shirt that still had sunny yellow paint dashed across the front from decorating the child's room. *The child.* William had named him Brett, but he'd never told anyone that. To everyone else, the baby was just that-thing-you-could-never-mention, particularly since William had also lost his wife at Bartlett General.

His green Nikes beat against the gravel, a blunt metronome as he left the porch and started along the road parallel to the Oval, what the townsfolk called the near hundred square miles of woods that had turned marshy wasteland when freeway construction had dammed the creeks downstream. Before William was born, those fifty or so unlucky folks who owned property inside the Oval had gotten some settlement from the developers when their houses flooded and were deemed uninhabitable. Now those homes were part of a ghost town, tucked well beyond the reach of prying eyes.

William's mother had called it a disgrace. William thought it might be the price of progress, though he'd never dared to tell her that. He'd also never told her that his fondest memory of the Oval was when his best friend Mike had beat the crap out of Kevin Pultzer for punching William in the eye. That was before Mike was the sheriff, back when they were all just "us" or "them" and William had always been a them, except when Mike was around. He might fit in somewhere else, some other place where the rest of the dorky goofballs lived, but here in Graybel he was just a little...odd. Oh well. People in this town gossiped far too much to trust them as friends anyway.

William sniffed at the marshy air, the closely-shorn grass sucking at his sneakers as he increased his pace. Somewhere near him a bird shrieked, sharp and high. He startled as it took flight above him with another aggravated scream.

Straight ahead, the car road leading into town was bathed in filtered dawn, the first rays of sun painting the gravel gold, though the road was slippery with moss and morning damp. To his right, deep shadows pulled at him from the trees; the tall pines crouched close together as if hiding a secret bundle in their underbrush. Dark but calm, quiet—comforting. Legs pumping, William headed off the road toward the pines.

A snap like that of a muted gunshot echoed through the morning air, somewhere deep inside the wooded stillness, and though it was surely just a fox, or maybe a raccoon, he paused, running in place, disquiet spreading through him like the worms of fog that were only now rolling out from under the trees to be burned off as the sun made its debut. Cops never got a moment off, although in this sleepy town the worst he'd see today would be an argument over cattle. He glanced up the road. Squinted. Should he continue up the brighter main street or escape into the shadows beneath the trees?

That was his moment.

William ran toward the woods.

As soon as he set foot inside the tree line, the

dark descended on him like a blanket, the cool air brushing his face as another hawk shrieked overhead. William nodded to it, as if the animal had sought his approval, then swiped his arm over his forehead and dodged a limb, pick-jogging his way down the path. A branch caught his ear. He winced. Six foot three was great for some things, but not for running in the woods. Either that or God was pissed at him, which wouldn't be surprising, though he wasn't clear on what he had done wrong. Probably for smirking at his memories of Kevin Pultzer with a torn T-shirt and a bloodied nose.

He smiled again, just a little one this time.

When the path opened up, he raised his gaze above the canopy. He had an hour before he needed to be at the precinct, but the pewter sky beckoned him to run quicker before the heat crept up. It was a good day to turn forty-two, he decided. He might not be the best-looking guy around, but he had his health. And there was a woman whom he adored, even if she wasn't sure about him yet.

William didn't blame her. He probably didn't deserve her, but he'd surely try to convince her that he did, like he had with Marianna...though he didn't think weird card tricks would help this time. But weird was what he had. Without it, he was just background noise, part of the wallpaper of this small town, and at forty-one—*no, forty-two, now*—he was running out of time to start over.

He was pondering this when he rounded the bend and saw the feet. Pale soles barely bigger than his hand, poking from behind a rust-colored boulder that sat a few feet from the edge of the trail. He stopped, his heart throbbing an erratic rhythm in his ears.

Please let it be a doll. But he saw the flies buzzing around the top of the boulder. Buzzing. Buzzing.

William crept forward along the path, reaching for his hip where his gun usually sat, but he touched only cloth. The dried yellow paint scratched his thumb. He thrust his hand into his pocket for his lucky coin. No quarter. Only his phone.

William approached the rock, the edges of his vision dark and unfocused as if he were looking through a telescope, but in the dirt around the stone he could make out deep paw prints. Probably from a dog or a coyote, though these were *enormous*—nearly the size of a salad plate, too big for anything he'd expect to find in these woods.

He frantically scanned the underbrush, trying to locate the animal, but saw only a cardinal appraising him from a nearby branch.

Someone's back there, someone needs my help.

He stepped closer to the boulder. *Please don't let it be what I think it is.* Two more steps and he'd be able to see beyond the rock, but he could not drag his gaze from the trees where he was certain canine eyes were watching. Still nothing there save the shaded bark of the surrounding woods. He took another step—cold oozed from the muddy earth into his shoe and around his left ankle, like a hand from the grave. William stumbled, pulling his gaze from the trees just in time to see the boulder rushing at his head and then he was on his side in the slimy filth to the right of the boulder, next to...

Oh god, oh god, oh god.

William had seen death in his twenty years as a deputy, but usually it was the result of a drunken accident, a car wreck, an old man found dead on his couch.

This was not that. The boy was no more than six, probably less. He lay on a carpet of rotting leaves, one arm draped over his chest, legs splayed haphazardly as if he, too, had tripped in the muck. But this wasn't an accident; the boy's throat was torn, jagged ribbons of flesh peeled back, drooping on either side of the muscle meat, the unwanted skin on a Thanksgiving turkey. Deep gouges permeated his chest and abdomen, black slashes against mottled green flesh, the wounds obscured behind his shredded clothing and bits of twigs and leaves.

William scrambled backward, clawing at the ground, his muddy shoe kicking the child's ruined calf, where the boy's shy white bones peeked from under congealing blackish tissue. The legs looked...*chewed on.*

His hand slipped in the muck. The child's face was turned to his, mouth open, black tongue lolling as if he were about to plead for help. *Not good, oh shit, not good.*

William finally clambered to standing, yanked his cell from his pocket, and tapped a button, barely registering his friend's answering bark. A fly lit on the boy's eyebrow above a single white mushroom that crept upward over the landscape of his cheek, rooted in the empty socket that had once contained an eye.

"Mike, it's William. I need a...tell Dr. Klinger to bring the wagon."

He stepped backward, toward the path, shoe sinking again, the mud trying to root him there, and he yanked his foot free with a squelching sound. Another step backward and he was on the path, and another step off the path again, and another, another, feet moving until his back slammed against a gnarled oak on the opposite side of the trail. He jerked his head up, squinting through the greening awning half convinced the boy's assailant would be perched there, ready to leap from the trees and lurch him into oblivion on flensing jaws. But there was no wretched animal. Blue leaked through the filtered haze of dawn.

William lowered his gaze, Mike's voice a distant crackle irritating the edges of his brain but not breaking through—he could not understand what his friend was saying. He stopped trying to decipher it and said, "I'm on the trails behind my house, found a body. Tell them to come in through the path on the Winchester side." He tried to listen to the receiver, but heard only the buzzing of flies across the trail—had they been so loud a moment ago? Their noise grew, amplified to unnatural volumes, filling his head until every other sound fell away—was Mike still talking? He pushed *End,* pocketed the phone, and then leaned back and slid down the tree trunk.

And William Shannahan, not recognizing the

event the rest of his life would hinge upon, sat at the base of a gnarled oak tree on Tuesday, the third of August, put his head into his hands, and wept.

GET *SHADOW'S KEEP* ON MEGHANOFLYNN.COM!

"MASTERFUL, STAGGERING, TWISTED... AND COMPLETELY UNPREDICTABLE."

~BESTSELLING AUTHOR WENDY HEARD

SALVATION

AN ASH PARK NOVEL

When Ed Petrosky stumbles across the body of his fiancée in the snow, he can tell that there are inconsistencies in her case even through his fog of grief. And when another body turns up, Ed realizes that Heather's death is far from an isolated incident...

GET *SALVATION* ON MEGHANOFLYNN.COM!

Edward Petrosky joined the Ash Park police force

with two goals in mind: escape the military and silence the demons that followed him home from the war. And no one soothes those traumas better than his fiancé, Heather—he doesn't even mind that she has a checkered past of her own.

But his dreams are obliterated when one night, on a routine call, Ed stumbles upon a scene as horrifying as any he's seen in combat: Heather's bloody body, half-buried in the snow. Though his superiors order him to stay away from the investigation, Ed can't help but notice the inconsistencies in Heather's case—her supposed cause of death doesn't mesh with what she's told him about her past.

When another body turns up, Ed realizes that Heather's murder wasn't an isolated act of violence; this new victim was connected to the same shelter where Heather volunteered and attended the same church where a kindly priest seems to know more about the murders than he should. And the detectives working the case seem indifferent to these links despite being no closer to finding Heather's killer.

Now Ed must choose whether to play by the rules or sacrifice his career to seek justice for the woman he was supposed to spend his life with. One thing's for certain: Ed can't go down without a fight, because Ed isn't the only one seeking vengeance.

And in Ash Park, the innocents aren't always who they appear to be.

GET *SALVATION* ON MEGHANOFLYNN.COM!

SALVATION: An Ash Park Novel
CHAPTER 1

The fuck you want to be, boy?

The drill sergeant's voice rang in Edward Petrosky's head, though it had been two years since he'd left the army, and six years since he'd had the question barked at him. Back then, the answer had been different. Even a year ago, he would have said "a cop," but that was more because it felt like an escape from the military, just like the Gulf War had been an escape from the loaded silence of his parents' house. But the urge to escape had passed. Now he would have said "Happy, sir," without a trace of irony. The future was shaping up to be good; better than the early nineties or the eighties, that was for damn sure.

Because of *her*.

Ed had met Heather six months before, in the spring before his twenty-fifth birthday, when the air in Ash Park still smelled like earthen death. Now he rolled over on the purple sheets she'd called "plum" and wrapped an arm over her shoulders, his gaze on the popcorn ceiling. A tiny half-smile played on her face with a strange twitch at one corner, almost a spasm, like her lips weren't sure whether to smile or frown. But the corners of her still-closed eyes were crinkled—definitely a smile. *Screw going out running*. The night he met her, she'd smiled like that. Barely forty degrees outside and she'd been taking off her leather coat, and by the time he rolled to a stop, she'd had the jacket wrapped around the homeless woman sitting on the walk. His last girlfriend used to stuff extra garlic bread in her purse when they went out to eat but refused to give even a quarter to the hungry, citing the degenerates' "lack of willpower." As if anyone would choose to starve.

Heather would never say something like that. Her breath was hot against his shoulder. Would his parents like her? He imagined driving the thirty minutes to Grosse Pointe for Thanksgiving next week, imagined sitting at their antique dining table, the one with the lace tablecloth that covered all the scars. "This is Heather," he'd say, and his father would nod, impassive, while his mother stiffly offered coffee, her steel-blue eyes silently judging, her lips pressed into a tight, bloodless line. His parents would ask thinly veiled questions, hoping Heather came from money—she didn't—hoping she'd make a good housewife or that she had dreams of becoming a teacher; of course, only until she bore his children. Dark ages shit. His parents didn't even like Hendrix, and that was saying something. You could get a read on anyone by asking their opinion on Jimi.

Ed planned to tell his folks Heather was self-employed and leave it at that. He'd not mention that he met her during a prostitution sting, or that the first bracelet he put on her wrist was made of steel. Some might argue that the start of a great love story couldn't possibly involve prostitution and near-hypothermia, but they'd be wrong.

Besides, if he hadn't put Heather in his squad car, one of the other units would have. Another time, another girl, he might have responded differently, but she'd been sniffling, crying so hard he could hear her teeth chattering. "You okay?" he had asked. "Do you need a drink of water or a tissue?" But when he glanced in the rearview of the squad car, her cheeks had been wet, her hands frantically rubbing her arms, and he'd realized her shaking was more from the cold.

Heather stretched now with a noise that was half groan, half meow, and snuggled farther under the covers. Ed smiled, letting his gaze drift past her shoulder and to his uniform on the chair in the corner. He still couldn't believe he'd uncuffed her in the supercenter parking lot and then left her sitting in the heated car while he headed into the store alone. When he came back with a thick yellow coat, her eyes had filled, and she'd smiled at him again in a way that made his heart feel four sizes bigger, made him feel taller like he was a hero and not the man who'd just tried to arrest her. They'd talked for hours after that, her whispering at first and looking out the windows like she could get in trouble just for speaking. She hadn't told him then that she hated yellow—he'd found out later. Not like there'd been a ton of options at that off-the-freeway supercenter anyway.

Ed let his vision relax, his black uniform blurring against the chair. Heather had told him she'd never talked to anyone that way before, so open, so easily, like they'd known each other forever. Then again, she'd also said it was the first time she'd ever walked the streets; the odds of that were slim, but Ed didn't care. If a person's past defined them, then he was a murderer; killing someone during wartime didn't make them any less dead. He and Heather were both starting over.

Heather moaned gently again and shifted closer to him, her light eyes hooded in the dimness. He brushed away the single mahogany tendril plastered to her forehead, accidentally snagging his calloused finger on the corner of the notebook under her pillow—she must have stayed up writing notes about the wedding again.

"Thanks for going with me yesterday," she whispered, her voice husky with sleep.

"No problem." They'd taken her father, Donald, to the grocery store, Donald's gnarled fingers shaking every time Ed looked down at the wheelchair. Congestive heart failure, arthritis—the man was a mess, hadn't been able to walk more than a few feet for over a decade, and by all accounts, shouldn't be alive now; usually, congestive heart failure took out its victims within five years. One more reason to get out of the house and enjoy each day, Heather always said. And they'd tried, even taken her father to the dog park, where the old man's miniature Doberman pinscher had yapped and run around Ed's ankles until Ed picked him up and scratched his fuzzy head.

He lowered himself to the pillow beside her, and she trailed her fingers over the hard muscles of his arm and across his chest, then nestled her head into his neck. Her hair still smelled like incense from church last night: spicy and sweet with the bitter hint of char over the gardenia shampoo she used. The church services and Donald's weekly bingo game were the only outings that Petrosky begged off. Something about that church bothered

Ed. His own family wasn't particularly religious, but he didn't think that was the problem; maybe it was how the pope wore fancy hats and golden briefs, while less fortunate folks starved. At least Father Norman, Heather's priest, gave as well as he got. Two weeks before, Petrosky and Heather had taken three garbage bags of clothes and shoes the father had collected to the homeless shelter where Heather volunteered. Then they'd made love in the newly empty back seat of his car. What woman could resist an old Grand Am with squealing brakes and an interior that stank of exhaust?

Heather kissed his neck just below his ear and sighed. "Daddy loves you, you know," she said. Her voice had the same raspy quality as the frigid autumn air that rustled the branches outside.

"Eh, he just thinks I'm a good guy because I volunteer at the shelter." Which Ed didn't. But weeks before Ed met the man, Heather told her dad that she and Ed worked at the shelter together, and even after he and Donald were introduced, she hadn't told her father they were dating. He could understand that though—the man was strict, especially about his only daughter, another parent from the "spare the rod, spoil the child" era. Like Ed's own father.

A curl fell into her eye, and she blew it away. "He thinks you guys have a lot in common."

Donald and Ed spent most of their time together talking about their posts in Vietnam and Kuwait, respectively, but they'd never discussed exactly what they'd done. Ed assumed this was another reason Donald liked Father Norman; the priest had been a soldier before he joined up with the church, and nothing turned men into brothers like the horrors of the battlefield. "I like your father too. And the offer is still open: if he needs a place to stay, we can take care of him here."

She shifted her weight, and gardenia and incense wafted into his nostrils again. "I know, and you're sweet for offering, but we don't need to do that."

But they would, eventually. Unease prickled deep in the back of Ed's brain, a little icicle of frost that spread down into the marrow of his spine. Donald had worked at the post office after the war, through Heather's early childhood, and through his wife's suicide, but his heart had put him out of commission when Heather was a teenager. The man had squirreled some money away, but if Heather had been desperate enough to sell her body, Donald's carefully laid nest egg must have been running out. "Heather, we might—"

"He'll be fine. I've been saving since my mom died, just in case. He has more than enough to support him until he...goes."

If she has all this money, why go out on the street? "But—"

She covered his mouth with hers, and he put his hand on her lower back and pulled her tighter against him. Was living in his own place her father's way to maintain independence? Or was it Heather's? Either way, intuition told him not to push it, and the military had taught him to listen to his gut. Her father was one subject Heather rarely broached. Probably why Ed hadn't known his relationship with Heather was a secret...until he'd let it slip. And the next day, he'd come home from work, and Heather's things were in his bedroom. *It's perfect for us, Ed. Can I stay?*

Forever, he'd said. *Forever.*

Were they moving too fast? He wasn't complaining, didn't want some long, drawn-out courtship, but it had only been six months, and he never wanted Heather to give him the same look his mother always gave his father: *God, why are you still alive? Go ahead and die already so I can have a few happy years alone before I kick off.*

"Are you happy here?" he asked her. "With me?" Maybe they should slow things down just a little. But Heather smiled in that twitchy, spastic way of hers, and his chest warmed, the icicle in his spine melting. He was sure. His gut said, "For god's sake, marry her already."

"Happier than I've ever been," she said.

Ed kissed the top of her head, and as she arched against him, he smiled in the subtle gray of the dawn. Everything smelled sweeter when you were twenty-five and done with active duty in the sand, when every path was still yours for the taking. He'd seen some shit, god knew he had, and it still came to him at night: the horror of comrades shot dead beside him, the burning smog of gunpowder in the air, the tang of blood. But all that seemed so damn far away these days, as if coming home had turned him into someone else, someone who'd never been a soldier at all—all that military shit was someone else's baggage.

He traced the gentle curve of Heather's spine and let the porcelain sheen of her skin in the dusky morning erase the last remnants of memory. Even with the streets covered in slush that froze your toes the moment you stepped outside, her smile—that quirky little smile—always warmed him up.

Yes, this year was going to be the best of Ed's life. He could feel it.

GET *SALVATION* ON MEGHANOFLYNN.COM!

"CHILLING, ADDICTIVE, WICKEDLY ENTERTAINING... *CRIMINAL MINDS* MEETS *GONE GIRL*."

~BESTSELLING AUTHOR KRISTEN MAE

PRAISE FOR BESTSELLING AUTHOR MEGHAN O'FLYNN

"Creepy and haunting...fully immersive thrillers. The Ash Park series should be everyone's next binge-read."

~New York Times Bestselling Author Andra Watkins

"Full of complex, engaging characters and evocative detail, *Wicked Sharp* is a white-knuckle thrill ride. O'Flynn is a master storyteller."

~Paul Austin Ardoin, USA Today Bestselling Author

"Nobody writes with such compelling and entrancing prose as O'Flynn. The perfectly executed twists and expertly crafted web woven into this serial killer series will captivate you. Born Bad is chilling, twisted, heart-pounding suspense that kept me

guessing all the way up to the jaw-dropping conclusion. This is my new favorite thriller series."

~Bestselling Author Emerald O'Brien

"Intense and suspenseful... *Conviction* captured me from the first chapter and held me enthralled until the final page."

~Susan Sewell, Reader's Favorite

"Visceral, fearless, and addictive, this series will keep you on the edge of your seat."

~Bestselling Author Mandi Castle

"Cunning, delightfully disturbing, and addictive, the Ash Park series is an expertly written labyrinth of twisted, unpredictable awesomeness!"

~Award-winning Author Beth Teliho

"Dark, gritty, and raw, O'Flynn's work will take your mind prisoner and keep you awake far into the morning hours."

~Bestselling Author Kristen Mae

"From the feverishly surreal to the downright demented, O'Flynn takes you on a twisted journey through the deepest and darkest corners of the human mind."

~Bestselling Author Mary Widdicks

"With unbearable tension and gripping, thought-provoking storytelling, O'Flynn explores fear in all the best—and creepiest—ways. Masterful psychological thrillers replete with staggering, unpredictable twists."

~Bestselling Author Wendy Heard

LEARN MORE ABOUT ALL OF MEGHAN'S BOOKS AT https://meghanoflynn.com!

Learn more about Meghan's novels on

https://meghanoflynn.com

ABOUT THE AUTHOR

With books deemed “visceral, haunting, and fully immersive” (*New York Times Bestseller Andra Watkins*), Meghan O’Flynn has made her mark on the thriller genre. Meghan is a clinical therapist who draws her character inspiration from her knowledge of the human psyche. She is the best-selling author of gritty crime novels and serial killer thrillers, all of which take readers on the dark, gripping, and unputdownable journey for which Meghan is notorious. Learn more at https://meghanoflynn.com! While you’re there, join Meghan’s reader group, and get exclusive bonuses just for signing up.

Want to connect with Meghan?
https://meghanoflynn.com

Milton Keynes UK
Ingram Content Group UK Ltd.
UKHW042141020823
426203UK00005B/343